The Light Bringer

The Ravenwood Trilogy Book III

Lora Deeprose

This is a work of fiction. Names, characters, places, and incidents are products of the author's imagination or are used fictitiously and are not to be construed as real. Any resemblance to actual events, locations, organizations, or persons, living or dead, is entirely coincidental.

World Castle Publishing, LLC
Pensacola, Florida
Copyright © 2025 Lora Deeprose
Hardback ISBN: 9798296061188
Paperback ISBN: 9798891264519
eBook ISBN: 9798891264526
First Edition World Castle Publishing, LLC, October 28, 2025
http://www.worldcastlepublishing.com

Cover: Cover Designs by Karen
Editor: Karen Fuller

To the misunderstood misfits,
To the sensitive dreamers,
To the introverted book dragons and
To those who still believe in magick,
I wrote this book
for You

CHAPTER ONE

Lizzie spotted the familiar Range Rover in her driveway before she noticed the two strangers on her front porch. The SUV was the make and color the Order consistently used. But why had members of the Order arrived at her doorstep unannounced? That wasn't how they usually operated.

Cathy. Had they found her at last? Was she okay? Was she alive? Her hand flew to her throat, her heart slamming against her ribcage.

The sound of knocking reverberated in the stillness of the surrounding forest. A man and woman stood on her porch, their backs towards her, shadowed by the steep overhang of the porch roof. The woman raised her hand to knock again, the sleeve of her oversized grey cardigan sliding down to reveal a thin, bony wrist. Lizzie's dog, Bear, darted from her side, the slight hitch in his gait the only remnant of his injury, although it didn't slow his steady progress towards the strangers.

Wren, who had gone with her on a hike in the forest, joined her at the edge of the clearing. Her dog greeted the newcomers with a loud woof, his great plume of a tail waving a happy hello. The couple turned towards the sound of the exuberant welcome, stepping to the edge of the porch where Lizzie could finally get a good look at them.

She inhaled sharply. From a distance, the young man looked much the same as he had the last time she had seen him. His chestnut hair was a bit longer than the crew cut he had sported back then, and he still wore his favorite navy wool coat over a well-worn pair of jeans. The woman's bright red hair was all the detail Lizzie needed to identify her.

As Bear nudged his nose against Madison's leg, she bent down to scratch behind his floppy ears. Gideon backed down the steps to get out of the path of Bear's swinging tail.

"Friends of yours?" Wren asked.

"In a manner of speaking." Lizzie took a deep breath to calm her nerves. "More like ghosts from my past." Squaring her shoulders, she started forwards to find out what had prompted Gideon and Madison to finally contact her after five months of silence.

She'd only taken a few steps before Wren grabbed her wrist and pulled her back into the shadows of the trees.

"What are you doing?" she asked, stumbling as he spun her around. "If you are worried about me, don't. I can handle—" She was about to go on, but something about the look on his face stopped her. When his arms encircled her waist and pulled her closer, she had to arch her neck to look up at him. When their eyes locked, her magick rose, dancing across her skin. Suddenly, she ached for him, needed him, wanted him.

He leaned into her, his mouth brushing hers, tenderly at first, then hungrily, seeking. His heart thundered against her palms as she trailed them up his chest, encircling his neck. Passion sparked then flamed as she angled her head to deepen the kiss when he suddenly pulled back.

"I'm so sorry, Elizabeth," he said breathlessly.

"For what?" She thought she saw something flash across his eyes; regret, longing?

"I thought we'd have more time."

Lizzie's eyebrows furrowed, and she shivered, suddenly feeling exposed. "What are you talking about?"

Instead of answering, Wren placed his index finger gently on her forehead. "I love you," he whispered before Lizzie's world went black.

Lizzie whirled around at the sound of her dog barking.

She could have sworn he'd been right by her side. She blinked furiously, the too-bright sunlight dazzling her eyes, and that's when she noticed the white SUV in her driveway. Bear was on the front porch getting his ears scratched by Madison as she cooed in a sing-song voice. And she wasn't alone. Gideon was there, standing on *her* porch steps. Lizzie stumbled forward and must have made a sound because Gideon turned, and their eyes locked.

She faltered as their eyes met, her hand automatically searching for the stone cross she'd worn since she was a little girl. Her fingers searched in vain. It had been lost in the forest the night she fled for her life. The night her handyman had been shot trying to save her. Without the necklace and the charm placed on it, Lizzie's power surged through her body as a tumult of emotions washed over her. The magick crackled along her skin, sending a faint scent of ozone into the air around her. She pushed down her power and, with it, all the feelings she'd thought she'd dealt with since they'd banished her from the only family she'd ever known.

Gideon stepped off the porch, his hand raised in greeting, his long strides quickly eating up the ground between them. Her mind had her turning around and running back into the safety of the forest, but her feet stayed firmly rooted to the earth.

"Thank the Goddess, you're home." He smiled broadly.

Lizzie felt the corners of her mouth turn upwards, mirroring his expression, but as he continued to speak, the smile died on her lips.

"I didn't think you'd ever show up. We've been waiting for hours. Where have you been?"

Where had she been? She shifted her weight, and the backs of her heels stung as they rubbed against the stiff leather of her hiking boots. Had she been heading out for a hike or returning from one? Everything seemed too bright, and she was getting a headache.

Thunder rumbled in the distance.

"Why are you here?" She hugged herself tightly, taking a step back.

"Because Madison needed to see you. I was already heading to Vancouver, so I had the plane diverted to Revelstoke and picked up one of our vehicles from there to drive her out to..." he glanced around, "the middle of nowhere, apparently."

"Why now? It's been months since I've heard from either of you." This time, she couldn't keep the hurt from her voice even while the thought of being needed tugged at her heart.

Gideon looked over his shoulder to where Madison was now crouched down in front of Bear before stepping closer to Lizzie. He spoke quietly, "Her dad died last week, and she's not coping well. She got it into her head that she needed to see you, and nothing I could say would change her mind. She's been obsessing about it."

"Oh." Lizzie looked over Gideon's shoulder towards her cottage. Even from a distance, Madison looked done in by her loss, her shoulders rounded, her body curved in on itself. She knew how close Madison had been to her father. She also knew firsthand what losing someone you cared about felt like. She straightened her shoulders, ignoring the ache she felt in her chest.

"I wasn't expecting visitors. And I have things to do."

"Just go over and talk to her, please. That's all I'm asking." Gideon ran his fingers through his hair, a familiar gesture he did when he was nervous, one she used to find endearing.

"Fine. Madison can say what she came to say, and then you both can leave." Lizzie didn't wait for Gideon's reply as she marched around him and headed for the cottage.

Her steps slowed as she mounted the porch. Bear had his meaty forehead pressed against Madison's. Lizzie watched as Madison's whole body relaxed, her shoulders dropped, and her breathing slowed down as the two sat for several minutes forehead to forehead in some kind of silent communion. Madison pulled away first, letting out a deep sigh as she sat back and gently stroked Bear's large ruff.

"You are a beautiful boy, aren't you?" Madison murmured.

"His name is Bear," Lizzie said.

"I can see why." Madison smiled, looking up at Lizzie. Gone was the vibrant young woman who worked and laughed alongside Lizzie at the flower shop, and in her place was a hollow-eyed creature with sharp cheekbones, the too-large cardigan swallowing up her thin frame.

Madison started to rise from her kneeling position, but she snagged her foot on the oversized cardigan and struggled to get up. Without thinking, Lizzie reached out her hand to help her. The moment their hands touched, Madison's grief moved up Lizzie's arm and straight into her chest like a bolt of lightning, opening up a deep well of sadness, overwhelming her with the intensity of emotions. Lizzie was still reeling from the unexpected deluge of sadness when Madison let go, severing their link.

Lizzie blinked furiously, trying to regain her equilibrium. "I'm sorry for your loss," she blurted out, the words sounding meaningless and almost callous to her own ears. Madison nodded her head, tears welling up. Her face crumpled, and much to Lizzie's alarm, Madison flung herself at Lizzie, wrapping her arms around her neck and trapping her in the embrace. Lizzie stiffened, her arms held out at her sides. The smell of Madison's unwashed hair mingled with the distinctly masculine scent of wool, stale pipe smoke, and engine grease that lingered in the scratchy fabric of the sweater she wore.

Lizzie felt Bear's weight against her leg as he leaned into both women. Only then did Lizzie wrap her arms lightly around Madison's trembling back. Her grief was silent, and Lizzie wouldn't have known she was crying if not for the quaking of her shoulders and the damp patch that was beginning to form on the back of Lizzie's collar. The weight of Madison's grief pressing against Lizzie made it hard for her to breathe.

Thunder rolled in the distance, and Madison flinched, tightening her grip around Lizzie's neck. She let go of Madison and, firmly but gently, grasped Madison's hands from around her neck and stepped back from the embrace.

"Come inside. You can freshen up. I'll put the kettle on," she said, releasing Madison's wrists. She turned away, digging in her pocket for the front door key and trying not to notice how Gideon had stepped in, his arm snaking around Madison's waist to support her.

"Thank you, I'd really like that," Madison said, swiping tears away with the sleeve of her sweater as she leaned into Gideon's side.

Lizzie fumbled the key in the lock as Bear stepped between her and the door, then promptly disappeared into thin air.

"Bear, why can't you be like other dogs and wait until I open the door?" Lizzie called out through the closed door as she twisted the key. Her hand trembled slightly as she turned the handle and stepped inside, inviting inside the two people who had hurt her the most. She thought she sensed a shift in the atmosphere of her cottage as she reluctantly invited her past into her sanctuary.

CHAPTER TWO

Lizzie headed straight for the fridge, where Bear was already waiting. She was grateful that the cottage was dark and a bit chilly because it hid the nervous heat blooming on her cheeks and the dampness prickling the back of her neck. "The bathroom is just down the hall, first door on the right," she called out over her shoulder as she slid the cookie jar from the top of the fridge. Popping off the lid, she plucked out a cookie and handed it to her dog. "You only get the one. You don't want to spoil your dinner," she said, booping him affectionately on the nose.

Grabbing the kettle, she began to fill it at the sink as Bear sat by the fridge, a hopeful look in his eye, having devoured the cookie in one greedy gulp.

"Your dog...he just, he just walked through a closed door." Gideon's voice rose. "That's incredible."

Turning off the faucet, she turned around. Her visitors stood just inside the door, Madison's eyes wide with wonder, Gideon's arm outstretched, pointing at Bear.

Lizzie looked from Madison to Gideon, confused by their reaction. "I can understand why Madison is surprised, but Gideon, surely this can't be the first magickal animal you've encountered, considering you were raised in an organization whose sole purpose is to train and protect people with powers?"

"People. Not animals." Gideon stepped further into the room, a feverish gleam in his eye. "The last magickal creature in captivity died in 1782. Has the Order been informed of his existence? Lizzie, do you have any idea what you have here?"

Her grip tightened on the kettle's handle, her knuckles turning white. "I have a loyal friend and companion." Slamming the kettle down on the stove, she flicked the knob and then spun around to face Gideon. "Someone who has been there for me, who risked his life to protect me. So yes, I know exactly what I have. And it's none of the Order's business to know about him." She wheeled around, her movements harsh, as she pulled down mugs and teabags from the cupboard.

"But the Order absolutely needs to know about this dog," he insisted. "You have in your possession a canine with magickal powers. And not just any magickal powers, but the rarest kind. Our scholars believed that phase shifting only manifested in three types of creatures and never in something as commonplace as a dog. This could change everything we thought we thought we knew."

His words stabbed fear into her heart. She blew out a breath and attempted to keep her voice steady. "He wasn't born with powers, so he is of no use to the Order. I gave them to him by accident. I found him on the side of the road where he'd been run over and left for dead."

"No," exclaimed Madison. At the sound of her voice, Bear trotted over to her side. Fresh tears slid down her cheeks as she ran her hands over the dog's head. "Who would do something like that to an innocent creature?" She whispered, swiping at her eyes with the sleeve of her cardigan.

"When I came across him lying in the ditch, I didn't know what to do, but I knew he needed help. When I used my powers, according to Vivienne, I must have gone too deep and ended up transferring some of my magick to him."

"Well, she's wrong. I can cite the texts housed in the archives that would tell you unequivocally that a human being cannot transfer magickal abilities to other people, much less an animal. It's not possible," Gideon said, his hands on his hips.

"Just because Lizzie and Vivienne believe something different from you doesn't make them wrong," Madison quipped, then sniffed loudly. "And just because there is no record of people transferring their powers to others in your archives doesn't mean it can't happen. It just means it hasn't been observed and recorded," she said, ignoring Gideon's exasperating sigh and looking over at Lizzie. "Has he demonstrated any other magical abilities?

Lizzie felt the sharp edges of her anger towards Madison soften. "He can turn on the faucet when he wants me to refill his water bowl. And although I haven't caught him in the act yet," she said with affection in her voice. "I suspect he can get his treat jar down from the top of the fridge and sneak cookies when I'm not looking."

At the word cookie, Bear cocked his head.

"If you believe you transferred your magick to Bear, then that would mean you also have the power to phase shift through solid objects. So, do you?" Gideon demanded.

"If you mean can I dematerialize and materialize, the answer is no, but —"

"There you go." Gideon interrupted, "You've just proven my point."

"Do you mean Bear is a kind of shifter?" Madison interjected as she dug through her satchel. Pulling out a notepad and pen, she looked up at Gideon expectantly.

"Yes, the dog is not just a shifter, but the rarest kind. Most people have heard about shapeshifters, werewolves, vampires, mermaids, selkies, and wyverns. Fantasy novels are full of them. Shapeshifters reconfigure their physical matter to change their appearance. Phase shifters are different. They can shift their physical matter back and forth between states, from solid, liquid, gas, and some speculate, even aether. Up until now, scholars believed the only animals capable of phase shifting are unicorns, Bigfoot, and phoenixes."

Madison stopped scribbling in her notebook to tap the pen

against her chin. "So, if there are only three types of animals that can phase shift, could Bear be doing something different, but on the surface, look similar? As in, could he be creating a portal to walk through a closed door?"

Gideon rolled his eyes. The gesture irritated Lizzie, the storm inside her building again. "No, they're completely different things. Portals are geological manifestations that have nothing to do with living beings."

Madison sniffed loudly as she wrote in her notebook, then tucked it under her arm so she could rummage through the pockets of her cardigan, coming up empty-handed. Grabbing her satchel from where it hung by her hip, she began rooting around in it before giving up with a frustrated sigh.

Lizzie seized the opportunity to put some space between herself and Gideon before she grabbed him by the collar and threw him out of her cottage. "Let me get you some tissues."

Madison sniffed again, looking up from her notes. "Thank you, I must have used all the ones I had with me."

Lizzie nodded and headed for the bathroom. Snagging the box from the top of the toilet tank, she stood for a moment with her eyes closed, forcing her breathing to slow down. She would go back out and calmly tell them she changed her mind, and they would have to leave. This was her home, and she had every right to decide who could be in her space. Opening her eyes, she turned around to find Gideon standing in the doorway, blocking her path. His eyes burned with a strange light.

"Lizzie, there's something you need to know," he whispered fiercely. "I shouldn't be telling you this because it's classified information, but if it helps you understand why Bear needs to come with me, I'm willing to break the rules. There's been an unexplained surge in dark energy and demonic activity over the last few months, not just here in Canada but globally. The heads of all the Mother Houses, including Vivienne, have set up task forces to figure out what's going on and how to stop it. And that's why I am heading to Vancouver. Madison thinks I'm going to an Archivists' convention, but I'm actually part of a think tank comprised of the top scholars whose expertise is studying the darkness."

Lizzie clutched the tissue box to her chest, the back of her neck prickling. "I still don't see what this has to do with Bear."

"Everything. He represents a huge breakthrough in our understanding of how phase shifting actually works. If we can study him, run tests, and isolate where his power lays, whether it is chemical or genetic, we could—hypothetically—replicate it in a lab and use it on ourselves or even on a pack of trained service dogs. Any weapon we can add to our arsenal that the dark side doesn't have means we have the upper hand. I have to take him to the Order today."

"Absolutely not," she said, crushing the tissue box in her hands, her anger blooming hot and fierce. "Bear will have nothing to do with you or the Order. And Vivienne agrees with me. She's known what he can do for several weeks now, and she's never asked me to bring Bear in to be studied. And I'll be telling her to order you to stop pestering me." Lizzie raised her chin, glaring at Gideon. "And let me make this perfectly clear: Bear. Is. Not. A. Weapon. He is part of my family. His home is here with me and Quinn. Now, I'm going back out there to hear what Madison came to tell me, and then the two of you are leaving." When Gideon didn't move, she pushed past him, shouldering him into the doorframe. "Get out of my way," she snarled, marching down the hallway and back into the kitchen, Gideon following close on her heels.

"Whose Quinn?"

"He's Quinn," she said, pointing the tissue box towards the back of the couch where Quinn perched. Madison sat on the couch next to the raven, gently running a finger down his breast. The bird was chortling deep in his throat, his tail feathers waggling with pleasure.

"He just flew in the window and made himself at home," Madison said in awe.

"I leave it open so he can come and go as he pleases. He befriended me when I first arrived at Halcyon and followed me here."

"Quinn's a crow?"

"Raven." Madison and Lizzie corrected him in unison.

"Hello, the house." Came a familiar voice from outside just as the kettle began to whistle shrilly, setting off Quinn, who flapped his wings in irritation, cawing madly.

Lizzie raised her voice over the din. "Gideon, make yourself useful and take the kettle off the stove," she ordered as she made for the open front door.

Relief washed over her as she scrambled out to the porch, greeting her friend just as the old woman was climbing the steps. Grandma Faye carried a large wicker basket. The aroma of warm baked goods scented the morning air.

"Good Morning." Grandma Faye leaned in and kissed Lizzie on the cheek. "I had an abundance of early summer strawberries and rhubarb that needed harvesting, so I baked several pies, and I thought you might like one."

"I'd never say no to your baking," Lizzie smiled.

"Is Vivienne here?" She asked, waving her hand towards the SUV parked in the driveway.

"No, former acquaintances I met during my brief stay with the Order. But they were just leaving."

"Oh?" Grandma Faye raised her eyebrows. "Well, if they plan on catching the ferry, they should hurry. If those clouds are any indication, the storm's going to be a big one, and ones that size usually delay the ferries."

Lizzie looked up, surprised to see how dark the sky

surrounding the property had turned in the brief time she'd been inside.

"I'll just drop this off so you can say your goodbyes then," Grandma Faye said, handing the basket over.

"No, please stay. I've just put a kettle on. Once they leave, you and I can have a nice visit, and I can tell you about my visitors because I can tell by the look on your face you are dying to know more," Lizzie sighed, suddenly feeling weary, "And I would really like a friendly ear right now."

The old woman placed a gentle hand on her arm. "Are you feeling okay?

"I'm fine. It's just a headache; it'll pass. Let's go in." As she stepped inside, Lizzie said with forced pleasantness, "I'd like you to meet—"

"Gideon York, as I live and breathe," Grandma Faye exclaimed. With a swirl of her voluminous skirts and the tinkling of bells she wore on her ankles, she swooped over to Gideon, wrapping her arms around him. Surprised, Lizzie watched as Gideon's face registered confusion, then panic as the old woman held tight to him. When she finally released him, he started to step backwards, but Grandma Faye snatched up his hands, holding his arms out from his sides. "Let me take a good look at you. My, you have grown into such a handsome young man!"

"Sorry," he said, shaking his head, "have we met?"

"Yes, we have, although you probably don't remember. You were only two when you came to live with me."

He stared blankly at her. "I don't remember. Are you sure you have the right person?"

Grandma Faye let go of his hands, and her expression softened. "Yes, I'm sure. Your parents brought you to me for safekeeping before they headed out on a mission."

He furrowed his eyebrows. "My father's last mission. He was killed during it, and I was about two when he died. And

Vivienne was with him? She never talks about it, or him for that matter." He looked at Grandma Faye properly for the first time. "You knew my father."

She nodded. "Your father was a dear friend. I knew him long before he joined the Order."

"You knew my father." He repeated, his voice faltering.

Smiling gently, she said, "He was an exceptional man, and I miss him every day. The world became a darker place when we lost his light." She reached out her hand, and Gideon gripped it tightly.

An unfamiliar pang hit Lizzie's chest, and she tightened her grip on the basket she still held, the wicker handle creaking loudly. She'd just assumed Grandma Faye and Vivienne had first met during the aftermath of the attempt on her life.

From the couch, Madison sniffed loudly. Gideon looked over at her, blinking as if he'd just woken from a dream. He dropped Grandma Faye's hand and stepped back as the old woman turned to face Madison.

"Sorry," she said, blowing her nose, then tucking the used tissue in her pocket.

"And who do we have here?" Grandma Faye made her way over to the couch, her hand outstretched.

"Madison Albright," she replied, trying to extricate herself from under Bear's bulk.

"Stay where you are. We don't stand on ceremony out here in the sticks," she said, shaking Madison's hand. "I'm Fayence Greene, but everyone calls me Grandma Faye."

"Gammee Fee," Gideon exclaimed, sitting down hard on a kitchen chair. "I remember you now."

"Lizzie," Grandma Faye said, looking over at Gideon, "perhaps now would be a good time for that tea you mentioned."

CHAPTER THREE

It was an awkward gathering assembled in Lizzie's living room. After pouring tea for everyone, Grandma Faye took her own cup and saucer and sat in the rocking chair by the fire Lizzie had lit moments earlier to take down the chill in the room. Gideon and Madison sat on either end of the sofa, with Gideon seated on the end closest to the front door. Lizzie took the remaining armchair while Bear curled up in front of the hearth and Quinn perched on the back of the sofa behind Madison's shoulder.

Madison stuffed forkfuls of pie into her mouth like her life depended on it, staring intently down at her plate. Gideon, on the other hand, left his pie untouched as he stared unseeing into the fire, his teacup clutched to his chest with both hands. Every once in a while, he would sneak a glance at Grandma Faye, his eyes searching her face, and then he would return to staring at the flames. All the while, Grandma Faye partook of her pie and tea, seemingly oblivious to the uncomfortable silence pressing down in the room.

Lizzie toyed with her pie, moving it around her plate while calculating how best to hurry along this unwanted tea party so Gideon and Madison could be on their way and out of her life when Gideon abruptly turned from staring at the fire to look at Grandma Faye. "What was he like?"

Grandma Faye's eyes softened. "Your father was brave and strong, but most of all, he was kind. I remember his laughter and the way he had of making anyone in his presence feel they were the most important person in his world."

Gideon lapsed into silence, his eyes shining. Lizzie held her breath, and Madison had her teacup to her lips but didn't take a sip. Grandma Faye tilted her head to the side, and with the same gentle tone, she said, "Never doubt that your father loved you, and if he were here today, he would tell you how proud he was of you and the young man you've grown up to be."

Gideon's eyes narrowed and abruptly turned to look at the fire again. "No, he wouldn't. I'm no longer a Guardian. I quit to join the Archivists."

And he used me to make the switch. Lizzie felt sick and embarrassed at the memory of their time together.

"Yes, I know. Vivienne told me about your entrance into the Archivists. That's why I know your father would be proud of you. He never wanted you to follow his career path. He hoped for you a life that felt right for you. He was an exceptional Guardian, but that's not where his heart lied."

Gideon's head snapped up, staring at Grandma Faye. "But he was a legend in the Guardians. I know because everyone in the Order keeps telling me."

"He was dedicated to his vows and obligations as a Guardian, but for as long as I knew him, his real joy and passion had always been books. That is until he met Vivienne, and then you were born. He had amassed quite a collection of antiquarian books on magick. He used to read to you, do you remember?"

"No, I don't." Gideon sounded crestfallen. "I don't know anything about him. No matter how many times I would ask Vivienne, she would never talk about him or what he was like, and then I just stopped asking."

"His death was extremely hard on her, and the only way she knew how to keep going was to avoid talking about him and cutting ties with people who knew and cared about him. Including me—until recently. And I think it wasn't just the grief of losing him. It's the guilt she carries about his death. You see, she blames herself for what happened, for not being able to save him." She leaned forward in the rocking chair. "It must have been very hard on you, growing up without a father and a mother who wouldn't speak of his memory, but I think you may find she's ready to take down those walls she built around herself — just give her a little more time."

Gideon's throat worked up and down as he returned to staring off into the fire.

Before the awkward silence in the cottage could grow any more uncomfortable, Grandma Faye leaned forward, her eyes sparkling in Madison's direction. "So," Grandma Faye said cheerfully, "Lizzie mentioned the three of you met at the Order." She placed her teacup gently in its saucer next to her now empty plate.

Madison answered, looking down at her almost empty plate. "Yes and no. I used to work for Lizzie at her flower shop before it burned down. But I do belong to the Order now. And Gideon was Lizzie's guardian."

Lizzie stared at Madison over her teacup, willing her to look up, but she remained staring at her plate.

"Yes, I noticed your tattoo." Grandma Faye motioned to Madison's wrist, where the tattoo of two crescent moons with a full moon in the center was outlined in indigo. "And if I am not mistaken, because it is not a solid design, that means you are a novice?"

"Yes." Madison poked at her pie with her fork, then stuffed the last piece in her mouth.

"Are you just down for the day?"

Suddenly, Gideon came to life again, "No, Madison wants to stay with Lizzie for a while. I'm just dropping her off before I head to Vancouver for a conference." Then he glanced back at the fire.

Lizzie's hand jerked, spilling hot tea down the front of her shirt. Madison inhaled sharply, then started choking on her mouthful of food. Shooting up from her chair, the cup and saucer in Lizzie's hand rattled as she hastily put them down on the side table while Madison continued to splutter and cough.

Grandma Faye calmly lifted her hand in Madison's direction, and with a quick flick of her wrist, Madison inhaled deeply. "That's better, but you might want to take a sip of tea, dear," she said to Madison, then turning to Lizzie, she continued, "How wonderful you have your first houseguest."

"I have to go change," Lizzie blurted out, then ran from the room.

***

Lizzie quickly exchanged her soiled shirt for a roomy sweatshirt, but she remained in her bedroom. Gideon had lied. Madison didn't just want to talk to her. She wanted to stay with her. She sat down on the edge of the bed, willing the familiar ache in her chest to go away. If Madison explained why she'd turned her back on Lizzie and had refused to see her, if she said she was sorry for the months of silence, maybe Lizzie would want her to stay. Then maybe they could be friends again. Or was it simply too late?

She blew out an exasperated breath and bent over, quickly unlacing her hiking boots. It troubled her that she couldn't remember going out into the woods. The blisters on her heels stung as she toed off her boots, a clear sign she had definitely been for a long walk, but when she tried to recall the details, all it did was make her head ache. Her socks were stuck to her heels, and when she gingerly peeled them off, she reopened her blisters, and they started to ooze again. Sliding her feet into open-backed slippers, she reluctantly headed back to her visitors.

"Well, that's settled then," Grandma Faye said, standing up and shaking out her skirt. Gathering up the soiled dishes, she then stacked them in the sink.

"What's settled?" Lizzie asked, stepping into the kitchen.

"Gideon is going to pop over to my place. I have a book

of his father's I'd like to give him, and he's volunteered to help me trim Mimi's hooves." She bustled around the kitchen, putting the leftover pie in the fridge and gathering up her basket. Gideon stood looking unsure at Grandma Faye. Lizzie twisted the bottom of her sweatshirt between her fingers. Panic bloomed as she realized what Grandma Faye was saying. She was going with Gideon in tow, leaving her alone with Madison.

"Are you sure that's such a great idea? Didn't you say the storm was coming and that if they wanted to catch the ferry, they should probably leave right away?"

Grandma Faye opened the door and peered out. "The storm seems to be holding off for now, and Mimi's the last of the goats to be trimmed. She's always been a challenge to do alone, and with Gideon's help, it can be done in a matter of minutes. We'll be back in plenty of time. Come along, Gideon, time's a wasting." She grabbed Gideon's sleeve and led him out the door. He gave one slightly frightened look over his shoulder before closing the door behind them.

Lizzie stood dumbfounded, staring at the closed door, the sound of Grandma Faye's truck fading in the distance, leaving only the sound of the fire crackling in its place.

The lid of the teapot rattled, and Lizzie watched as Madison fiddled with the lid, having discovered the pot empty.

"I'll make more."

As Lizzie reached for the pot, Madison quickly pulled her hands back, resting them in her lap. Lizzie scooped up the pot, rinsed it out at the sink then return the kettle to the stove. She kept her back to Madison as she pulled out a tin of chamomile tea and filled a tea ball with the dried leaves. Lizzie could feel the growing silence like an uninvited guest taking up all the space and air in her tiny cottage. Her shoulders tightened as she gripped the edge of the sink, waiting for the water to boil. She heard the rustle of fabric as Madison shifted on the couch.

Outside the kitchen window, the trees began to sway and dance to the strong wind that had kicked up. The afternoon light had taken on a strange, menacing glow, matching Lizzie's growing irritation. As soon as the water began to boil, Lizzie snatched it off the stove and filled the teapot. The silence grew. Clattering the lid roughly on the teapot, she stared out the window at the storm, her magick sparking down her arms.

"Why did you refuse to see me or take my calls?"

A log shifted in the hearth as the wind snaked in through the open living room window, brushing the back of Lizzie's neck. She stared out the window, tears burning her eyes and blurring her vision. She spun around. "Well?" she spat out.

Madison was slumped over the armrest of the couch, her head cradled in her arm, fast asleep. Lizzie blew out a sigh as she padded across the room. Gently lifting Madison's legs, she swung them onto the couch, then covered her with the quilt she kept folded over the back of the couch. She took a needlepoint cushion from the rocking chair and tucked it under Madison's head. Returning to the kitchen, she filled a heavy stoneware mug full of tea, grabbed a cookie for Bear and a handful of raisins for Quinn, and went outside to watch the storm. Bear followed her out the door as Quinn hopped out the window to join them.

She took a seat at the small table where she could safely watch the distant lightning and wait for Gideon and Grandma Faye to return. Quinn perched himself on the back of the empty chair across from her while Bear laid down by her feet as soon as he demolished his cookie. By the time she'd finished her tea, there was still no sign of the old woman's truck, and it had begun to rain in earnest.

As she tracked the storm, she noticed something odd. Above her, the cloud cover was a light grey, but circling around her property, dark purple clouds roiled and churned in a counterclockwise spiral, seeming to move closer, then spiraling outward again. Lighting flashed, illuminating the bruised clouds, momentarily changing their color to lavender, the thunder a deep rumble echoing off the mountainsides.

She'd never seen a storm behave in such a way, and she wasn't sure if it had something to do with the way air currents moved through the mountains or if the proximity to the lake affected its path, but something felt off to her. The storm was spiraling in again. Lizzie pondered whether to call Grandma Faye to see if they were going to be much longer when a lightning strike zig zagged down through the sky, hitting just beyond the front gate. The crack of thunder seconds behind the flash reverberated in her chest.

The skies opened up, rain pelting the ground just as Madison started screaming. Before Lizzie could even stand up, Bear blinked out of sight, and Wren flew through the open window. Fast behind them, she flung open the door, scrambling over the threshold and into a nightmare.

CHAPTER FOUR

Lizzie flattened herself against the wall as a book whizzed through the air, narrowly missing her head. A blizzard of loose pages and paperbacks from the bookshelves filled the air. The coffee table rocked back and forth, thumping the floor with angry knocks as cupboard doors in the kitchen rattled in their frames. Quinn clung to the edge of the mantle, flapping his wings as Bear stood his ground in the center of the paper storm, slowly inching towards Madison while dodging the flying books. Madison's eyes were wide and unseeing, her voice high with terror. "Please don't, Richard. Don't hurt me. Please. Please." She was pushed up against the corner of the sofa, her legs pulled up against her chest, her arms over her head.

Lizzie quickly drew up her magick and cut a swath through the airborne books and pages. She ran to Madison's side, shouting over the chaos. "Madison, it's just a storm. You're safe. No one is going to hurt you." She placed a gentle hand on Madison's shoulder.

"No," Madison screamed, "Don't hurt me." Pale yellow sparks of magick exploded around her as Madison's arms flailed out, hitting Lizzie square in the face. Lizzie ducked, avoiding a second blow, her cheek blooming with pain. There was the screech of wood on wood, and then something clattered to the ground. She managed to grab Madison's wrists before she got hit again, feeling the sting of Madison's magick on her palms.

"Madison, listen to me. You need to get your magick under control! You are in my cottage, and you're safe. It's just a thunderstorm."

Wind barreled through the open window, whipping

Lizzie's hair into her eyes. A paperback and several loose pages landed in the fireplace, where they caught fire. The burning flash danced elongated shadows around the room. Lizzie flinched as the thunder following the next flash of lightning shook the house, but she managed to keep her hold of Madison's wrists.

Pushing down her own rising panic, she drew her magick around Madison, trying her best to infuse a feeling of calm. But it wasn't working. Madison kicked out with her feet as she tried to push Lizzie away. Bear approached the sofa and placed his muzzle next to Madison's ear, and let out three loud barks. Madison jerked away from the sound, her head snapping back, her magick winking out. The books instantly drop to the floor, the loose pages fluttering in lazy arcs to settle silently with the paperback. The coffee table remained with all four feet on the floor, and the cupboards ceased banging. Lizzie released Madison's wrists.

"Bear?" Madison blinked, looking from the dog to Lizzie as if waking from a dream. In answer, Bear started vigorously licking her face. Madison let out a startled laugh and turned her head, but he kept at it until she gently pushed his face away.

Lizzie sat back on her heels, watching and waiting. Madison's breathing had slowed, but her arms trembled as she reached out to pet Bear. The next roll of thunder came from behind the house as the storm circled around in its strange spiral. Madison tightened her hold on Bear's fur, but she remained calm.

Getting slowly to her feet, Lizzie plucked the quilt off the floor where Madison had kicked it in her panic. She gave it a quick shake, creating a gentle eddy of loose pages skittering across the floor. She draped it around Madison's quaking shoulders, then reached over and closed the window, muffling the sound of the storm. Stepping over the debris scattered across the floor, Lizzie grabbed a mug from the kitchen cupboard and filled it with the chamomile tea, adding a generous dollop of honey.

By the time she picked her way back across the room, Madison was sitting upright, her feet on the floor with Bear lying next to her, his head in her lap.

"Drink this. It's still warm but not hot."

Madison took the mug and nodded. It shook in her hand. She sipped tentatively as she looked around the room while Lizzie gathered handfuls of pages and fed them into the fire. "L-l-lizzie, your books. What have I d-d-done to your precious books?" Madison said through chattering teeth. She cradled the mug against her chest with one hand while the other continued to absently stroke the top of Bear's head. Quinn flew down from the mantle and settled in his preferred spot on the back of the couch.

"They were just second-hand paperbacks, no great loss, and easily replaced." Lizzie tossed another handful of pages into the fire. *Not like her first edition Jane Austen's she'd lost in the fire that destroyed her flower shop.*

"D-d-did I do that-t-t?" Madison asked, pointing to Lizzie's cheek.

"I'm fine," she said, lightly touching the side of her face. It was tender, but Lizzie's unique ability to heal quickly meant she knew by tomorrow there would be no bruise or pain to mark where she'd been hit. "Nothing's broken."

The kitchen window lit up with the next lightning strike, followed immediately by an ear-shattering boom. Both Lizzie and Madison yelped in alarm as the sound wave shook the house. Then the lights went out.

"Does this happen often?" Madison said, snuggling closer to Bear.

"The storm or the power going out?"

"Both?"

"There have been a few spring storms since I moved in, but none as violent as this one." Lizzie carefully picked her way over to the mantle and lit several candles she had placed there when she'd decorated her cottage. "Oh wait, that's not true." She crossed over to the kitchen to retrieve the box of emergency candles she kept in one of the drawers. "There was that one storm where lightning actually hit the driveway." She kept talking, hoping to distract Madison from what was happening outside. "It created a piece of lightning glass. It's that lumpy bit of glass on the mantle." Lizzie lit a candle, dripped wax onto several saucers, and began affixing candles to the hot wax. "But that wasn't a natural storm but a demon storm sent by Jon. It could've been worse, but Emma protected the cottage from any damage." Once Lizzie tested the candles were solidly stuck in each saucer, she lit each one, placing several on the kitchen table.

"Demon storm? And who are Jon and Emma?"

Lizzie carried two candles over to the coffee table, then perched on the edge of the sofa. "Jon was my contractor who installed my new kitchen. He tried to scare me off and sent a demon to visit. Turns out Jon wasn't just a contractor but a warlock and the head of a drug cartel who was running a secret pot farm and drug running operation out of my barn." Lizzie tracked the storm as she told her tale, noticing it was circling around to the front of the property again. She also noticed Madison barely reacted to the flashes of light and rumbling thunder.

She hadn't intended on going into the details of what had happened, but as she talked, she felt something lighten inside her as if a heavy weight had been lifted off her whole being. She and Grandma Faye hadn't spoken of any of it since that night, and sharing what had happened to someone who wasn't there seemed to make it all real. She could see it outside herself more clearly now.

"But he died when Grandma Faye called in the Order when I got shot, and my handyman was murdered. The Order tracked him down, and there was a car chase, and he ran off the road and down the mountainside."

The whites of Madison's eyes glowed eerily in the candlelight. "You were shot?"

"Yes."

"I had no idea. Gideon mentioned that the Order had been called out here, something about another demon being detected, but nothing about you being hurt or a murder or drug runners."

Lizzie shrugged. "He probably didn't know the details. Like he didn't know about Bear's powers. For whatever reason, Vivienne didn't tell him."

"Was it Jon who shot you?"

"No, one of his henchmen, a corrupt cop, as it turns out."

And Emma?" she asked a little breathlessly. She'd stopped petting Bear and was leaning forward.

"She was the spirit of the witch who first lived here. Her name was Emma Hawksworth. This is her cottage. The villagers locked her in the cellar and starved her to death. They also put an enchantment in the cellar to trap her down there, but Grandma Faye and I managed to release her into the light. We located her remains, and we exhumed them. We buried her out in the yard. The apple sapling marks her grave." Lizzie turned to look out the window at the young tree bending in the fierce wind, hoping it would weather the storm. "That reminds me, it was Gideon who located the spell to reverse the binding, and I haven't thanked him yet." As if speaking his name had conjured his presence, Lizzie noticed headlights arcing through the front gate.

"Finally, they're back," she said, leaning over Bear's bulk to get a closer look at Grandma Faye's truck as it struggled up the drive. As it approached the cottage, the truck fishtailed, spraying an arc of sand high in the air. Two separate bursts of magick followed, engulfing the vehicle, straightening out its path, and pushing it up the mess of sand and rain, the truck coming to rest next to Gideon's SUV.

"Stay here," Lizzie ordered, and quickly exchanged her slippers for rubber boots. Swinging her slicker over her shoulders, she grabbed an umbrella and stepped out into the storm. And quickly wished she hadn't. With each step, her raw blisters rubbed painfully in her boots, the rain coming down in sheets being driven at an angle so that the porch offered no protection at all. She struggled to open the umbrella, only to have the wind grab it and turn it inside out before she even got off the porch. Tossing aside the now useless umbrella, she managed only a few sliding steps across the driveway when Grandma Faye jumped out of the truck.

She didn't have an umbrella, and instead, the old woman quickly raised her arms and brought them down in an arc over her head. Lizzie watched the magick flare briefly as the spell took hold. Grandma Faye reached inside the cab of the truck, retrieving a lantern and the basket she'd brought with her earlier that day.

"Stay where you are, Lizzie," the old woman shouted over the storm. As she dashed for the cottage, the passenger door swung open, and Gideon sprinted for the back of his SUV. As he disappeared behind his vehicle, Lizzie caught a glimpse of what he was wearing; something pink and short. And did it have ruffles?

Lizzie backtracked up the porch and held the door open as Grandma Faye hastened inside. She held onto the door, peering out into the storm. "Did I just see Gideon wearing a housecoat?"

Grandma Faye handed Lizzie the wicker basket and flashlight before removing the rain-repelling spell. She was just hanging up her dry raincoat when Gideon appeared in the doorway dragging two suitcases behind him. He was soaking wet, and Lizzie hadn't been seeing things. He was definitely not wearing the clothes he'd left in. He wore only a housecoat in an extravagant pink cabbage rose print and large ruffles at the hem and sleeves. On Grandma Faye, it would have come to her ankles, but on Gideon's tall frame, it barely brushed his knees.

"Don't either of you say a word," he growled, then looked about the room. "What the hell happened here?" he asked, parking the pink suitcase up against the wall.

Madison clamped a hand over her mouth the sound she made a cross between a snort and a cough. Gideon glared at her.

"The power went out," Lizzie replied, fighting to keep the laughter from bubbling up and offering no explanation for the chaos littering the floor.

Letting out a huff, he grabbed his suitcase and the flashlight Lizzie held and stomped down the hallway to the bathroom. His sneakers squeaked with each step as he dripped water across Lizzie's floor.

"What happened?" Lizzie turned to Grandma Faye, no longer holding back her mirth.

"He had a small misunderstanding with Mimi, and then he did the one thing you should never do around an angry goat. He turned his back on her, and, well," Grandma Faye shrugged, "he ended up face first in the mud. He had a quick shower at my place, but his clothes were ruined, and the only thing of mine that would fit him was my housecoat. It was either that or a towel."

This time, Madison didn't hold back her laughter.

"It's not funny!" Gideon shouted from the bathroom.

"Oh, yes it is," Grandma Faye shouted back as the three women dissolved into fits of laughter.

CHAPTER FIVE

Lizzie added a rain hat to the slicker and rubber boots she already had on before venturing back out into the storm. Grandma Faye had suggested Lizzie close up the coop and check to make sure the hens had enough feed and water before the storm got worse. The old woman had offered to do it, but Lizzie insisted on going out herself. In truth because she needed a few minutes alone to process what Grandma Faye had said earlier after their laughter had subsided. The three of them were going to have to weather the storm together in Lizzie's cottage.

While Gideon was taking a shower at Grandma Faye's place, the old woman had checked the emergency lines and discovered there had been reports of flash flooding and power outages all the way from Halcyon to Cherryville, and the ferries weren't running either due to the severity of the storm. Grandma Faye's original plan had been to collect Lizzie and Madison and spend the night at her place as her cabin was off-grid and the power outages wouldn't affect her place, but on the drive over to Lizzie's, it became apparent that the road was quickly becoming treacherous even with the help of magick. "

"So," Grandma Faye had announced matter-of-factly, "The safest thing to do is to hunker down here until the storm plays itself out and the ferries are back up and running."

It took a moment for what Grandma Faye had said to sink in before the back of Lizzie's neck started to burn, and she couldn't catch her breath. She needed some air and some distance, and securing the coop offered both.

As she navigated the short distance to the coop, her feet leaving deep impressions in the saturated ground, she slipped and fell to her knees just as she was reaching up to unlatch the door to the chicken run, soaking her pant legs. After shutting the hatch, she went around to the coop itself and through the larger door just to check on the hens. They were all warm and safe, either tucked up in their nesting boxes or perched on the roosting poles. She topped up their feed, but instead of heading back to the house, she took a seat on the metal feed barrel. The coop was surprisingly cozy, and the sound of the chickens humming and cooing mixed with the staccato rhythm of the rain beating on the tin roof was oddly soothing. She'd cleaned out the coop a few days earlier, and the air was redolent with the smell of the fresh straw lining the nesting boxes and pine shaving strewn across the floor.

Lizzie felt her shoulders slowly relax for the first time since she'd spied Gideon and Madison on her front porch. She closed her eyes and let her mind wander, hoping to work out the tangled emotions warring for dominance in her heart; the shock of seeing the two of them standing on her front porch after months of silence, the anger at being abandoned by the people she once considered family, the unexpected compassion that surged in her when she saw the raw grief in Madison's eyes over the death of her father and witnessing Madison's panic during the storm. Lizzie was beginning to realize just how much Madison had been through and was *still* going through.

She knew she couldn't hide out in the coop forever, and replaying the day wasn't going to stop the storm of emotions raging inside her. Reluctantly, she left the quiet comfort of her chickens and stepped back out into the rain, bolting the door behind her. She leaned back under the short overhang of the coop, hoping for a break in the wind gusts before making a dash for the cottage when she spotted movement out of the corner of her eye. It was the young apple tree swaying and bowing as the wind battered it relentlessly. She worried that it would get uprooted in the storm, but for now, it was upright.

She started to push off from the wall when a thought occurred to her. She looked from the young tree to the cottage and back again. The last thing she remembered before spotting Gideon and Madison on her porch was taking a break from planting the tree. She'd been sitting on the grass next to the sapling, looking down at her vegetable garden with a clear view of the front gate.

Her scalp prickled. She would have seen them pull up to the gate, but she hadn't. She'd only noticed the car when it had already been parked, pretty much where it stood now. And Gideon and Madison were already standing on her porch. So where had she been coming from, and what had she been doing?

More importantly, why couldn't she remember?

The sensible thing would be to get out of the storm and back to the cottage. But she couldn't let it go; like a too-stiff tag on the back of a T-shirt, the blank space in her mind scratched and poked at her, refusing to be ignored. In the past, when she'd experienced walking into a room only to forget why she'd come into it in the first place, the simple solution had been to retrace her steps, and inevitably, she'd remember what it was she'd gone into the room for. She hoped the same thing would hold true now.

She dashed across the yard, not towards the comfort of her cottage but towards the barn. She wasn't sure if that was where she'd been coming from, but it seemed like the obvious place.

The rain pounded down, making it hard to see. Rivulets had formed on the path up to the barn, washing away the sandy topsoil, exposing rocks, and leaving deep grooves in their wake. She slid around as the soles of her rubber boots failed to gain any purchase on the washboard ground, but she managed to make it to the barn without falling again. Turning the handle on the door, she let out a growl of frustration as a stream of rainwater made it past the upturned collar of her slicker, soaking her back. The rain had swollen the door in its frame. She shouldered it, but the bottom corner of the door held firm.

Stepping back to ground herself before calling up her magick, she stumbled into a puddle formed in the small depression in the ground. An electric jolt made her jump back. This was the exact spot where she'd found Audley's body face down in a similar puddle of rainwater. Lizzie looked down at her feet, scanning the soggy earth, trying to detect any evidence of where her handyman had lain, but there was only flattened down grass and small streams of rainwater washing down the path. Nothing remained of that night. She tried to recall the events around finding Audley lying lifeless on the ground, but the details were vague. She remembered begging someone to save Audley, she remembered a bright light and Grandma Faye, but they were only flashes of memory like they were held behind a gossamer curtain.

Squeezing her eyes shut, she quickly grounded herself and called up her magick. She opened her eyes as she flung her magick towards the door. It swung open with such force it bounced back against the doorframe but remained unstuck. She scrambled inside, leaving the door open to provide what little light was available from the darkened skies to light her way. She pawed at the wall until she located the light switch. She toggled the switch up, but there was only the sound of a soft, ineffectual click. She chided herself, remembering the power was out. Murky darkness surrounded her as she stood dripping water on the concrete floor, waiting for her memory to return. Nothing. Wood creaked as the wind battered against the timbers. As her eyes adjusted to the gloom, she could make out the layout of the space around her, although the corners disappeared into impenetrable darkness.

In front of her, on the wall hanging from hooks, were an

assortment of ancient-looking hand tools. She remembered that night, grabbing a pitchfork off the wall in her panic to defend herself, only to have the tines fall off the rotted wooden handle. She could see the empty hook where the pitchfork once was, but the broken tool was nowhere to be found. The floor around her was bare. To her left was a large center aisle that led to the opposite end of the barn with several box stalls on either side, plus a ladder leading up to the hayloft. She started to walk in that direction, but when the faint musk of pot hit her, she stopped in her tracks. She couldn't imagine she would have gone down that part of the barn as even now, the memory of waking up in the empty stall, tied up, her fate resting in the hands of Jon's henchmen, had a cold dread flooding her body. She shivered again.

When the Order had descended upon her property after the ordeal, and she was tucked safely away in the in-between while her body healed, they must have removed any evidence of the grow op that had been hidden below the barn, but they obviously could do nothing about the lingering aroma of what had been here.

Turning around, she wandered past the wall of tools, and for the first time, she noticed a door at the very end of the wall. She moved to the door and turned the handle. It turned stiffly in her hand, the hinges letting out a shivering creak as it opened. Beyond was the inky black of nightmares.

She conjured a blue ball of light in her left palm and flung it into the room, where it floated and bobbed about six feet off the ground. It cast its cold wintery light, allowing Lizzie to see that the room was empty. The floor was covered in a thick layer of undisturbed dust.

"This was a stupid idea," she muttered to herself. Not only did coming into the barn not trigger her memory from this morning, but she was now soaking wet and cold, and the only memories that rose up in the gloom of the barn were from that horrible night. She retraced her steps, the ball of light gently bobbing in front of her when the air around her shimmered, the edges of her vision rippling. The barn walls were undulating as if she were seeing the sturdy timbers and planking from deep underwater. A wave of dizziness engulfed her, and she bent over, hands on her thighs. Her nose filled with the smell of lemon polish and roses.

When the light-headedness passed, she slowly lifted her head and let out a yelp of surprise. She blinked furiously, willing her brain to comprehend what she was seeing. A warm light poured into the barn from a wall of glass where the solid wall had been moments before. All around her was a hive of activity as women she didn't recognize moved with purpose. But none of them seemed to notice her. Some of the women carried wooden boxes, others had baskets filled with produce and flowers scenting the air with the perfume of high summer, and still, others were empty-handed, but all of them were smiling and laughing. Whatever the women were preparing for, Lizzie could sense an air of celebration. A kaleidoscope of color danced across their faces as they moved around, and large pools of rainbow light danced across the floor, which was now not only clean but the concrete had been sealed and polished.

Lizzie looked up and discovered the source of the many-hued spots of light was an enormous chandelier, or perhaps it was a mobile. From a wire frame of copper hung what had to be hundreds of crystals of every color and shape. Four large ceiling fans hung at a slightly higher level moved the air, causing the mobile to slowly move and the crystals to dance and shiver.

Her pulse thumped at her temples, and she couldn't catch her breath.

"Lizzie, are you ready to go?" came a voice behind her. She spun around and spotted the young woman who'd spoken.

She cradled two leather-bound books in her arms, a wide smile on her face. She was looking past Lizzie and up towards the loft.

Birdie? It couldn't be, could it? It sounded like her and sort of looked like her, but a happier, more relaxed version. Gone was Birdie's signature thick kohl eyeliner, and she looked tanned and fit in a pale blue summer frock printed with what looked like birds of all things. But what stood out was the young woman's hair. Instead of the glossy black tresses Lizzie was used to seeing, Birdie's hair was a blinding white, except for one lock of black. The contrast between her youthful face and her snow-white hair gave her an otherworldly look.

"I'll be right down," someone answered from the hayloft. The sound of that voice made the hairs on the back of her neck stand on end. It was *her* voice. Lizzie slowly turned and looked up towards the loft and gasped. She was looking at herself, leaning over a hand-turned railing instead of the makeshift railing of two-by-fours that should be there. And instead of a wooden ladder leading to the second story, a proper staircase gently curved down to the main floor.

Just like Birdie, the other version of Lizzie looked happy, her skin sun-kissed, but unlike Birdie, her hair was still its original color. It was the other Lizzie's eyes that grabbed her attention; one was grey, the other golden. Before she had a chance to ponder what that meant, Bear, who had been standing next to the other Lizzie, thrust his head through the spindles and looked down. He turned his head, looking straight down at her, and barked, his tail wagging enthusiastically. He saw her.

"Bear?" Lizzie called up at him. He barked in reply, pulling his head back from in between the spindles and prancing towards the staircase.

"Lizzie, what are you doing in here?" Grandma Faye asked.

Lizzie spun around, expecting to see an older version of

Grandma Faye addressing the other Lizzie, who was now making her way down the stairs to join Birdie. But it was *her* Grandma Faye standing in the gloom of the empty barn, a look of concern on her face.

"I think I'm going to be sick," Lizzie mumbled, then bent over and retched onto the dusty floor. When her stomach stopped cramping, she wiped her mouth with the back of her hand, took a shaky step towards the door, then gave up and plopped clumsily onto the ground.

"What's happened? You'd been gone a long time, and when I went to see what was keeping you, you weren't in the coop." Grandma Faye crouched next to her.

"I'm not exactly sure."

"Why did you come in here?"

She vigorously scrubbed her face with her hands. "You're going to think I'm ridiculous, but I came out here to see if I could jog my memory?"

"Why? Have you forgotten something?"

"Yes, and it's really not that important, but it is driving me crazy that I can't remember what I was doing right before Gideon and Madison arrived. I first saw them when I was walking across the yard towards the cottage, so it makes sense that I had been in the barn or coming back from the forest. Anyway, I thought I would try the barn first and the woods after this stupid storm stops."

"And did it work?"

"No, in fact, something even stranger happened." She twisted around to look at the loft. It was just a hayloft, with a simple wooden ladder leading up it and rusted tools hung on the far wall. Turning back to Grandma Faye, she said, "I had decided to go back to the cottage when suddenly, it was like the air around me shivered, and then everything changed. It was a sunny day, and the front wall of the barn was all glass windows, and there were several people moving around down here, and then I saw Birdie."

"Birdie?"

Lizzie nodded. "She didn't look much older than she is now, but her hair was completely white, and I was struck by how happy she looked. But the weirdest part was I saw myself. Up there," She pointed behind her, "in the loft. I heard you call my name, and it all disappeared, and the barn was back to normal." Her fingers automatically sought out her necklace that wasn't there. She rubbed at her collarbone instead. "It was so real. I could feel the warmth of the sunlight coming through the windows and smell flowers and lemon polish." She searched the old woman's face for reassurance. "It felt so real."

"It sounds like you had a vision of the future or potential future."

"Potential future?"

"Our future isn't set in stone. It can change based on the decisions we make in the present."

Lizzie nodded her understanding.

"Have you had anything like this happen before?"

Shifting her weight, she curled her legs underneath her to find a more comfortable position on the hard floor. "No, never. But this is the first time I've been without my necklace. And I know Vivienne said without its enchantments holding down my powers, they would start to emerge, but it never occurred to me that it would include something like seeing into the future. I guess I assumed it would just mean having more power available to cast spells."

"It can be both." Grandma Faye placed a gentle hand on her shoulder. "You have such a natural ability to work with your energy. I forgot you've skipped the normal progression a witch goes through when they come into their power. It usually happens slowly, over time. The Order usually finds these people early and is able to train and teach them as their abilities emerge. You've had no time to be taught or to explore your capabilities with someone to guide you."

"Could my memory problems have to do with my abilities waking up? Could I be having trouble with my memory because there's just too much going on inside me right now?" She looked hopefully at Grandma Faye. She wanted desperately to be reassured that she wasn't losing her mind.

"It could explain it," Grandma Faye hesitated. "Is it just this morning you're having trouble remembering?"

Lizzie closed her eyes, thinking back over the past few weeks. She blew out a frustrated sigh when she felt yet another headache building behind her eyes. "I don't know," she said, rubbing her temples.

"You've been through lately, and there hasn't really been time for you to catch your breath and process everything." She hesitated. "And I take it you have a less than cordial relationship with Madison and Gideon."

"That's one way of putting it."

They were both startled when a flash of lightning lit up the gaps between the barn boards, the thunder that followed reverberating in the floor.

"We should probably head back to the cottage. I've left those two in charge of preparing dinner, and I'm not sure either of them knows their way around a kitchen. Do you feel steady enough to stand up?" Grandma Faye stood, shaking out the dust from her skirts.

"Yes, I actually feel fine now, missing time notwithstanding," she said, grasping Grandma Faye's outstretched hand and standing up.

Grandma Faye held tight to Lizzie's hand. "When we get back to the cottage, I'll make you up a tonic that may help. But you need to let me know if the forgetfulness persists or if you get your memory back from this morning."

"I will, I promise," she said, squeezing Grandma Faye's hand. "And thank you."

"For what?"

"For everything. I don't think I've told you how much I've appreciated everything you've done for me since I arrived here. And for being here now."

Grandma Faye waved away Lizzie's words. "That's what family does. We look after each other." A frown suddenly furrowed the old woman's brow, and she stepped back, holding Lizzie's arm out as she looked her up and down. "Lizzie dear, you look like you've been dragged through a hedge backwards. How did you manage to get so bedraggled in an empty barn?"

Lizzie looked down at herself. Her damp clothes were filthy. The dust from the barn now added to the mud from when she fell earlier. "I slipped and fell going to the chicken coop. But at least I didn't lose a fight with a goat."

Grandma Faye laughed as they both peered out the open door at the deluge outside. "How would you like your first lesson in magick? I'm thinking a simple rain-repelling spell?"

"I would like that a lot," Lizzie said, her throat suddenly tight with emotions. And so began Lizzie's formal training in magick. She followed Grandma Faye's instructions on casting the spell as a warmth bloomed in her chest and spread through her entire being. Not from the power the two women called forth, but from the simple word the old woman had spoken; family. Lizzie held the feeling close, protecting it like a precious gem as she stepped out with Grandma Faye into the storm, protected by magick, surrounded by love.

CHAPTER SIX

Dressed in clean, dry clothes and a pair of thick socks to ward off the chill that had settled in her bones, Lizzie stepped into the kitchen to the smell of frying bacon, her stomach growling. The sight greeting her clutched strangely at her heart, a strange mix of comfort and longing. A cheery fire crackled in the fireplace. Small golden orbs of magick, like strings of faerie lights, floated in swags along the walls of the cottage. Larger ones glowed in a row along the fireplace mantle, bathing Gideon in a warm glow as he sat on the edge of the sofa. He was dressed in jeans and a long-sleeved shirt. An old-fashioned rotary phone sat next to him, the receiver pressed tightly to his ear as he listened intently. Grandma Faye had dug up the telephonic relic at her place and brought it to Lizzie, knowing her cordless phone would be useless with the power out.

In the kitchen, the largest of the golden orbs hovered a few feet above the table where Madison and Grandma Faye were preparing food. Quinn perched on the back of Madison's chair, and Bear sat at her other side, both bird and dog following Madison's every move. Someone, Grandma Faye Lizzie suspected, had fired up the wood cookstove, adding to the homey warmth of the cottage.

The storm still raged outside, but inside the thick stone wall of her cottage, golden lights glowed, bacon sizzling on the woodstove scented the air, and her cottage was filled with people. The illusion was so strong she could almost believe she was looking at a homey family scene, even if she was unsure of Madison's and Gideon's place in her life and heart.

"It smells amazing in here. What can I do to help?"

"Nothing, Madison and I have things pretty much under control," Grandma Faye said as she stood at the table cracking eggs into a large earthenware bowl, while Madison sat at the head of the table grating cheese onto a plate, stopping occasionally to pluck a few orange curls from the plate to feed to the animals flanking her. Lizzie felt her own smile spreading across her face as she pulled out a chair and sat down.

"I hope you don't mind that I had a little rummage around in your kitchen," Grandma said briskly, whisking the eggs.

"I don't mind at all, especially seeing as you managed to conjure up a meal for four when I could have sworn I had nothing in my cupboards, and during a power outage, no less."

"It's nothing fancy, but I have yet to meet anyone who doesn't like eating breakfast for dinner." Grandma Faye stopped whisking the eggs and stepped over to the cookstove to flip the bacon. "How are you feeling?" She asked, turning from the stove.

"Fine."

Madison stopped grating the cheese and looked from Grandma Faye to Lizzie. "What happened? Did you hurt yourself when you fell outside?"

Instead of feeling any warmth at Madison's concern, a spike of irritation tightened Lizzie's shoulders. Where was this concern for her well-being six months ago, when what she really needed was for Madison to be there for her? "It's nothing. When I went to check on the chickens, I had a little dizzy spell. Probably just low blood sugar from not eating all day."

"That reminds me," Grandma Faye said, moving to the kitchen counter to retrieve a glass containing a few ounces of amber liquid. "I've mixed that tonic for you. You had most of the herbs I needed to make it in your cupboards. The rest I took from around the cottage." She handed the glass to Lizzie and took a seat at the table.

"It's best if it is allowed to steep for a day or two, so I've infused it with a charm to boost its efficacy. But there is nothing I can do to mask the bitterness. It's best if you just drink it down in one shot."

"Thank you," Lizzie said, raising the glass to her lips. She hesitated for a second when the strong medicinal smell hit her, then squeezed her eyes shut and swallowed it down in one gulp. "Phew, you weren't kidding," Lizzie gasped, shaking her head. The astringent taste made her eyes water. She swiped at them with her sleeve to clear her vision.

"What does it do?" Madison asked, eyeing the empty glass.

"Helps reset the body during a stressful time or after a shock. Also helps in getting a good night's rest."

"Is it only for physical stress?"

"No, it's also very helpful for emotional trauma. I could make up a dose for you if you'd like."

"No, no, I wasn't asking for myself. I was just curious," Madison said hastily, then picked up the grater, focusing her attention on adding to the mountain of cheese already grated on the plate.

"Argh," Gideon groaned, slamming the receiver down with a bang. He leaned his forearms on his knees and hung his head.

"Gideon, I told you the ferries wouldn't arrive until morning at the earliest," Grandma Faye said as she moved to the stove, transferring the bacon to a plate, then sliding the plate into the warming drawer at the top of the stove. "And you calling the information line every few minutes isn't going to change that." She retrieved the bowl of sliced potatoes and onions, adding them to the frying pan.

"There must be another way to get back onto the highway other than the ferries. I'd look it up myself, but I can't get cell service in this stupid backwater town." Gideon raised his head, running his fingers through his hair.

Lizzie bristled at his words but kept her mouth shut. She wasn't happy that he was going to have to spend the night in her cottage either, but there was nothing anyone could do about that.

Madison let out an exasperated sigh and rolled her eyes. "He's been dialing that information line over and over since Grandma Faye plugged in the phone. He thinks if he keeps calling, somehow the recording will have changed in the last 30 seconds from the last time he called."

Grandma Faye turned slowly from the stove, a wooden spoon she was using to stir the potatoes in her hand. "The fastest route to Kelowna is by taking the ferry to the highway, which isn't an option. The only other way is to drive six hours in the opposite direction, making your trip a twelve-hour journey. And there is no way of knowing if the roads are even passable with this amount of rain. You've seen what the rain has done to the driveway outside." She brandished her wooden spoon, jabbing the air to make her point. "Nor will I allow you to drive twelve hours by yourself in which more than half of it will be in the dark on unfamiliar roads. Then there's the Monashee. That mountain pass is not for the faint-hearted, and you won't have cell service through that stretch of road. And no amount of magick will help you if you take a switchback too fast and plunge off the mountainside. You," she jabbed the spoon in Gideon's direction, "will be spending the night here with us: end of discussion. And besides, this will give us more time to catch up, and I can tell you more stories about your father," she said, her tone softening.

"Wait, how far is it to Nelson?" Gideon asked as if he hadn't heard a word Grandma Faye had said. "The Order has a helicopter pad. If I call them now, I may be able to charter a flight."

Grandma Faye put a hand on her hip, but before she could say anything, Madison burst out laughing. "Oh, Gideon, I doubt very much the Order is going to authorize the use of their helicopter just so you can keep your date with Annabelle, even if you are Vivienne's son."

"What are you talking about?" Gideon spluttered. "I don't have a date with Annabelle. She's an archivist and is part of the conference in Vancouver. I agreed to pick her up as it's on my way. Nothing more."

"Oh please, my whole training section knew you had the hots for her by the time she and her parents finished touring the mother house this spring. How could we not, with you following her around like a puppy, giving her moon eyes the whole time."

Gideon's face went a deep crimson. He looked wildly around as if trying to find an escape route.

Lizzie felt like she was a step behind. She'd thought Madison and Gideon were an item. Wasn't it Vivienne who had said as much when she'd talked to her shortly after arriving in Barton? Could she have misunderstood? And if they'd broken up, why was Madison acting more like — like a little sister teasing her brother than an ex-girlfriend?

"Well," Grandma Faye said softly, turning back to the stove, "now I understand your urgency." Over her shoulder, she looked at Gideon, pointing her wooden spoon at him again. "But you're still not going. If this Annabelle shares your feelings, then she would understand why you have to reschedule your date, and if she doesn't, then she's not worth risking your life over.

"Fine," he said to Grandma Faye, then turned to Madison. "And I was not following her around like a puppy. And what are moon eyes? What a stupid saying. It doesn't make any sense."

Madison laced her fingers under her chin and tilting her head up to Gideon, she opened her eyes wide.

"Oh, moon eyes," Lizzie bit down on an unexpected laugh, "Now I get it."

"Cut it out," he said in exasperation, his face turning an

even darker shade of red.

"In my day, we called that look making cow eyes," Grandma Faye said.

"Grandma Faye!" Gideon exclaimed.

Grandma Faye chuckled. "Don't get mad at me. I wasn't the one making cow eyes at a young lady. Speaking of which, why don't you call this Annabelle person to let her know what's going on so we can sit down to dinner before the potatoes get overcooked?" Her lips curled up in a smile again.

"I would, but there's no cell service out here. And we're not supposed to call another member of the Order on an unsecured line. So now she's going to think I stood her up."

"You can call her on that," Grandma Faye said, pointing to the phone next to Gideon. "It doesn't have your fancy encryption tech, but the spell I placed on it works just as well."

He picked up the receiver but didn't dial the number. Instead, he just looked around the kitchen at the three women, all of whom were now staring back at him. Lizzie surprised herself when she not only felt a little sorry for him but said, "You are more than welcome to use my bedroom if you want some privacy. There's a phone jack next to the nightstand."

"Thanks," he said with relief. Unplugging the phone and cradling it in his arms, he dashed down the hallway.

"Don't be too long. Dinner will be ready in about twenty minutes," Grandma Faye called out.

"Yeah, Gideon, don't keep us waiting. I'm starving," Madison cupped her hands to her mouth and shouted, "Moooo — ve it along, little doggy."

"Shut up!" Gideon yelled from down the hall.

Lizzie threw back her head and let out a surprisingly accurate imitation of a mournful low.

Madison's eyes went wide before she burst into giggles. The three women were laughing so hard none of them heard the door to the bedroom slam shut.

***

It was almost midnight when Lizzie let Bear out in the yard before she turned in for the night. The others had gone to bed an hour ago. The sleeping arrangements, much to Lizzie's relief, had been decided by Madison of all people, and everyone had agreed without any argument. Madison and Grandma Faye were sharing the queen-sized bed in Lizzie's room, Gideon took the antique bed up in the loft, and Lizzie happily agreed to sleep on the couch in the living room.

She wanted Gideon to be as far away as possible from Bear. Even with the storm, she didn't trust him to be alone with her dog. Also, she didn't want to share a bed with anyone. She wanted time to think and to process the strangeness of the day, including, surprisingly, how much she'd enjoyed the evening. Even though there were moments where her old resentments rose up as she watched the ease and familiarity in which Madison and Gideon interacted and a few awkward silences when the conversation stalled overall, she'd actually enjoyed the meal and the company. It helped that Grandma Faye kept the conversation going, recounting stories of Gideon's father as a young boy and her time with him. Grandma Faye, it turned out, was an amazing storyteller, and Lizzie found herself being swept up in her tales, only feeling a slight twinge of guilt that she'd never bothered to ask the woman sitting across from her about her past.

Bear's aversion to getting wet meant he went quickly about his business and just as quickly stepped back inside when Lizzie opened the door for him. She didn't follow but lingered on the porch, watching the lightning flash in the night sky. With everyone asleep, her thoughts returned to the strangeness of the storm. She'd forgotten to ask Grandma Faye about it. Stifling a yawn, she followed Bear inside, making a mental note to ask Grandma Faye about the storm in the morning.

CHAPTER SEVEN

Lizzie perched on the front porch step with her morning coffee, surveying the storm damage while Bear and Quinn played their stick game on the wet grass that had been pummeled flat by the rain. The forest beyond sparkled with moisture, still clinging to the needles and branches. She couldn't spot any downed trees, but she knew she'd have to walk her property to be sure, but that could wait. Even the chicken coop and its residents had come through the storm unscathed. When she'd let her chickens out earlier, they happily set about eating their morning feed she'd scattered in their run. And just as important as her chickens, the apple sapling was intact, standing straight and true, much to Lizzie's relief. The only real damage was to the path leading to the barn and her driveway, except where Grandma Faye's truck had been, the rain having carved deep runnels in the sand.

Tipping her head back, she let the morning sun warm her face as she breathed in a lungful of clean, watery, scented air. Lizzie raised her cup to her lips, the aroma of strong black coffee filling her senses before she took a careful sip.

Cowboy coffee, Grandma Faye had called it. The old woman had been the first one up, heading straight to the cookstove, expertly bringing the banked coals to life. Lizzie joined her in the kitchen, momentarily dismayed to find the power still out and at a loss as to how to make her much needed morning coffee without a proper heatproof coffee pot, having only an electric drip coffeemaker. Grandma Faye had waved away Lizzie's concern and filled a pot with water and coffee grounds, setting it on the stove to boil. The resulting coffee was surprisingly good.

Before Grandma Faye nipped back to her place to feed and

let out her own animals, she'd peppered Lizzie with questions on how she was feeling, how she'd slept, and if she'd gotten her missing memories back. Lizzie hadn't been completely truthful with Grandma Faye when she'd said she felt fine. Although she'd slept well after taking the nerve tonic, and she hadn't experienced any more missing blocks of time, nor had she had any more visions, she still felt something was off deep inside herself. And she still couldn't remember what she'd been doing before Gideon and Madison had arrived.

Seeing first-hand how trauma affected Madison, she could easily explain the oddness she felt as her particular response to the recent events in her own life. She'd been physically assaulted more than once, drugged, kidnapped, shot, and witnessed the death of Audley, her handyman. But that rationalization just didn't feel right to her, no matter how many times she tried to convince herself. Not knowing why she felt wrong inside just added a layer of frustration to her already overburdened thoughts.

Satisfied with Lizzie's answers, Grandma Faye announced it was time for Lizzie's second lesson in magick.

"Your driveway was so rain-soaked yesterday, even with Gideon and I using magick to get us up to the cottage, my truck is sitting in some fairly deep ruts. How would you go about getting it unstuck?" Grandma Faye asked, the two of them standing near the front tires.

"Could you use a levitation spell to lift the tires out?"

"It's possible, but it would take a great deal of magick and focus. You'd have to have years of experience to harness that kind of magick, and even then, it would be draining. That truck weighs quite a bit."

Lizzie pondered what Grandma Faye had said as she circled around the truck.

"So, if it's not levitating the truck, what if you shifted the sand?"

"You've almost got it. Shifting the sand wouldn't be enough force to budge those tires up and out because you're still dealing with the weight of the vehicle. At least not using your magick alone and a spell, which is what you used to cast the rain repel spell. For this, we are going to use Elemental Magick." Grandma Faye stood with her feet apart, her arms out in front of her, palms facing up. "Your ability to see a magick will make this so much easier to explain." She called up her magick into her palms. "What color do you see?"

"Green, a beautiful apple green."

"And why is my power that color?"

Lizzie didn't know why she'd never considered the question before, as almost from the start of her powers emerging, she could see the color of magick as it was being wielded, and everyone she'd seen cast had a different color. "Oh, it has something to do with the earth element."

"Correct. Each witch, as they come into their full power, will find she or he has a particular affinity to one of the four elements. The elements feel it, too. They're attracted to that alignment, and when they sense the person is ready, they will invite the witch to bond with it. That bond strengthens every spell and enchantment we cast, but it also allows us a special relationship with that particular element."

"Has there ever been an instance where a witch has never bonded?"

"Not that I know of, but a witch doesn't have to accept the invitation once it is offered, so I guess technically there could be a witch who hasn't bonded, but it would be because they chose not to, not because the elements refused."

Lizzie nodded her understanding.

"Back to the truck. What I am going to do is connect with the sand in the driveway by sending my energy to it. Once the connection is made, I ask for what I would like to have happen using a language we both understand." Grandma Faye turned her palms to face the ground.

Lizzie could see Grandma Faye's energy shoot out and down into the sand around the truck. Then, the old woman began to draw a sigil in the air. Lizzie saw the symbol take shape in the air in front of Grandma Faye—it shimmered green and then dissolved.

"Sigils are a type of language, a symbolic and energetic one that the elements understand. So, I have asked for the sand to help. The symbol roughly equates with releasing or getting something unstuck. Now, I am also sending my intention of what I would like to have happen because it never hurts to add as much detail of what you need as possible because you have no control over what the sand is going to choose to do to help or if they will help at all. Now we wait for a response."

Lizzie focused on the sand around the tires. It lit up briefly with a sparkling green energy, and then the golden web she'd seen when she'd first arrived at Rose Cottage came alive. She watched the interplay of energy not just between Grandma Faye and the ground but with Gaia herself.

"Oh," she gasped as the earth shifted under the tires of the truck, gently raising it up, the sand flattening out underneath each tire. "The sand pulled energy from the earth herself to boost their own power so they could lift the truck and rearrange themselves underneath it."

Grandma Faye smiled broadly. "Exactly. Now, before we release the connection, we give thanks for their assistance. You must always remember they do not work for us. This is an equal partnership and one built on respect and gratitude." She placed her palms together in prayer and bowed her head.

Lizzie felt the warmth and gratitude flowing from the old woman into the earth and was surprised and delighted when she felt the earth respond back.

Bear barked, chasing after Quinn, who now had the stick, the sound bringing Lizzie back to the present. Putting her coffee down on the step next to her, she looked at the palms of her hands and then up at the driveway. The once hard-packed sand was rippled with deeper groves where Grandma Faye's truck had driven up the night before.

She called up her magick, the blue orbs strong and clear in the palms of her hands. She sent her energy down and *felt* into the sand itself. When a corresponding resonance reached out and touched her own power, she let out a startled laugh and deepened the connection.

"Now what?" she whispered under her breath. The sigil Grandma Faye had shown her was to unstick something. But that wasn't what she wanted to do. She wanted the level out the driveway. Quickly glancing over her shoulder to make sure she was still alone, she then spoke to the sand. "Good morning. That was quite the storm we had last night." She thought she felt a change in the vibration, like the sand was responding. She felt a bit foolish talking to sand, but in for a penny in for a pound, as Sister Collette would have said. "I would like the driveway to be smooth again like it was before all the rain. Do you think we could work together to do that?" Her power shifted suddenly, its clear blue color morphing into a bright green just as she felt the responding ripple of energy from the sand. Her pulse raced with excitement, but as minutes ticked by, the sand didn't shift or levitate, nor did she feel the sand connect with Gaia like it had for Grandma Faye. The driveway remained as it was. "Well, it was worth a try. Thanks anyway," she said softly, trying to keep the disappointment out of her voice. She pulled back her energy, which had returned to its familiar blue color. This was the second time her energy had changed color. She was pretty sure that just before she had the vision in the barn, her magick had changed to a bright yellow.

Retrieving her cup from the stoop, she took a large gulp. She needed to ask Grandma Faye what this meant. She hadn't mentioned to Lizzie that her energy would change. But is that the process of the elements checking her out to see if they wanted to bond with her? Could that be affecting her memory, too?

The breeze shifted suddenly, bringing down the comforting smell of wood smoke from the chimney above her. Steam began to rise in curling wisps from the water-logged earth as the sun's heat penetrated the ground. They looked like eerie phantoms escaping their underground lairs to dance in the sun before disappearing into the ether. Despite the warmth of the sun, a shiver raced from the top of her head and down her spine.

She was about to head inside to refresh her coffee when she heard someone moving around inside the cottage. Her time alone was over. Annoyance slithered in around her heart, filling her limbs with a static-y restlessness. She shifted around to face the open door just as Gideon stepped out onto the porch, a cup of coffee in his hand.

"Good morning."

"Morning," he mumbled as he shuffled across the porch. His hair stuck out at odd angles, and he rubbed his eyes one-handed, holding his own mug of coffee in the other.

"Is Madison awake?" She asked hopefully, not wanting to spend any time alone with Gideon, whose past actions still confused and angered her.

He leaned his forearms on the railing, head hanging over the steaming mug he cradled in his hands. Keeping his head down, he replied, "No, still sleeping. At least someone got a good night's rest. That storm just wouldn't quit. Between the noise of the rain on the roof and the thunder, I hardly slept at all." He yawned loudly, then took a sip of his coffee. "Do you have any cream for this?" He spluttered, his face contorting in a grimace.

"Sorry, no," she replied evenly, gripping her own mug tightly. "I take it black, and I wasn't expecting visitors, so I didn't think to pick any up on my last trip into town. And nothing would be open at this time of day."

He looked at Lizzie, confused, then down at his cup. "Do you at least have any milk?"

"Nope, you're just going to have to make do. Or you could drive over to Grandma Faye's and ask Mimi if she'd give you some." Lizzie took a huge swig of coffee to hide her smile.

"Ha ha, very funny." Gideon put his mug down on the railing. Raising his arms above his head, he arched his back in a stretch, then stood with his hands on his hips looking out into the yard, just as Bear and Quinn disappeared behind the chicken coop, still battling over the stick.

"Grandma Faye's gone?" he asked, the disappointment clear in his voice when he noticed the empty space where her truck should be. "She didn't wait to say goodbye?"

"She just went home to let out her animals. And she mentioned before she left that the ferries are running again. She's coming back to make your favorite breakfast. Something she called Battered Beasts?"

"Battered Beasts? Oh," he chuckled, his face lighting up, "I remember now. She used to make me pancakes in the shape of magickal creatures; unicorns, dragons, griffins. I called them battered beasts as in pancake batter." Gideon looked off into the middle distance.

"I'm happy for you. That the two of you reconnected after all this time." She genuinely meant what she said.

"Me too," Gideon beamed, continuing to look off into the treeline. "I hope she gets back soon. I'd like to head off as soon as possible."

Lizzie shifted positions on the step, unwilling to say she hadn't decided if Madison could stay or not, when she noticed the driveway. Stifling a gasp, she leaned forward, scanning the driveway. It was pristine, with no ruts or gouges, just smooth, hard-packed sand.

"Thank you."

"For what?" Gideon asked, turning to look at her.

She didn't think she'd spoken aloud, but the expectant look on Gideon's face told her otherwise. "Umh." She searched frantically for something she would want to thank him for. "I meant to thank you earlier for—for finding the counter spell for the binding placed in my cellar."

"What are you talking about?"

"The scroll you found in the archives. You know, the one containing the counter spell allowing me to release the spirit who was trapped there."

"Oh, that. I never got around to looking into it. That's when the increase in dark energy started happening, and I had other things that took priority."

"Then where did it come from?" Lizzie slowly lowered her coffee cup onto the porch beside her.

"I could take a look at it if you want. All of our archival documents have magickal watermarks placed on them, so I can tell you which archives they came from. From there, we could trace who sent it to you."

"I don't have it anymore. Vivienne must have taken it back with her after she and the Order had finished placing the wards around my property. I'll give her a call later and thank her." It could have been Vivienne or some other member who had taken the scroll back with them, but that didn't explain who put it in her cottage to begin with. Yet another memory she was unclear of. Lizzie could feel the beginning of a headache behind her eyes.

Just then, Quinn exploded from around the other side of the coop, flying low and fast, a blur of black feathers flashing iridescent in the light, a stick clamped firmly in his beak. Bear was hot on his tail, his hitching gait not slowing him down. When he was mere inches from Quinn's tail feathers, the raven swooped upwards out of his reach, soaring higher with each powerful beat of his wings. Lizzie craned her neck to follow his trajectory, marveling at Quinn's swiftness, when suddenly, he stopped. From Lizzie's viewpoint, it looked like he was suspended in the air, not hovering, not flying, but as if he'd stopped time itself. Then, just before he hurtled himself down to earth, he flicked his head back, releasing the stick. It flew off in a wide arc as Quinn plummeted to the ground in a spiral, aiming for Bear's head.

"Better luck next time," Lizzie shouted to her dog. Bear glanced at her, then at the stick plunging to the ground, and just before Quinn made contact with Bear's head, her dog disappeared.

She let out a startled laugh when Bear instantly appeared right below the stick. Before it hit the ground, he simply opened his mouth, clamping his teeth around it, then took off running towards the barn, Quinn flying after him, cawing loudly.

"How?" Gideon stuttered, "How did he do that?" He raced down the porch step, his eyes intense.

"I already told you," Lizzie said, standing up. "I accidentally gave him some of my power when I healed him."

"No," he said, waving his hand dismissively as he took another step down. "That's not what I meant. How did he calculate the angle of the trajectory of the stick so that he could reappear at just the right spot? And if it is like what Madison speculated, how is he creating portals at both ends in such a short time and with such accuracy?" He took another step down, looking off towards the barn where the two animals had disappeared. Bear's barking carrying down to the cottage.

"I don't know."

"But don't you want to?"

"Of course I do, but it's not like I could just ask him."

"And that's why he needs to be studied at our labs. The

magick techs could run tests, take samples, and run computer models. They could figure out how he does it and what he is actually doing. Your dog is the first one we know of in modern times. I have to take him back with me."

Lizzie blinked hard several times, her fingertips buzzing. "Absolutely not. I've already told you, Bear is not going anywhere, and you are not going to tell anyone in the Order he exists."

"Why can't you grasp the importance of this discovery? It could expand our understanding of magick and its existence in this world. All we have are written accounts of magickal animals, and you have an actual living specimen."

"Bear. Is. Not. A. Specimen," Lizzie spat out, clenching her hands. "I was given a choice whether or not I wanted to stay in your organization. And I chose to leave, to come here. If you had your way, Bear wouldn't be given that choice. And if you locked him up, took him away from here, how are you going to stop him from using his magick to come back home? How far would *your* people go to keep him in your labs?" Anger sang in her veins. "And just because Bear doesn't have a human voice doesn't make him any less sentient or deserving of freedom. He's not a thing. He's my friend." Gideon tried to interrupt, but Lizzie talked over him, raising her voice. "And what happened to all those ancient magickal creatures documented in your books?" She stomped down the steps to stand face-to-face with him. "How did they die out?"

Gideon crossed his arms over his chest.

"Answer my question, Gideon, how did they die?"

"They were either hunted for specimens or died in captivity," he mumbled.

"Exactly. As long as I am breathing, you and the Order will *never* get your hands on him. And you," she said, poking him in the chest, blood pounding at her temples, "will never speak of his existence to anyone. Do I make myself clear?"

"Whoa, calm down," Gideon said, holding out his hands and backing up the stairs in retreat.

"Don't you dare tell me to calm down." Rage seared white hot in her chest. She started forward after him, but Bear appeared, blocking her path, leaning his considerable weight into her legs.

"Well, you need to. You're allowing your emotions to cloud your judgement. And if you aren't going to listen to reason…."

"You need to leave now!" She shouted, cutting him off. A red haze clouded her vision as she shot out her hands. Crimson orbs, sparking erratically, glowed in her hands. Instead of responding, Gideon shifted his weight to his back leg, bent his knees, and brought his hands up, palms facing her.

"Get your stuff and get off my property before I—"

"Before you what, Lizzie," Gideon yelled back, instantly calling up his magick, "put me in a coma like you did to Richard?"

His words struck her like a slap, penetrating her rage. She stumbled back in shock, her hands flying to her throat.

"No," she cried. The look on Gideon's face made her turn and run from him. Bear followed fast on her heels. For it wasn't anger she saw reflected in his eyes, but fear.

CHAPTER EIGHT

He trailed behind her as she stumbled blindly through the trees. He knew where she was going even if she didn't; the stones always called to her when her need was great. His nostrils flared, and the back of his throat burned from the acrid scent of her fear. She tripped, stepping into the stone circle, and fell hard on her hands and knees. Checking to make sure she hadn't injured herself, he prodded her gently until she sat up. When she wrapped her arms around him in a fierce hug, he wiped her tears away, the hot iron tang burning the tip of his tongue.

He waited by her side until the tears played themselves out, and the soothing resonance of the ground beneath them worked its magick on her frayed nerves. When she lowered herself onto the damp grass, he joined her, nestling the bulk of his body into the curve of hers, and waited. He waited until he felt the rise and fall of her breath against his back syncopate with the lullaby of the earth.

He waited until he heard Gideon's vehicle roar down the driveway before he stood up. He cocked his head, listening intently. He could hear Madison moving about in the cottage, anxiously pacing back and forth. The last thing he needed was for Madison to come looking for Lizzie and find them, or worse, seeing where he went and following. Rising to his full height, he summoned his powers, and when they'd reached their zenith, he dropped to all fours, sending out a wave of energy. It rippled outward, stopping just outside the stones.

Satisfied, Bear glanced down at Lizzie's sleeping form. He'd failed to protect her, realizing too late what had been done to her. In time, he was sure he'd be able to safely restore her memory, but after what Quinn had told him, he'd discovered last night, Bear no longer had that luxury. The darkness had found them and was closing in. If he was to fulfill his sacred duty, he needed to act fast. He knew there was a chance he'd not return, but to protect Lizzie and the rest of humanity, it was a risk he was more than willing to take. With a nod to Quinn, he turned, striding purposefully to the center of the circle, then disappeared.

CHAPTER NINE

Lizzie sat up, uncertain as to what had jolted her awake. She quickly scanned her surroundings. "You have got to be kidding me," she growled, standing up and brushing at her pant legs in vain. "So now I can add taking naps on the forest floor to lapses in my memory and having visions," she said to Quinn, stomping over to where he was perched on a nearby branch.

Shivering, she let out a frustrated sigh, looking in the direction of the cottage. "I suppose we should go back." She needed to change out of her wet clothes, and if Gideon hadn't heeded her warning, she was going to have to have it out with him *again*. Her eyes were gritty and swollen. What Gideon had said echoed in her head, making her eyes burn with fresh tears.

His words were weapons enough, but the man who'd once protected her, whom she'd had once felt an attraction to, had also been ready to use his powers against her. Against *her*. She rubbed her temples, trying to clear her thoughts. She couldn't shake the feeling that something was off, more than just being upset with Gideon. What had she done or said to make him resort to such cruelty?

She'd been so angry everything had been awash in a haze of red, the whole argument a blur, except for the fear she'd seen in his eyes. That look was etched in her memory. And then she'd run away like a child, too scared and hurt to face the situation head-on.

She looked around for Bear, trying to shake off the strange, empty sensation growing in her chest. This was *her* home, and if Gideon hadn't left yet, she would deal with him without losing her temper. If she was lucky, he was already gone. If not, perhaps

Grandma Faye had returned, and at least she would have her calming presence as a buffer.

"Bear, come. It's time to go." She waited a beat, expecting to hear him moving through the underbrush, but all she heard was a lone thrush calling through the trees. "Bear, playtime is over. Come on, let's go inside and get you some breakfast." She scanned the forest for a glimpse of his white and buff fur, but he was nowhere in sight. "Bear," she yelled, her voice cracking, "Bear, come!"

Her heart hammered in her chest. The off-kilter sensation she felt wasn't from her fight with Gideon, but because something was missing from deep inside her, a connection that was so much a part of her, she didn't realize it until it was no longer there.

She raced towards the cottage, pushing her powers farther out, desperately trying to detect even a faint signature of her dog. By the time she'd reached the driveway, tears of panic blurred her vision. Lizzie froze in her tracks and let out an anguished scream. Gideon's car was gone.

Madison flew down the porch steps, the oversized grey cardigan flaring out behind her like a cloak. Under it, she wore only a large t-shirt, her bare legs ending in fluffy pink slippers. "What's happened?" She smelled of sleep. "Are you hurt?"

"When did Gideon leave?" Lizzie demanded, cutting her off.

Madison blinked at her in confusion. Lizzie grabbed her by the shoulders and shook her, "Answer me, Madison! When did he leave?"

"I don't know, I wasn't looking at the clock. Forty-five minutes? An hour ago? I'm not sure." She shrugged off Lizzie's grip and took a step back. "What's going on? Gideon woke me up to tell me he was leaving, that you ordered him to go. Is that true?"

"Maybe I could catch him at the ferry."

"Or he might still be at Grandma Faye's." Madison put her hands on her hips, blocking Lizzie's path. "He said he was going to say goodbye to her before he drove to the ferry." Madison stood her ground. "What happened between the two of you?"

"Then I still have a chance to stop him." Lizzie shoved Madison aside and raced into the house.

"Hey, there's no need to push," she exclaimed, following Lizzie inside, her slippers thwapping on the hardwood floor. "Tell me what's going on," she insisted.

"Gideon's stolen Bear. My keys, where are my car keys?" Lizzie frantically checked the pockets of her coat that hung by the front door, but came up empty-handed. "Gideon's kidnapped Bear." She was heading for the mudroom to check her other jackets when she spied the phone. She quickly dialed Grandma Faye's number, her hand shaking as she punched the keypad.

"Pick up, pick up," Lizzie chanted as the phone continued to ring. When the call went to voicemail, she slammed the receiver down and turned to head to the mudroom.

"Gideon didn't take Bear," Madison said, blocking Lizzie's path again.

"You heard what Gideon said about taking him to the Order so they could study him. He started in again about that this morning. That's why I told him to leave. And now Gideon is gone, Bear is gone. Who else would have taken him?"

"I don't know, but it wasn't Gideon," said Madison. "I followed him out to the car, and I was there when he put his suitcase in the back. The lift gate was open, and I could see all the way through to the front. Bear was not in there. Gideon was alone when he left."

"He could have put Bear in the car before he woke you and cloaked Bear with an invisibility ward." Lizzie had seen Gideon use such a ward in the past when he had been protecting her.

"He didn't use a ward."

"How would you know? You barely have any magick."

"I would have sensed it. It's one of the first things they train you in. Which you would have known if you'd joined. And my magick has gotten stronger."

"I don't have time for this. I need to find my keys."

"And speaking of wards, yours would have stopped Gideon from taking your dog. I'm assuming you included Bear in the protection spell."

Lizzie's eyes widened in surprise.

"Yes, I know about the wards on your property because, like I've just told you, I'm trained to detect them," she shot back.

Lizzie was about to push past Madison when the familiar rattling cough of Grandma Faye's ancient truck drifted through the open door. She raced outside, flinging open the driver's side door before Grandma Faye had even shut off the engine.

"I need your help. We have to stop Gideon. He's kidnapped Bear, and I can't find my car keys. We need to go, now." Lizzie's words spilled out in a torrent.

"Whoa, slow down," the old woman said as she stepped nimbly down from the cab of the truck, "Your energy is zipping around like an angry bee in a bottle." She gently placed a hand on Lizzie's arm. "Take a breath and start at the beginning. Why do you think Gideon has taken Bear?"

"But he didn't because her wards wouldn't have allowed him to," Madison insisted before Lizzie had a chance to speak. "I keep trying to tell her, but she won't listen."

"Of course, you'd take his side."

"And what is that supposed to mean?"

"Do I have to spell it out for you?"

"Ladies, enough. If Bear has gone missing, you two sniping at each other isn't going to help." She turned to Lizzie. "Now tell me why you think it was Gideon who took Bear?"

"As soon as Gideon saw what Bear could do, he's been

obsessed about taking him to the Order's labs to be studied. This morning, he started in on it again. We argued, and that's when I told him to leave. Bear was with me in the forest, but when I woke up, he was gone." Her heart pounded in her throat, making it difficult to breathe. Tears slipped down her cheeks. "I can't feel him here," she said, pressing a hand to her chest, "I can't feel him anymore."

"Madison is right about the wards. He wouldn't have been able to take Bear off the property, and I can say without a doubt Bear wasn't in Gideon's car because he'd stopped by my place before catching the ferry." Grandma Faye paused. "Did you say you *woke up* in the forest, and that's when you noticed Bear was gone?"

Lizzie nodded her head as tears continued to track down her cheeks, the hollowness inside her growing.

"Did you faint or have another episode like in the barn?"

"No," she said impatiently, "I didn't pass out, and I didn't have another vision. I was pissed off at Gideon, and I just wanted to get away, so I ran into the forest, and Bear followed me," Lizzie faltered. Why did she go to sleep on the wet ground when she wasn't feeling tired? She was angry and very much awake when she'd stalked off into the forest. A prickle of fear seared a band of heat across the back of her neck. "I don't remember lying down, just waking up, and Bear was gone. Something happened to him. I can't feel my connection to him anymore. He could be seriously injured or dead, and we're wasting time standing around talking." Lizzie turned on her heels and ran back towards the trees

Grandma Faye caught up to her just as she entered the forest. "He is not dead. I don't know why you can't feel him right now, but the one thing I do know for sure is he's still alive," the old woman said, easily keeping pace with Lizzie, the tiny bells she always wore around her ankles chiming with each step.

"How do you know?" Lizzie asked, sparing Grandma Faye a sideways glance as they continued deeper into the forest.

"Because if Bear were dead, the moment his spirit left his body, the magick you gave him would return to you. And you would know, without question, if that had happened even if you'd been asleep."

"But maybe I did feel it, and that's what woke me up." Her grief threatened to swallow her whole, so she focused on the ground ahead.

"No, you would know without a doubt. You wouldn't have thought that Gideon had taken him. You would've known in every fiber of your being." When Lizzie didn't reply, Grandma Faye grabbed her arm, stopping her in her tracks. "Do. You. Understand. Me?" The old woman punctuated each word with a firm squeeze of Lizzie's arm.

Only when Lizzie nodded did Grandma Faye release her grip on Lizzie's arm.

"Wait up, you two, I can't run in these stupid slippers," Madison called out from behind them.

A prickle of irritation bloomed on the back of Lizzie's neck when Grandma Faye turned and retraced her steps back through the trees. Lizzie was about to go on without them when she heard Grandma Faye's belled anklets chiming closer again, and then she spotted the old woman with Madison trailing behind her, holding her soggy slippers in her hands.

"You should have stayed back at the cottage."

"But I can help."

"How, by slowing us down?" Lizzie didn't wait for Madison to reply and pushed through the trees, calling Bear's name.

The stone circle was empty, but not the trees surrounding the clearing. Quinn was where she'd left him in his perch high up in a tree, but now he was joined with hundreds of his kin.

They roosted in the trees surrounding the stone circle, all their attention focused at its center, dark sentinels watching and waiting. A shiver of déjà vu passed down her spine.

"Is this where you saw—" Madison trailed off as she caught up with the other two women, her eyes wide. Stepping further into the clearing, she craned her head up at the black birds that hung like strange fruit on the boughs of every tree.

"I've never seen anything like this, have you?" Madison said, awestruck.

"No," replied Grandma Faye.

"Yes," said Lizzie at the same time.

Madison and Grandma Faye stared at her. "It was in the forest near Halcyon when I went after the demon. They showed up just like this," she explained. "It felt like they protected me and strengthened my powers when I fought the demon."

"I take it they weren't here when you woke up?" Madison asked, still focused on the black birds.

Seeing all the ravens gathered again, all focused on the stone circle instead of comforting her, filled Lizzie's heart with dread.

"No, it was just Quinn," Lizzie said, pointing to her feathered friend, who was positioned on the same branch he'd been perched on when she'd left the clearing.

"Lizzie, the last time a flock of ravens gathered like this, you said it was when a demon was present."

Lizzie nodded.

"Ladies, send out your magick and see if you detect dark energies or magick of any kind."

All three women held out their hands, calling up their magick. Their magick spread across the meadow in waves of color; Grandma Faye's a bright green, Madison's a pale wavering yellow, and Lizzie's a deep blue. Lizzie pushed her magick out until it reached the boundaries of her property, then sent it out farther. She felt nothing out of the ordinary, nor did she feel the presence of her furry friend.

"I'm not picking up any dark magick, did you?" Grandma Faye asked, lowering her arms and grounding her magick.

"No, no darkness of any kind," Madison replied.

"Me neither," Lizzie said, "What do we do now?"

"You'll cast a tracking spell from when you and he entered the clearing. And it will show us where he went."

"Me? But I don't know how to cast one. Shouldn't you do it?"

"No, you are the one who has a deep heart connection and magickal bond with Bear. Also, your gift of being able to see magick means we don't need to use dowsing rods or a pendulum to follow his trail. You'll be able to see his exact route. You already know the basics of casting. Trust me, Lizzie, you can do this."

Lizzie nodded hesitantly, then pulled back her shoulders. "Okay, show me what to do."

Grandma Faye walked Lizzie through the incantation, and as soon as she repeated the words the old woman said, drawing the sigils in the air, a bright green line of energy shot across the meadow and around the perimeter of the stone circle.

Lizzie gasped. "It's working, I can see the trail. The line stops where I fell down, and Bear came over to comfort me. Now it's moving away from where I was and...." Lizzie trailed off, confused by what she was seeing. She cocked her head to one side as she watched the green line tracing a clockwise path around the inside of the circle, then briefly stopping before zipping to the center, where it remained unmoving.

"What do you see?" Madison asked.

"I'm not sure. It showed Bear walking around the inside of the stone circle, then the line tracked to the center, and it just stopped. It's not moving anymore." She looked at Grandma Faye. "What does that mean?"

Grandma Faye and Madison exchanged puzzled glances, then looked at Lizzie, confusion on both their faces.

"Lizzie," Grandma Faye said, her tone spreading a cold dread through Lizzie. "There is no stone circle in the meadow. No stones or rocks of any kind."

"What are you talking about? They're right here." Lizzie insisted, touching one of the stones with her foot. When the old woman shook her head slowly, Lizzie felt an odd buzzing in her head. "The circle is right in front of you. It's right here," she said again, pointing down. "Madison, you're standing right next to a stone the size of a melon."

Madison looked down at her foot, then up at Lizzie, shaking her head. "There're no rocks by my foot, not even a small pebble."

"I tripped over them this morning," she said, panic rising in her voice. "That's why I am soaking wet again, and the knees of my pants are stained. The tracking spell stops in the center of it. Just over here," Lizzie marched over the stones and into the circle, a low hum enveloping her. It radiated up from the earth, soft and insistent. And with it came the pull of sleep. She wanted to succumb to the siren's call of the music thrumming up through the soles of her shoes, up her legs, pulling her down, inviting her to slumber. And she would have, except that's when Madison started to scream.

CHAPTER TEN

Lizzie spun around just in time to see Madison launch herself into the circle. Grandma Faye lurched forward to pull Madison back, but she wasn't fast enough, and her hand closed on empty air. As soon as Madison's foot crossed over the stones, she winked out of sight. Lizzie whirled around, spotting Madison just as she reappeared several feet on the opposite side of the circle from where she entered, her momentum carrying her forward, her hands windmilling for balance as she stumbled headlong towards a large pine tree. There was no time to go after her. Instinctively, Lizzie threw out her hands, her magick stopping Madison mere inches away from her face, smashing into the rough bark of the tree.

Lizzie crossed the circle, racing to Madison's side. When she grasped Madison's arm to pull her upright, Madison shrieked and spun around. "Holy shit," she exclaimed, looking wide-eyed at Lizzie. "What the hell was that?"

"I don't know. That's never happened before."

"Are either of you hurt?" Grandma Faye called frantically, moving towards them.

Madison waved away her concern. "I'm good, no harm done," she said breathlessly. There were two bright spots of color high on her cheeks, and her eyes shone with excitement.

"I'm fine. Stay where you are. We'll come to you," Lizzie said when Grandma Faye moved to join them. "Take my hand and stay to the right of me," Lizzie said, holding out her hand to Madison.

"Hold on a sec." Looking around by her feet, Madison grabbed a foot-long fallen branch. "Grandma Faye, see if you can detect anything when I throw this. Heads up," she hollered, then hurtled the stick at the center of the meadow. It arced through the air, then winked out of sight, reappearing in a downward trajectory, landing several feet away from where the old woman stood.

Madison looked to where the stick lay, then back at Lizzie, her eyes wide. "Okay, let's go." Hand-in-hand, they quickly skirted the circle and came to stand with Grandma Faye, whose face had gone a ghostly shade of white.

"Anything?" Madison asked breathlessly.

"It's not a ward or an enchantment, but there's definitely a concentration of earth energy that spiked when the twig vanished and again when it reappeared," Grandma Faye said, lowering her arms and shifting her weight slightly. "And there is a rather strong ley line running along here." She pointed off to her left.

"What does that mean?" Tears burned behind Lizzie's eyes, and when her vision blurred, she swiped at them angrily with the back of her hand. "Because whatever caused the stone circle to do what it did, it did something to him."

"And why did it just spit me out on the other side but not do anything to Lizzie?" Madison chimed in. "And why did the ravens all show up?"

"I don't know," Grandma Fay said, her eyes narrowing as she scanned the meadow, "Something has drastically changed since the Order was called in to sweep the area. Because this involves Bear, Vivienne needs to know immediately what's happened. And until we figure out what is going on, it'll be safer for us back at the cottage."

Lizzie didn't want to leave, but she didn't know what else to do, so when Grandma Faye took hold of her arm, she allowed herself to be led away from the clearing and back through the woods. She felt numb inside, her limbs heavy.

She was first through the cottage door. The aroma of

scorched coffee singed the air, bringing Lizzie abruptly back to her senses. Grandma Faye scooted around Lizzie, immediately grabbing a pot holder and removing the coffee pot from the stove, placing it in the sink.

Lizzie stumbled over to one of the kitchen chairs, sinking down on it right before her knees gave way, her hands limp at her sides. He can't be gone, he can't be gone. She kept repeating the words in her head as if they would bring him back.

Grandma Faye joined Lizzie at the kitchen table. "Before I call Vivienne, you need to tell me everything and anything about that stone circle you can think of."

Lizzie blinked, trying to focus on the old woman's words. "Like what?"

"Like, when did you first discover it?" Madison asked.

Lizzie startled, having forgotten Madison was there. She stood by the woodstove, her bare legs covered in bloody scratches, her feet caked in dirt.

"Um," Lizzie furrowed her brows, "it was just a few days after I'd moved in, I think."

"And when was the first time Bear went with you inside it?" Grandma Faye asked.

"Wait, someone should be writing this down," Madison said before Lizzie could answer. She dashed from the kitchen and down the hall, returning moments later holding her notepad and pen. She took a seat at the table with the others, pen poised. "Okay, I'm ready. So, when did you and Bear first visit the circle?"

Lizzie thought back through her time since moving into Rose Cottage, finding Bear injured on the side of the road and bringing him home after his surgery and recuperation. She clenched her fists under the table, fighting down fear as she encountered more blank spots in her memory. "I can't recall. But I know he's been there with me, and nothing strange ever happened to him.

"Has anyone else gone with you inside the circle?" Grandma Faye asked.

"No, it's always been just Bear and me," she replied. But as she spoke, her mind bumped up against a wall of blackness where she sensed a memory should be. Had anyone else been with them inside the circle? Had she ever been there with someone other than her dog? "Wait, Quinn was with me when I first discovered it. He saw the stones because I distinctly remember him hopping on them. But he never crossed over them. In fact, he always waits outside the circle when Bear and I have stepped inside. And I'm pretty sure he could see us when we were inside it."

"Curious. So, Quinn either has the ability to see through whatever is making the stones invisible to the two of us," Madison said, gesturing to the old woman and herself. "Or the stones and whoever steps inside the circle were at one time visible." Madison absently tapped her pencil on the table. "Was today the first time other people have been with you in the clearing?"

Lizzie was about to say no when images of the night Audley was killed flashed in her mind. She'd been running away from the gunman. A bullet had hit her in the shoulder, and she'd fallen into the circle. Bear had been with her. Sharp knives of pain stabbed her temples, but she pushed through it, chasing the memory.

"Yes. The night I was shot," she said haltingly, "I ended up in the circle with Bear. The man who shot me caught up to us. He was standing near the tree where Quinn was today and..." She rubbed her temples. "He was wearing night vision goggles, and he found us. He aimed his gun right at me, and if Bear hadn't leapt at him, he would have finished me off."

Something else had happened, something significant, but she couldn't remember. She pushed harder when a searing pain flared at her temples, blinding her. Lizzie held her head in her hands, and when she felt the cool touch of Grandma Faye's hand on the back of her neck, the pain disappeared along with the tendrils of the memory she was so close to recalling. She inhaled slowly at the sweet relief from the pain.

"Are you okay?" Madison asked in alarm.

"Yes, yes, I'm fine. It's just a stress headache," she said, still holding her head in her hands. "Just give me a second."

Madison nodded and stood up. She paced between the table and the row of cabinets, rereading her notes. When Lizzie slowly raised her head, Madison stopped pacing and spun on her heels to face her. "The gunman aimed his gun at you. And Bear attacked him. He aimed his gun at you because he saw you," she said slowly.

Madison's words hit home. "He *saw* me while I was *inside* the circle."

"Bingo," Madison shouted, pointing her finger at her.

Lizzie raised her eyebrows. "The stone circle is behaving differently since that night. If we could figure out what caused it to change and what is actually happening, we at least have a chance of figuring out what it did to Bear." She looked at both women. "But where do we start?"

"Vivienne might be able to shed some light on the problem," Grandma Faye replied, going to get the phone. She picked up the handset but didn't punch in Vivienne's number. "Is there anything else any of us can add before I call?"

"I'm not sure," she replied slowly as she tugged at her memory. "Other than the humming was much louder this time."

"The circle hums?"

"No, the ground does. I can feel the pulse of the land here all the time, but inside the circle, the resonance has always been more concentrated and more vibrant. I've always found the sensation comforting, but today, both times, it was incredibly strong, and instead of soothing, it felt more intoxicating, like a sleeping drug. If you hadn't screamed, I probably would have fallen asleep again."

Madison rubbed her knuckles against her chin. "So, the energy in the circle has become stronger." She resumed pacing between the kitchen table and the counter. "Maybe that's what drew all the ravens this time as opposed to when they came to you when you fought the demon, because none of us detected any dark entities, wards, or enchantments in the clearing." She stopped pacing and looked from Lizzie to Grandma Faye. "But what could have caused the Earth's energy to increase?"

Grandma Faye spoke up. "The stronger energy could be coming from that ley line I felt. I bet if we could dowse the area, we'd find several ley lines converging inside the circle."

"It's a vortex," Madison exclaimed.

"That would make sense," Lizzie piped up, "because when I fought the demon and the ravens were there, the place I chose contained a vortex. And now that I think about it, the energy feels similar. Although the one here is much stronger."

"Yes, and that's probably why the stones were placed there in the first place by the First Nations people who were living here at the time. They knew it was a vortex and marked it as a sacred sight," Grandma Faye said. "And the sudden increase in the humming you felt," she said to Lizzie, "could be explained by the energy of that ley line being unbound recently."

"The barn," Lizzie whispered, slowly putting together what the old woman was saying. "That energy line goes right under the barn."

"Right," Grandma Faye said.

"Why was the energy line bound to the barn? I don't understand." Not for the first time, Lizzie felt more than a mild regret for not staying with the Order. There was so much she didn't know about how magick worked, things she should know that could help Bear when he needed her. Lizzie looked quizzically between the women.

"It has to do with the clandestine drug operation running out of Lizzie's barn, right?"

"Yes," Grandma Faye confirmed. "Jon used several types of wards on the barn to obscure its actual size. He also placed a kind of memory fog on it to stop curious trespassers from wanting to see what was inside and then forgetting it was there as soon as they left," Grandma Faye continued. "When the Order was called in, they dismantled all the dark magick attached to the barn."

"Oh, that makes sense," Madison said, gazing off in the middle distance and absently running the knuckles of one hand over her chin again.

"Well, it doesn't make sense to me. Can someone explain?"

"In order to maintain the wards on a building or, say, a piece of land, you need a steady supply of energy to maintain them," Grandma Faye explained. "In the case of your property, the Order used magickally imbued crystals because their energy is more stable and controlled than using a naturally occurring earth line, but even your crystal-powered wards will need to be reset on a regular basis."

Lizzie nodded her understanding. She vaguely recalled being told that the wards surrounding her property would need to be reset twice a year. "But the wards I placed on the cottage don't have an energy supply."

"Yes, they do. They are using the vibration of the stones in the walls. That's one advantage of living in a stone structure. The energy supply is built in. But the complicated wards and enchantments Jon placed on the barn would take a great deal more energy and would need several warlocks with high-level magick constantly maintaining and resetting them. So he tapped into a ley line and diverted it to the barn to continually power the spells. It's not ideal, but he had to work with what he had. That's probably why he chose this location in the first place. It had everything he needed. It's remote and isolated and had the added bonus of powerful, accessible earth energy. But when the Order dismantled the spells on the barn, they released the flow of energy back into that ley line, and that's probably why the energy, or the hum as you call it, feels stronger because it is." Grandma Faye looked from Lizzie to Madison. "But that doesn't explain what happened today. That circle isn't behaving like a vortex. It's acting more like—"

"A portal. A very small one, but you're right." Madison looked down at her notes, flipped back a few pages, and then huffed in frustration. "But that can't happen. A portal needs several, what did Gideon say, cataclysmic natural events to occur simultaneously for a portal to be created. And unbinding one ley line wouldn't be enough. And it doesn't explain why it doesn't affect Lizzie and only affects Bear once he is inside it?" Madison scrubbed her face with her hands. "This is giving *me* a headache. We need more resources. We need to call in a team from the Order."

"No," Grandma Faye and Lizzie said at the same time. Lizzie was surprised by the old woman's agreement.

"Why not?" Madison looked from Grandma Faye to Lizzie, confusion etched on her face. "They have the manpower and expertise we don't."

"Because we are talking about a dog who has magickal powers. Vivienne and I both agreed after we saw what Bear could do, it would have to remain a secret. She feels like you do, Lizzie, about Bear having a right to autonomy, and he wouldn't have that if the rest of the Order knew about him. I had assumed Vivienne had spoken to you about it, but I see from the expression on your face she didn't. With all that was going on at the time, it must have slipped her memory."

"Oh," was all Lizzie said as she processed what Grandma Faye had revealed. Until Gideon had brought up the idea of

Bear needing to be studied, the thought had never occurred to Lizzie. She realized now that not training under the organization meant she didn't understand how the Order would have reacted to finding out about Bear's abilities until Gideon had shown up. That he would be considered a discovery to be studied and nothing more.

"But," Grandma Faye continued, "Vivienne may still be able to help, and at the very least, she needs to know what happened. While I'm talking to Vivienne, why don't the two of you get changed?"

Madison looked down at herself as if just realizing she was still only wearing a sleep shirt and cardigan. "Oh, right," she said, disappearing down the hallway.

Lizzie remained behind. "Grandma Faye, Gideon mentioned that there has been a surge in dark energy worldwide. Could that be related to what happened today?"

"I don't know, but I'll ask Vivienne. Go on and get changed." She smiled gently at Lizzie before finally punching in Vivienne's number.

When Lizzie entered the bedroom, she found Madison sitting cross-legged on the unmade bed, scribbling in her small notebook. There were dark streaks of dried blood on the rumpled sheets from the scratches on her legs, and a smear of what Lizzie speculated was dirt on the duvet cover Lizzie had just washed the day before. She didn't look up when Lizzie walked past her to get to the dresser.

Lizzie clenched her jaw as she flung open the drawers, snagging a clean t-shirt, socks, and underthings. She slammed the drawers shut, then moved to the wardrobe to grab a pair of jeans, her irritation growing. Shivering as she peeled off her wet clothes, she dressed quickly and, after glancing out the window, pulled on a thick sweatshirt. The sight of the darkening skies added to her mood, and she let out a huff as she gathered up her dirty clothes.

She'd just stepped out of the bedroom when Madison called out to her. Lizzie rolled her eyes before turning around and heading back into the room.

"What?"

"How far has Bear managed to phase shift?"

Lizzie thought for a moment. "The farthest I've seen him use his powers is from the house to the barn, so a few hundred yards."

Instead of continuing the conversation, Madison bent over her notebook and started to furiously write.

Lizzie took the hint, heading down the hall to dump her wet clothes in the mudroom sink. The back door rattled in its frame as the wind picked up. She shivered, wrapping her arms around herself. Grandma Faye's voice floated down the hall, but Lizzie remained staring out the window at the growing storm.

She'd almost snapped at Madison for carelessly soiling the bedclothes as if that was what mattered after all that had happened, after all Madison had done, was doing, to help find Bear. Madison's father had just died, yet she'd put her fresh grief aside to do what she could to help without being asked. When Madison thought Lizzie was in danger, without any thought for her own safety, she had gone after her into the circle.

And how was Lizzie repaying the favor? By getting upset over dirty sheets? Lizzie shook her head, ashamed of herself. She wasn't annoyed at Madison, she was terrified she'd lost Bear, and even now, she couldn't stand to think about it. Hastily, she returned to the kitchen, pushing down her fears before they paralyzed her.

"Will do. Call me at my number if you find anything, and I'll keep you updated at our end. We'll see you soon," Grandma Faye said and returned the handset to its cradle.

"What did she say?" Lizzie asked, gripping the back of the

kitchen chair for support.

"She pulled the report from that night and confirmed that the stone circle marks an energy vortex. The Sweepers found it after they removed the wards on the barn, and they were clearing the area. It's a mid-level positive spin vortex of no significance. When I told her that it now seemed to be operating like a portal, she'd never heard that happening to a vortex either, but she was going to look into it. She's right in the middle of an urgent matter; otherwise, she'd be on the first plane out, but she expects to be here in a couple of days. In the meantime, she'll confer with members of the Order who are experts on portals and get back to us as soon as she knows anything. As for the rise in the darkness, there haven't been any reports of any activities in our area, but she'll have the Watchers look into it."

"Does she have any idea what might have happened to Bear?"

Grandma Faye shook her head, "No, but—"

"I think I do," Madison exclaimed, appearing from the hallway. She had her satchel over her shoulder, and she was holding her notebook high in the air like a prize. "Well, I have a theory, at least," she said, lowering her notebook and referring to its pages. "When we first arrived, you mentioned Bear's favorite game is the stick thing he plays with Quinn, and he phase shifts when he's playing. And I'm going to bet he was playing that game this morning before you went to the circle."

"Yes, but what does that have to do with his disappearance?"

"If I'm right, it has everything to do with his disappearance. What if, after you fell asleep, he and Quinn started to play the stick game, and he phase shifted just as he stepped over the stones and into the portal. Maybe the portal doesn't affect him when he is in his physical form, the way it doesn't affect you, but it does when he is in between states?"

"If he phase-shifted as he crossed over the portal, what do

you think happened to him?"

"Well," she said, flipping through her notebook until she found the page she was looking for, "you saw what happened to me. It flung me at least six feet on the other side of the circle, and if you hadn't used your magick to stop me, I would have whacked right into that tree. Imagine how far the portal would have pushed Bear if he was in a pure energy state. Best case scenario is that he might be miles away from here. He could be trying to get back to you right now, but he may not be familiar with where he ended up and is lost."

"And worst case?"

"He may be trapped inside the portal, unable to move through it because he is not in a solid form."

Lizzie's stomach dropped.

"This helps us. It really does because we know to widen our search first, and if he isn't in this plane of existence, we can focus on how to get him out of the portal."

"And it will narrow down what spell to use," Grandma Faye added. "A Lost and Found may do the trick for the first part.

"But if he's trapped inside the liminal space of the portal," Lizzie said softly, her dread increasing, "how do we get him out?"

"By using what you can do naturally," Grandma Faye said. "You called the inside of the portal a liminal space, and it's a good description because it is like a threshold of a door. It's not inside the circle nor outside, but the in-between space connecting the two. Not unlike the liminal space you created and go to when you are healing.

"The in-between," Lizzie repeated, the realization dawning on her.

"Okay, you've lost me," Madison said, looking at Lizzie. "You can create a space out of time?"

"Yes, I guess you could describe it like that. But more importantly, I know how to travel to and come back from an in-between space. If Bear is trapped in a similar type of space, Grandma Faye thinks I can go and get him." Butterflies erupted in Lizzie's stomach. Could she really do what she just said?

"Exactly," Grandma Faye said. Madison stood, mouth hanging open as the old woman continued. "I have a few spells in mind to ensure your safety if that is where Bear is trapped. And I may not have the resources the Order has, but I do have extensive tools at my disposal. That means we need to perform the spells at my place."

"No, we can't leave. What if Bear comes back while we're gone? What if he's injured, and I'm not here to help him?"

"We'll only be at my place just long enough to determine where he is. If he's just been flung farther from your place than he can get back to, we'll drive out to get him. If he's in the portal, we'll come back here to the circle. And while we're at my place, you sense Bear has returned, we will come back immediately. It really is the most efficient use of our time." She held Lizzie's hand. "I know you're scared, but we are going to get him back. And Quinn and the other ravens are watching over the circle. I have no doubt Quinn will let us know if anything changes."

Lizzie nodded, the sudden lump in her throat preventing her from speaking.

"If Bear is stuck in the portal," Madison murmured as she scribbled furiously in her notebook, then looked up abruptly, "are you thinking of casting a Guiding Light spell?"

"That or a Beacon spell," Grandma Faye replied.

"Oh yes, that might be a better one to start with." Madison stuffed her notebook in her satchel and headed for the door. When Lizzie and Grandma Faye didn't follow, she stopped and turned around. "What are we waiting for? Shouldn't we get going?"

Grandma Faye looked pointedly at Madison.

"What?" Madison asked, confused.

"Aren't you forgetting something?" Lizzie replied

pointedly, looking down at Madison's bare legs.

Madison followed her gaze and looked down. "Oh, right, I need some shoes," she said, making her way over to where she'd left them by the front door.

"Pants might also be a good idea," Grandma Faye chuckled, the corners of her mouth turning up into a smile.

Lizzie returned the old woman's smile with a faint one of her own as Madison scrambled back to the bedroom to get dressed. They had a plan, a way forward, to bring Bear home. And for the first time since he'd disappeared, she felt something other than overwhelming fear; she felt hope.

CHAPTER ELEVEN

No one spoke as Grandma Faye raced the truck headlong down the country road. Madison sat in the middle, her bag spilling across her lap and onto Lizzie's. Inside the satchel, something with a sharp corner dug painfully into Lizzie's thigh. As she carefully repositioned the bag, the objects shifted, clanking dully together. She looked up in time to see a wall of trees filling the windshield as the truck barreled down a dead-end road. She flailed for the truck's grab bar with one hand while instinctively flinging her other arm across Madison's chest. The rough bark of a massive cedar loomed large in the windscreen, and Lizzie squeezed her eyes shut, letting out a shriek of alarm.

But the collision metal never came.

Instead, the truck kept moving forward as Madison let out a whoop of delight. Lizzie's eyes flew open, and to her astonishment, the truck was continuing down a road that hadn't been there moments before. Madison struggled to twist around to look out the rear window, but with three adults squeezed into the small truck, there just wasn't room. She sighed and settled back down, facing forward again.

"When this is all over, and we have Bear back, you are definitely going to have to teach me that glamour. That was amazing," Madison said.

"It would be my pleasure," Grandma Faye said as she maneuvered the truck down a long tree-lined lane.

When Lizzie's heart finally left her throat, she added, "Some of us would have appreciated a bit of warning we were driving through an illusion and not to our deaths."

"My apologies, my mind was on what spell we need to

use," Grandma Faye said, following a road that skirted around a large garden and parking under a rustic wooden carport.

As soon as Lizzie stepped out of the truck, she held out her hand to take Madison's satchel to make it easier for Madison to scoot across the seat. Surprised by the weight of the bag, Lizzie fumbled with the strap, almost dropping it before recovering her hold.

"Be careful," Madison said, scooting across the seat and jumping out of the truck. She snatched her satchel from Lizzie's hands. She effortlessly lifted the strap over her head and onto her shoulder so it hung across her body, the satchel resting against her hip. Flipping open its leather flap, she searched around inside. Reassured the contents were undamaged, she hip-checked the truck door closed. Lizzie stood back, feeling the sting of Madison's words.

"This way, ladies," Grandma Faye called out, then headed briskly down the path towards the house.

As Lizzie stepped out of the shadow of the carport and into the sunshine, the prickle of irritation ignited by Madison's words softened as she drank in the view of the garden. A series of dry-stone beds were laid out in concentric circles with a large fountain in the center and walkways bisecting them into four equal sections. The beds were planted with a tapestry of vegetables, flowers, and herbs. She let her hand trail over the leaves and petals as she walked past them, the air perfumed with layers of scent, butterflies taking flight as she disturbed their resting places. The sound of bird songs filled the air and seemed to be concentrated in the middle of the garden. Crystal-clear water burbled from the top of the rough-hewn stone fountain in the center of the garden, the water gently flowing down into the basin below. Robins, sparrows, and plump little towes flitted around the fountain as a large thrush drank from the basin.

On her own property, she'd glimpsed the golden web

of connection, but here she was seeing the flow of each being from plant, bird, insect, and even the stone comprising the raised beds. It was a constant swirl of soft colors that moved with ease through the concentric circles of the garden. There was a balance and harmony everywhere she looked. Instead of soothing her frazzled nerves, without Bear by her side, the hole in the center of her grew. Turning her back on the garden, she followed Madison down the curving path to the cabin.

The house, it turned out, was just as unconventional as the garden. Lizzie had imagined Grandma Faye's house to be similar to hers, rough-hewn grey stones or at least the traditional log cabin, but the structure was neither. The front of the house was floor to ceiling windows framed by large timbers that supported an undulating roof that swooped gracefully like the wing of a bird, creating a deep overhang shading the house from the heat of the midday sun.

Grandma Faye led them into a small vestibule where Lizzie and the old woman hung up their coats while Madison kept her oversized grey cardigan on. Lizzie took a moment to get her bearings as Grandma Faye ushered them into a large room that doubled as both living and dining room. The wall of windows and the high ceiling made the room bright and airy, but the soft furnishings, which included an overstuffed green velvet couch, a worn leather chair, and an ottoman, lent the space an air of cozy comfort. The curved plaster walls were painted a soft ochre, and the floors were covered in several brightly colored woven rugs, but what caught Lizzie's eye was the floor-to-ceiling bookcases flanking a fieldstone fireplace at the opposite end of the room. The back of her neck began to tingle, and she rubbed at it absently. It felt like something in the house was calling to her. She took an unconscious step forward, realizing the pull was coming from a closed door between the bookcase and the wall of windows.

"This is an amazing place you've got here," Madison said, taking in the view from the windows as she placed her satchel on the round teak dining table situated in front of them.

"Thank you. The house and I have treated each other well over the years," Grandma Faye said as she walked over to the bookcases and removed a large book bound in dark blue leather. "I think we should do the spell right here and use the coffee table as our altar. We can pull it out from the couch to give us more space." She took a seat on the couch, opening the book on her lap. "I just need to check a few things in my grimoire before we start."

"What can we do to help set up?" Lizzie asked, trying to ignore the energetic tugging pulling at her attention.

"Do you know what's needed to call a circle?" Grandma Faye looked up from her grimoire, not at Lizzie but at Madison.

"Yes, I've even cast a few circles in class, so I know the basic setup."

"Good. You and Lizzie can collect the items to cast a circle. The things you'll need are in the still room through that door there," the old woman said, pointing to a door between one of the bookcases and the wall of windows.

It was where Lizzie had felt the strange, compelling pull coming from.

"My ritual tools you'll find in a black lacquered box on the back wall, third shelf from the bottom. I think we'll use the large wrought-iron candlestick for the circle, and there are handled baskets to carry everything out just under the butcher block table," she said before going back to her grimoire.

Scrubbing the back of her neck, Lizzie followed Madison into the still room. As she stepped over the threshold, the tingling sensation spread through her whole body. Something in the room was calling to her. No, not calling, shouting.

The wall of windows continued into the small room, providing more than enough light to see, while the deep overhanging roof kept out the glare of the sun. Madison let out a slow whistle as they walked further into the room while Lizzie did her best to ignore the tingling that was growing stronger by the minute.

"This place is like Disneyland for witches," Madison said, running her finger over a long stainless-steel workbench directly to the left of the door. It would have been right at home in a laboratory, complete with a deep sink and drawers below. Three copper stills of various sizes rested on the benchtop, and above them were narrow shelves filled with tiny amber bottles.

"So that's why it's called the still room—she makes her own essential oils," Madison said, closely examining the stills before moving on to inspect the rest of the room.

There were floor-to-ceiling shelves on the two remaining walls, complete with a library ladder on rails. The shelves were stocked with tins of herbs and tinctures in amber apothecary bottles, some with glass stoppers, others with cork. There were candles of every size and color imaginable, neatly stacked bowls sorted by type: wood, porcelain, metal, and heavy earthenware. The lower shelves held white enameled canisters of different sizes, their contents clearly marked with handwritten labels, while the upper shelves held an array of crystals, rocks, and shells.

Lizzie scanned the shelves, trying to narrow down where the magnetic pull was coming from. "Do you feel anything in here?"

"Like what?"

"I don't know, it feels like something is trying to get my attention, like something is pulling me towards it. You don't feel anything like that?"

"No, I mean it feels great in here with all these magickally charged items, the crystals, and those lovely essential oils," she said as she read out the labels on the shelves, "It's very soothing. But nothing feels like it is calling to me. But who knows what

Grandma Faye has in here that you might be picking up on."

Lizzie paced over to the other wall of shelves, finally honing in on the location of whatever was calling out to her.

"I'll get the salt if you want to grab the candles," Madison said, pointing to a shelf of candles before bending to retrieve a large canister from one of the lower shelves. She placed it on the butcher block table, scurried over to another shelf, and selected an earthenware bowl from a large array, returning to the table where she began scooping the salt into the bowl.

Instead of getting the candles, Lizzie curled her hands around the rolling ladder, sliding it across the rail until it was positioned next to the top shelf of crystals. Madison continued to scoop salt as Lizzie nimbly scrambled up the rungs, stopping when she was chest height to the shelf. What she was looking for was coming from the very back. She slid a large amethyst geode out of the way and searched with her fingers as far back as she could reach, the pulse so close, her fingertips throbbed with it. Rising on her tiptoes, she held tight to the ladder with one hand as she leaned as far as she could, reaching into the corner with her free hand. Her fingertips brushed against something hard, and she scrabbled to inch it forward on the shelf until it was in front of her. It was a small, plain wooden box. Leaning her weight against the ladder, she used both hands to lift off the lid and peered inside. She gently picked up the object. It was warm to the touch and pulsed ever so slightly, like a gently beating heart.

She was about to climb down when an image flashed across her vision, so clear and detailed that she startled and almost let go of the ladder. There was a voice, too, in her left ear telling her she had to be the one to end it, that he couldn't be the one to do it. And just as quickly as the vision had descended on her, it was gone.

Her heart thudded against her ribcage, and for a second,

she thought she was going to be overcome by vertigo. Pressing herself against the ladder, she rested her head against a rung when the ladder suddenly shifted on its rails. Lizzie fumbled the object in her hand, clutching it to her chest while gripping the rung with her other hand.

"What are you doing?" She yelled down at Madison, who was holding the ladder.

"Sorry, I didn't realize it would move that easily on the rails. I was just trying to help."

"I didn't ask for your help," she shot back. "And I don't need it. I've dealt with far more dangerous things over the last six months on my own than climbing down a ladder. So, stop interfering where you're not wanted."

Madison's eyes went wide, then blank. "Fine," she said, walking away.

As Lizzie descended one-handed, not willing to let go of her find, Madison finished scooping out the salt and then bustled about below, gathering up the other items and placing them in a large wicker basket.

By the time Lizzie had both feet on the ground, Madison had filled the basket, and all that was left to bring out were the large wrought iron candlesticks. The sun dimmed, throwing the still room into shadow. The basket creaked as Madison lifted it, resting on her hip.

"I'm going to help rescue Bear whether you want me to or not because I know what it's like to lose someone you love," she whispered, "And I'll do anything to stop that from happening to you." She marched out, leaving Lizzie alone in the half-light of the empty room.

CHAPTER TWELVE

Moments later, when Lizzie returned to the living room carrying the candlesticks, the other two women were kneeling at the coffee table, setting up the altar. On the tabletop was a bowl of water, a dish of salt, and two maps spread out. It only took a few minutes for Lizzie to place the candlesticks in the four directions a few feet beyond the makeshift altar, so she was left to stand off to the side waiting, watching as Grandma Faye placed the lacquered box on her lap and lifted out the items one by one, handing them over to Madison. She, in turn, placed the athame, a chalice, incense, a wand, and a brass pentacle in what Lizzie had to assume were the correct positions without having to be told where they go. Lizzie crossed her arms over her chest, shifting her weight onto one foot. She avoided looking at Madison.

When they were done, Grandma Faye surveyed the items on the table. "I almost forgot the most important tool, the pendulum." She narrowed her eyes, looking towards the still room. "I haven't used it in so long I can't remember exactly where I put it."

"We could use mine," Madison ran to retrieve her satchel from the dining table and brought it over to the couch, where she took a seat. She carefully removed a flat rectangular object wrapped protectively in a silk scarf. When she laid it aside next to her, the scarf shifted to reveal a silver picture frame. From where Lizzie was standing, she couldn't see what the picture was, but she had no doubt that was what had been poking her leg in the truck ride over.

Next, Madison pulled out a metal first aid kit that had to be older than she was. The red cross on the lid faded to a soft pink, the white paint scratched and scored. It was about a third of the size of Grandma Faye's lacquered box. When Madison flipped the catches and opened the lid, Lizzie stepped in closer to peer inside. The lid housed three rows of tiny glass vials held in place by elastic loops. The bottom of the tin was filled with a variety of smaller tins, from the original adhesive bandage tin to a Sucrets and even an Altoids container. Despite their different sizes and shapes, they fit snuggly together like a Tetris game.

"A portable apothecary," Grandma Faye said, leaning over to look inside, "how ingenious. Did you design it yourself?"

Madison looked up at Grandma Faye, pride written across her face. "Yes, I called it my witch's kit, but I like portable apothecary better. When I knew I was coming to visit Lizzie, I wanted to be able to keep up my studies, so I threw it together last minute from containers I found at a local thrift store." Reaching in, she nimbly plucked out a pale green and gold tin with a red Lucky Strike logo printed on the center. Madison gently placed the tin on the table, removed the lid, and, with her forefinger and thumb, plucked out a thin silver chain. Suspended from the other end was a silver pendulum in a rounded shape of a gourd, except it ended in a needle-thin point.

"May I?" Grandma Faye asked.

Madison nodded, holding the pendulum out as the old woman carefully draped the chain across her hand so the pendulum rested in her palm.

"This is very well crafted. Mmmm," she said, closing her eyes. "And I see you, and it have bonded strongly." She opened her eyes and smiled at Madison.

"I do like dowsing with a pendulum."

"Yes, that would make sense, as your connection to air is very strong. And because of that, I think you should be the one to cast the spell and use the pendulum. You do know how to do a Lost and Found spell?"

"Me? Yes, no. I mean, yes, I know how to do the spell, but I'm still a novice. I couldn't possibly."

"Yes, you could. In fact, I think you are the exact right person to do the casting." The old woman looked down at the coffee table, up at the candles waiting to be lit, then to Madison, and finally resting her gaze on Lizzie. "We place the symbols of our craft on the altar before casting a spell, we light candles and incense, and ask for the elements to join us in our rite to add power to each step, to layer and imbue the sacred circle with as much power and protection as we can. The three of us," she said, sweeping her hand out in an inclusive gesture, "each bring unique skills and talents, and we should use those to our advantage."

"Madison, you are a far more powerful dowser than I am. I can feel it just by holding your pendulum. My power lies in healing and my bond to the earth and this land in particular." She looked at Lizzie. "Your magick is your unique ability to call the Elementals into the circle, boosting the power of what we do here beyond what Madison and I could do by just calling the elements alone. And although your deep heart connection to Bear would cloud your use of the pendulum, it will be the most powerful magick at your disposal if it turns out you need to go into the liminal space of the portal to get him." She turned back to Madison. "You see, we each have a role to play. We each contribute to the success and power of the spell. So, will you be the one to use the pendulum?" She held it out by its chain so it swung gently.

Madison looked over at Lizzie, her expression guarded. Shame washed over Lizzie. She was sick to her stomach, recalling how she'd spoken to Madison in the still room. This wasn't about how Madison had treated her in the past. This was about rescuing Bear. With the force of her will, she pushed her feelings down. "Grandma Faye is right. We need each other's particular magick to successfully rescue Bear. He needs your help." She drew in a deep breath. "*I* need your help."

Madison's face lit up. "I will," she said, taking back her pendulum and holding it tight against her chest.

It was at that moment the stone Lizzie had slipped into her pocket sent out a jolt of energy, startling her. "I almost forgot about this." She pulled out the strangely shaped stone for Grandma Faye to see. This was in your still room, and I think we need to use it in the spell."

"What did you find?"

"I didn't just find it. I felt it calling to me the second I stepped through the front door. The pull was so strong when I entered the still room that I didn't think and just climbed the ladder and found it. I apologize for rummaging around in your things without asking, but I felt this stone calling to me, and I couldn't ignore it." Lizzie hesitated for a moment, not wanting to share her find with anyone, not even Grandma Faye. She forced herself to stretch out her hand and slowly uncurled her fingers to reveal the object in her palm.

Grandma Faye leaned into Lizzie's outstretched hand. A look of confusion passed briefly over her face, quickly replaced by recognition. "Oh, I'd forgotten I had that. If it called to you, it is best to respect its wishes."

The stone was an amorphous shape as if a soft grey mud had been dripped into a puddle, left to harden, and then another smaller dollop had been plopped on top of it where it, too, had solidified. But it wasn't clay. It was way too heavy to be just that.

"It looks like the mud pies I used to make as a kid." Madison craned her neck to get a better look at the stone in Lizzie's palm. "What is it?"

"It's a piece of petrified clay. It's called a faerie stone. I found it years ago when I was digging the foundation for the house."

Lizzie gently placed the stone amongst the other ritual

items and knelt down at the coffee table. Her fingers tingled, and she clasped them tightly in her lap, fighting the urge to snatch the stone back.

"Grandma Faye? Madison asked as she peered at the map opened on the coffee table. "Could you point out exactly where Lizzie's property is on the survey map? I can't find Rock Island Road. This map doesn't have any of the side roads marked, just the highway and the road leading to the ferry."

Grandma Faye scanned the map for a second, then outlined a small circle with her finger. "The property would be about here and..." she pondered the map, "and Rose Cottage would sit about here, so the stone circle would be in this area." As Grandma Faye pointed out each area, Madison used her gold mechanical pencil to draw a boundary and mark the cottage with an X and the stone circle with a small circle.

"Okay, is everyone ready to cast the circle?" When the other two women nodded, the old woman raised her hand. With a flick of her wrist, a thin stream of salt rose from the bowl on the coffee table, flowing across the room and landing on the outside of the wrought-iron candlesticks in a perfect circle. "Lizzie, if you want to call down the circle and invite the Elementals to join us, we can begin."

Without need of any of the ritual tools, Lizzie stood up and walked over to the first candlestick positioned to the east. In a clear voice, she called the directions, inviting in the Elementals to assist and protect them as they weaved their spell. She moved with confidence in a clockwise direction, the clear blue light of her magic igniting each candle as her hand passed over the wicks. As she invited in the Sylph, Salamander, Undine, and Gnome, orbs of yellow, red, blue, and green followed in her wake, swirling around the sacred circle.

"When you said Elementals, you really meant Elementals, not Elements," Madison whispered to the old woman.

When Lizzie rejoined the women at the table, Grandma Faye said to Madison, "With the Lost and Found spell, the pendulum will act like a dowsing rod and start swinging in the direction of where he's gone. You'll have to keep moving your hand in the direction of the swing. If it stops swinging, you'll know to try another direction. If it shows he's gone beyond the surrounding area, we'll switch to the provincial map." She patted the folded map, sitting off to the side. "We'll know we've found him when the pendulum starts swinging in a circle instead of an arc."

"Got it," Madison replied.

Grasping the pendulum chain between her thumb and forefinger, Madison held it in front of her a few inches above the coffee table. She closed her eyes and drew in a slow, deep breath.

"Wait," Lizzie said, her heart pounding.

Madison's eyes flew open, the pendulum swinging erratically in her outstretched hand. She lowered the pendulum to the table.

"Could you ask it a question first," Lizzie's voice faltered, "before you cast the spell?"

"Of course. What's the question?"

"I need to know if he is alive." Her heart raced. She'd finally said it. She'd placed her fear on the table like a dark stone visible for the other two to see, the fear she could no longer deny. She rubbed her sweaty palms on the thighs of her jeans.

Grandma Faye opened her mouth to say something, but Lizzie held up her hand to stop her. "I know what you said earlier, but I need to know for sure. I need to know if this is a rescue mission or—" Lizzie cleared her throat, staring down at the circle Madison had drawn on the map, "a recovery."

Madison raised the pendulum, her arm steady. "Is the dog known to us as Bear alive? Yes or No?"

Outside the wall of windows, the sky darkened, and

thunder rumbled in the distance.

Lizzie watched the pendulum, but when it started to sway, she squeezed her eyes shut. Blood pounded in her ears, and she couldn't catch her breath. It was less than a minute before Madison spoke, but to Lizzie, time seemed to have slowed down. Tears burned behind her closed eyelids as the fear inside her grew.

"It's a yes, it's a yes," Madison exclaimed.

Lizzie opened her eyes, staring at the pendulum as it swung forward and back, then up at Madison. "He's alive?" She needed to hear the words from Madison.

"Yes," she smiled, "he is alive, and we are going to find him." The pendulum continued to swing as Madison returned her attention to it. "Thank you," she said, and the pendulum stilled instantly. "Shall I cast the spell now?" She looked at Lizzie.

Lizzie sat up straighter. "Yes, cast the spell."

"To the Elements—sorry, to the Elementals," Madison said, looking up at the circle of swirling colors that surrounded them, "who have joined us here, through this pendulum, assist us to find what we hold dear, the beloved dog known as Bear. Show us now, by Earth, Fire, Water, and Air."

Lizzie stared at the pendulum, gripping the edge of the coffee table, willing it to start swinging. Instead, the silver bob flew across the table, yanking its chain from Madison's fingers. The needle-end of the bob shot down into the penciled circle on the map, piercing the paper and making a dull thud as it stabbed into the wood table underneath. The objects on the table rattled from the force. There was a moment of shocked silence as the three women stared at the pendulum, now stuck solidly upright.

"Well, that was unexpected," Madison said, eyeing the pendulum.

"That means he's stuck in the in-between of the portal, doesn't it?" Lizzie asked.

"Yes, it does appear so," Grandma said with surprising calm. "But we need to confirm it by asking yes or no questions."

Madison reached across the table, gingerly wiggling the silver bob back and forth. It didn't budge. Grasping it with both hands, she gave it a tug, but it remained firmly stuck into the table. She let out an exasperated huff and yanked at the pendulum again, this time adding her magick to the effort, but it stayed stubbornly imbedded into the table.

"May I?" Grandma Faye asked.

"Sure," replied Madison, letting go of her hold on the pendulum.

Grandma Faye placed the palm of her hand not on the pendulum but on the surface of the table next to it. A sparkle of magick spread from her fingertips and over the tabletop. "Now try."

When Madison pulled up on the pendulum, it released its hold on the table with barely any effort on her part. Madison examined the end, checking for damage. "Doesn't look any worse for wear. Thank you."

Madison squared her shoulders and grasped the chain of the pendulum in her fingers again and let the silver plumb bob hang over the penciled circle in the map.

"Is Bear inside the liminal space of the portal?" The pendulum immediately began swinging up and down. "That's a yes," Madison said. She thanked the pendulum, and it immediately stopped moving.

"There's our confirmation." Lizzie started to move. "I'll open the circle."

"Wait," Grandma Faye said, "I'd like to ask a few more questions to plan out how we are going to get him out."

"We already have a plan. We go to the circle, and I use my ability to enter the portal's in-between, and if I can't feel his energy in there, I'll use those spells you mentioned. I don't understand why we are wasting precious time asking questions when we already know where he is!"

"Because we'll waste more time performing a spell that won't work in this situation than asking the pendulum which one to use."

"Oh," Lizzie replied, chaffing under the old woman's chastisement.

"Madison, ask which of the two spells will work best."

"Will a Beacon spell assist us in retrieving Bear from the portal and returning him to this realm?" The pendulum swung left to right. "That's a no," Madison said and stilled the pendulum. "Will a Guiding Light spell assist us in retrieving Bear from the portal and returning him to this realm?" Again, the pendulum indicated a no.

Lizzie threw up her hands and pushed back from the table, determined to head to the circle when Madison asked her own question.

"Can we retrieve Bear from where he is now?" The pendulum hung motionless from the silver chain.

"Why isn't it moving?"

"I don't know?" Madison frowned, looking up at Lizzie and then at Grandma Faye.

"Do you think it got damaged when it got stuck in the table?" Lizzie asked.

"No, it's working fine. My connection with it is strong, and it answered the other question right away. Maybe it is the question that's the problem." Madison shifted her gaze back down to the pendulum. "Can Bear return to this realm?"

The pendulum swung yes, then stopped abruptly, switching to the no direction.

Lizzie stared at the arc of the pendulum as it kept alternating between yes and no. The prickling heat of her magick raked down her arms. She balled her hands into fists to stop herself from snatching the pendulum and throwing it against a wall.

"This is a waste of time," she barked. "We should never have come here in the first place. We should have tried to get him back from the portal as soon as Madison guessed what had happened to Bear and not played around with that stupid pendulum." Something knocked against the table. "I'm going back to the circle now, with or without you two." Lizzie started to rise from the floor, but Grandma Faye grabbed her arm, stopping her.

"I understand how hard this is on you and that you're scared, but just give me a few minutes to think of any other spells that may help us."

"No, you don't understand," Lizzie said, wrenching her arm back. "You can't possibly understand." The knocking from the table got louder. "It's all my fault he's stuck."

"You guys?" Madison said, a note of alarm in her voice.

"If I hadn't lost my temper and ran away to the circle, he wouldn't have followed me. He'd never have been there in the first place!" Lizzie cried, the guilt and pain warring inside her.

"Guys!" Madison shouted.

"What?" Lizzie growled, glaring across the table at Madison. But Madison wasn't looking at Lizzie. Her terrified gaze was directed down at the table. Lizzie looked down at the altar at the faerie stone. It rocked back and forth, moving faster and faster until the stone became a blur of grey. The ritual tools jumped and rattled across the table, the brass goblet tipping over and spreading its contents across the map like a bloodstain. A high-pitched whine emanated from the stone as it spun.

"Why is it doing that?" Madison exclaimed, leaning across the table to get a better look.

"Madison, move away from the stone now," shouted Grandma Faye. Lizzie could barely hear her over the wail from the stone. The sound pierced Lizzie's eardrums like a hot poker, and an intense pressure pushed on her temples. She tried to cover her ears but discovered she couldn't move her arms.

"We need to get out of here. Move." Grandma Faye ordered.

Lizzie tried to move, but when she went to shift her weight, she discovered she was rooted to the floor. When she tried to move her head, the air was like moving through treacle. She managed to turn her head just enough to see Grandma Faye. Adrenaline surged through Lizzie, electric panic overtaking her senses.

Madison shouted, but Lizzie couldn't make out the words over the incessant piercing whine of the stone. She struggled to breathe as the air pressed down on her, but she managed to shift her gaze to see what had caught Madison's attention.

The Elementals, Lizzie had called to protect the circle, were spinning in synchronicity with the grey stone, their colors blending until they were a blinding white sheet of light growing and converging above them. Lizzie watched in fascinated horror as the white light bent inwards like a funnel reaching into the center of the spinning stone, then out through the bottom, down through the table. Amidst the chaos of sight and sound whipping around her, Lizzie heard singing emanating from the Elementals.

She tried to open her mouth to tell Grandma Faye and Madison what the Elementals were doing, but the pressure around her was so strong she couldn't speak.

A flash of green light seared her eyes. At the same time, a loud boom shook the air more like a sonic wave than a crack of thunder, followed by a wave of energy. Her limbs now free of whatever force the stone possessed, she flung them up instinctively, trying to protect her face, squeezing her eyes shut. Instead of knocking her to the ground, she felt the pressure wave pass through her like a warm, electrified current. She heard someone scream, high and terrified.

What followed was a deep, penetrating silence. Her ears no longer rang with the vibration of the stone, but they felt like they were wadded in cotton. Slowly lowering her arms, she blinked, trying to make sense of what she was seeing. Within the circle of protection, it was snowing. Grey particles floated in the air, slowly settling down to the ground. She sought out Grandma Faye through the dust fall.

The old woman was on her back, her arms flung out from her sides. Lizzie scrambled on her hands and knees, batting the altar items out of her way that lay strewn across her path from the explosion, and all but collapsed with relief when Grandma Faye moved and opened her eyes. She was covered in a dusting of the powder. The whites of her eyes and the blueness of her irises glowed strangely against the greyness of her face.

"Are you hurt?" Lizzie asked, her voice sounding far away as she helped her friend sit up.

Grandma Faye shook her head, slowly raising it to look at Lizzie, a single tear spilling out of her eye. Lizzie watched, mesmerized, as the tear snaked a muddy trail down the grey ash on the old woman's cheek.

"Are you okay?" Grandma Faye asked hoarsely.

Before Lizzie could answer, a moan came from the side of the table where Madison should have been.

"Madison, oh my god, Madison," Lizzie said, struggling to move.

A hand rose up from below the coffee table. Like Lizzie and Grandma Faye, it was coated in grey dust, and it looked more like the hand of a newly risen corpse than a young woman's. Fingers grasped the edge of the table, and Madison pulled herself upright.

"What the fuck was that?" she said, a dazed expression on her face. Neither woman answered, staring at her in horror. "And where did all this dust come from? Do I look as ridiculous as you two? Madison looked from Lizzie to Grandma Faye. "What's wrong? Have I suddenly grown two heads? She raised her arms to pat her head, but she yelped in pain when she moved her left arm. "Oh," she said, looking down at her arm, "That's not good."

The athame that had been sitting on the table before the stone exploded was now embedded almost to the hilt in Madison's upper arm. She slowly raised her head, her eyes wide and unfocused. "No, that's not good at all," she said before her eyes rolled back in her head, and Madison fell face-first on the coffee table in a dead faint.

CHAPTER THIRTEEN

Somehow, the old woman got to Madison's side before Lizzie could even move; her legs had gone to sleep from kneeling so long during the spell casting. She reached to put her hand on the coffee table to push herself up.

"Don't touch the table," Grandma Faye snapped as she swept her hands down Madison's injured arm, keeping them a few inches away from actually touching her. "Stay where you are. We can't risk accidentally dislodging the knife."

Lizzie sat back on her heels, staring in shock at the obscenity of the deeply imbedded knife and the blooming rose of blood—Madison's blood—seeping outward from the athame's handle, staining the sleeve of Madison's cardigan.

"I just need to immobilize her arm and the knife before I can assess the damage." Grandma Faye murmured a spell, the green light of her energy pouring from her palms, encasing Madison's arm in a sleeve of jade light. She kept her hands raised and gently placed them on either side of the athame.

"How bad is it?"

Grandma Faye bowed her head, shifting her hands slightly. "Oh, dear Goddess," she murmured.

Lizzie didn't know what frightened her more, the growing crimson stain around the knife handle or the desperation she heard in the old woman's voice.

Grandma Faye's head snapped up. "We need to move fast and get her on her back on the floor. As soon as I get her upright, you need to stand next to her while I clear some space and get rid of this dust." She cast another spell as she gently lifted Madison's head off the table. "Move now."

Lizzie pushed up from the floor, using her own magick to assist her. As soon as she reached Madison, the old woman leapt into action. Raising her arms up and out, she built up her magick, then with a slashing motion, she brought her hands down. Everything that had gone flying when the faerie stone exploded; the ritual tools, the salt, candles, candle holders, and the grey dust that was still drifting in the air was swept away to the far edges of the room. Grandma Faye's magick even removed the stone dust from each of them. It felt like a thousand tiny spiders were crawling and leaping off Lizzie's skin as the dust rose and scattered to the corners of the room.

Grandma Faye spun around to face Lizzie. "We need to levitate her onto her back on the floor like we did Bear."

As soon as they'd carefully shifted Madison to the center of the rug, Grandma Faye knelt down next to Madison's arm and ran her pointer finger up the sleeve of her cardigan. It fell away as if sliced by a laser, exposing the wound. Placing her hands around where the knife pierced Madison's skin, she began pouring magick into the wound. Beads of sweat dotted her forehead as she continued to work, whispering incantation after incantation.

Lizzie stood frozen, watching Madison's breathing get more and more shallow, her skin going from an already ghostly pale to a deathly grey.

"It won't stop. I can't get the bleeding under control," the old woman said through gritted teeth.

Lizzie snapped into action, kneeling down and placing her hands on Madison's good arm, her magick surging forward, her heart in her throat.

"Stop, your power is too unfocused. You're making it worse," Grandma Faye shouted.

Lizzie released Madison's arm, breaking the energetic connection and pulling back her magick as fast as she could. She held her hands up, too afraid to let her power accidentally make contact with Madison's body. She tried to rein in her fear, but she couldn't catch her breath as a panic attack overwhelmed what little control she had left. Looking around wildly, she searched for a way to stop what was unfolding in front of her, as if the answer would be sitting in the room.

"I can't get the artery to close with the knife cutting through it, and I can't get the knife out because it's stuck in the bone," Grandma Faye's voice rising in panic.

"Can't you remove the knife like you did with the pendulum?"

"No, it's not the same thing."

"I'll call 911. We have to get her to a hospital." Lizzie stood up abruptly and stumbled towards the kitchen with the vague notion of finding a phone there.

"There's not enough time. I've managed to slow the blood loss a bit, but not enough, and the hospital is three hours away. Even if they sent a medivac, she'd bleed out before the helicopter even gets here."

Lizzie stopped in her tracks and spun around to look at the old woman. The green of Grandma Faye's magick, as she continued to pour it into Madison's wound, had faded to a sickly shade of green, tendrils of hair were plastered against her forehead and cheeks, her cotton blouse darkened with sweat. But it was the look of despair in her eyes that made Lizzie's anger flair.

"I'm so sorry, Lizzie. I don't know what else to do."

"No, don't you dare. Don't you dare give up on her!"

Lizzie called up all of her powers, then drew up more, her body vibrating with energy. She looked around, her intention to call upon the Elementals to help, but they weren't there. Then, she caught movement coming from above. Craning her neck, she saw they were still joined as one intense white light, billowing and shifting like summer clouds across the ceiling. She released her energy into the light.

"Help her," she pleaded to them, "Please. Don't let her die. It's not her time. It can't be." The Elementals continued to swirl across the ceiling, seemingly oblivious to Lizzie's plea.

"Lizzie, she doesn't have much time left. Come be with her." Grandma Faye said softly, gently.

"No, she's not going to die. I won't let her." Lizzie shouted, swiping tears from her eyes. "Take me instead," she screamed up at the ceiling. "If you need to balance the scales, then take my life instead."

The Elementals began to coalesce, spiraling above Lizzie's head, accelerating so quickly that Lizzie had no time to react as a funnel of energy whipped down from the center of the spiral and pierced her heart.

In one blinding flash, she was pulled from her body, her consciousness flying into the light. Then everything stopped. She was floating in a void, not of darkness but of light. It was such an odd sensation; she knew who she was and could feel the edges of her*self* even though she didn't have a physical body. And at the same time, she was of the light, eternal, endless. She was surprisingly calm, more curious than afraid, when a tendril of light seemed to detach itself and reach out to her.

"We have been waiting for you, Elizabeth."

She was hearing the words inside what she still thought of as her mind, even in her formless state, and when she spoke, it felt as effortless as when she had been in a body. "Am I dead?" She was startled by a low, rumbling chuckle emanating from the light.

"No, you are not dead. We simply removed you from the flow of time to respond to your invitation."

"Does that mean you will save Madison?"

"Yes. We would have assisted you earlier, but you had not

invited us in until now."

Lizzie was confused. Who had she inadvertently invited in? She didn't feel any malevolence coming from the light being, just the opposite, in fact. "Who are you?

"We are all that is and all that will ever be. We are the one where all things are born before they merge into matter. And we accept your invitation to bond."

Wait? What? "*You* accept *my* invitation?" Hadn't Grandma Faye said it was the other way around, that it was the elements that extended the invitation to bond with them?

"Yes, and we are pleased and honored to be in a relationship with you."

"Umh," she said, unsure of what to say. It felt like she needed to reply to the Elemental in some formal way, but all she could think about was getting back to Madison. "Me too."

The light undulated forward, engulfing Lizzie, merging with her. A joy she'd never experienced in life infused her being. If she were in her body, she would have fallen to her knees and wept at the sheer intensity of the love pouring into her from the light. When the Elemental pulled back, the bonding complete, she could feel her connection to it, the joy and wonder still there, but not the intensity it was a moment ago. She longed, craved to feel those emotions again, to remain completely merged with the light.

Her desire frightened her. She knew if given the choice to remain here she would, she would abandon Madison to die just to feel that deep connection once more. "So, what happens now?" she forced herself to say, "How do I get back and save Madison. What do I need to do?"

"We will return you to the flow of time. Go to the sister of the light you call Madison and place your hands on her. Call upon your power, and we will assist you."

"Okay," she said quickly, not giving herself the chance to

think about what leaving the light would mean.

"I'm so sorry, Lizzie. I don't know what else to do."

Lizzie whirled around to face Grandma Faye, the déjà vu so strong it raised the hairs on her arms. As she rushed to the old woman's side, she realized what the Elemental had done. It had placed her back a few minutes before she'd begged for help.

She didn't have time to think about how it had done such a thing. Madison didn't have that kind of time. Instead, she did what the Elemental had told her to do.

"Lizzie, there's nothing more we can do."

"Yes, there is," she elbowed Grandma Faye out of the way. Calling up her magick, she connected to Madison's energy, and she and her newly bonded Elemental got to work.

Lizzie became one with the amalgamation of bone and sinew, of artery and corpuscle. She became the cells. She and her magick went deeper, becoming the vibration of all matter and then the space between the vibration. She became the eternal silence. And in that silence between the space of things, she knew what to do.

Withdrawing from the stillness to merge with Madison's physical body, she quickly searched around, then, finding what she was looking for, wrapped her magick around a gossamer thread. She gently tugged on it, and at first, it resisted, pulling upwards, but when she pulled again, the tension on the filament relaxed like a sigh, and Lizzie immediately anchored it to Madison's body. Lizzie switched her focus to Madison's heart, infusing it with magick, keeping its beats steady but slower to reduce the blood loss from the wound. Satisfied with what she'd done, she turned her attention to her biggest challenge; removing the blade from the bone.

Lizzie was aware she was speaking to Grandma Faye, but it sounded far away. The song of Madison's physical body was by far the loudest vibration, filling her senses.

"You need to grasp the hilt of the knife. When I say 'now,' you have to pull it out as fast as you can. Do you understand?" She felt more than heard Grandma Faye's reply, and as soon as she sensed the old woman's energy withdraw from Madison's body and grip the knife handle, she focused on the blade of the athame.

Following the same path as she'd done with Madison, she went into the blade until she reached the space between the vibration, but instead of slowing the vibration down, she sped it up, faster and faster, until the blade was less matter more energy, less there than it had been moments ago.

"Now! Pull it out now!" She ordered.

As soon as she felt the blade slip out of the bone, Lizzie split her focus between the bone and artery, knitting together bone and mending torn tissue. When it was done, she slipped back into Madison's heart and nudged it back up to its proper rhythm. Satisfied that all was as it should be, she withdrew back into her own body.

The jarring contrast from being pure energy to being flesh and bone again overwhelmed her. She slumped over Madison as the weight of her own body caught her by surprise. Grandma Faye grabbed her by the shoulders, pulling her back as Lizzie drew in a deep breath, only to be overcome again when her senses kicked in. She smelled the lingering fear in the old woman's sweat, the metallic tang of spilled blood, and the sound of her own heartbeat boomed in her ears.

When Madison sighed softly, Lizzie slowly raised her head, relief washing over her when she spied the healthy glow returning to Madison's face, the steady, strong rise and fall of her chest. As long as Lizzie didn't look at the blood staining the carpet next to her or the angry red scar on Madison's arm where the gaping wound had been, Lizzie could almost convince herself Madison had merely fallen asleep and had not been a hair's breadth away from dying. Almost, but not quite. *"And whose fault was it that Madison had been put in harm's way in the first place?"* her fear whispered to her as Madison sighed once more, her eyes darting back and forth beneath her closed lids as if she were dreaming.

CHAPTER FOURTEEN

After transferring Madison to the bedroom, they washed the dried blood from her arm, changed her into one of Grandma Faye's cotton nightgowns, and put her to bed, where she was still soundly sleeping. Grandma Faye sat on the edge of the bed, checking Madison's vital signs.

"How is she doing?" Lizzie asked, bundling up Madison's soiled clothes in her arms.

Grandma Faye pulled back her magick from Madison's once-injured arm and leaned back against the headboard. "She's doing just fine. All of her injuries are fully healed, and there is no sign of infection setting in."

"How long do you think she'll be asleep?"

"It's hard to say, at least a few hours, maybe more. Although she's completely healed, her nervous system needs to reset itself. Normally, healing takes time, and that time is necessary for the body to recover, not just from the physical injury, but from the shock."

Lizzie's gaze lingered on Madison's arm resting on top of the bedcovers. The scar left behind from the stab wound had faded even more and was now a pale pink line. The coppery scent of dried blood from the clothes she held made bile rise in the back of her throat. "Why did the stone explode?"

"I've been thinking about that too. There could've been an air pocket inside the stone, or it could've had a hairline crack along its surface, making it fragile. The resonance of our combined magick must have matched the frequency of the stone itself, causing it to vibrate. And because of its structural weakness, it exploded, like a piece of flawed pottery in a kiln."

Lizzie nodded, looking down at the bundle in her arms. "Is it possible to mend this?" She asked, holding up the unraveled, blood-soaked sleeve of the cardigan. "I think this was her father's."

Grandma Faye rested her head against the headboard, her eyes heavy with exhaustion. "Yes, just leave it over there, and I'll get to it later," she said, motioning to a chair in the corner of the room.

Lizzie carefully draped the cardigan over the arm of the chair, making sure that the bloodstain didn't touch the upholstery. "What should I do with the rest of these?"

"There's a laundry hamper in the bathroom." Grandma Faye scrubbed her face with her hands.

Lizzie had just crossed over the threshold to the bathroom when Grandma Faye spoke again. "How did you do it?"

Lizzie leaned against the doorframe. "I'm not really sure. It's all a bit hazy. I remember using my magick and the Elemental's magick to increase the vibration of the knife's "matter" so that it was less "there." Then, when you pulled out the knife, I repaired the damaged bone and tissue."

"You altered the knife from a solid object to pure energy?" she asked, sitting forward.

"Not entirely, just enough to make it small enough it could slide out of the bone. Did I do it wrong?"

Grandma Faye shook her head, a look of wonder in her tired eyes. "No, what you did wasn't wrong. It was *impossible*."

"But I did exactly what you did with the pendulum when it got stuck in the table."

"That's not what I did at all. I merely called upon the Fire element and had it dry out the wood around the pendulum point so that the wood fibers contracted, loosening the pendulum. And how did you heal all that damage and close up the artery in mere seconds?"

"I'm not sure exactly. Everything happened so fast. When I called on the Elementals for help, one of them bonded with me, and they showed me what to do. And I think they may have stopped time or turned it back somehow." She furrowed her brows. "I'm still a bit foggy on that part."

"So, you bonded with an Elemental instead of one of the elements," Grandma Faye said more to herself than to Lizzie, "That should have occurred to me as a possibility based on your relationship with them. And I've never heard of an Elemental being able to alter time. Curious." The old woman rested her head back on the headboard again. "I'll make us some tea, and you can go over what you did in detail while we wait for Madison to wake. And I'm thinking we may be able to use your new bond to figure out a way to open the portal and find Bear." Moving slowly, Grandma Faye swung one leg off the bed.

"No, you stay and watch Madison. I'll make the tea." Lizzie willed herself to stand up straight, swaying a little until she found her footing.

"You'll find the kettle on the stove and the tea things in the cupboard to the left of it," she said, settling back on the bed.

After depositing Madison's clothes in the hamper, Lizzie headed into the kitchen. She skirted the living room, trailing her hand along the wall for support, deliberately averting her gaze at the chaos on the other side of the room. While she waited for the kettle to boil, she leaned against the counter, looking out the window into the forest. The sky had darkened considerably since they'd arrived at the cabin, the rumble of thunder sounding closer, although no flashes of lightning lit up the sky.

She should be relieved Madison was alright and no harm had come to Grandma Faye. She should be relieved, if not ecstatic, considering the circumstances of her bonding, at least hopeful she had another ally in her quest to rescue Bear. But alone in the kitchen, watching the wind stir the branches of the trees and the darkness staining the sky, nothing felt right. She wasn't right.

She hugged herself tightly, squeezing her eyes shut to stop the tears. She was the one who led Bear into the circle. She was the one who found the Faerie stone and insisted it had to be part of the spell. If she hadn't bought Rose Cottage, Audley wouldn't have been killed trying to save her. If she hadn't fought with Ian, he would never have stormed out of the apartment and been killed in the bus accident. And what about Richard? Could she justify what she'd done to him because she was saving Madison? Could she admit she'd gone too far, lost control in her anger and rage? Richard was technically alive, but he wasn't living.

Everything she touched, she broke, everyone who came into her life, she hurt. She couldn't deny it anymore; there was a darkness inside her, poisoning everything and everyone she came in contact with. And the nuns must have known, seen it growing in her. That's why they had to be paid to take her in, and when she'd turned eighteen and their obligation fulfilled, they had kicked her out, turned their backs on her, because they knew exactly what she was.

The kettle whistled, and Lizzie opened her eyes, quickly snagging the kettle off the burner to silence the shrill sound before it woke the two women in the other room. As she fixed the tea in two earthenware mugs, she turned over in her mind what she could recall from the moment the Elemental approached her in that in-between space. What she'd felt in that space, emanating from the Elemental, was the opposite of what was inside her. It was the light to her dark, the joy to her despair. She couldn't change who she was, but...she almost didn't want to finish the thought for fear she would somehow jinx her bonding. But maybe her bonding with the Elemental could, if not rid her of her darkness, maybe override it. Maybe, just maybe, this time, things would be different.

As she carried the mugs of tea into the bedroom, she

hoped Grandma Faye could shed some light on what Elemental she was now aligned with. It had said it was the one that all other Elementals come from, but with Lizzie's limited knowledge, she had no idea what that would be. She thought there were only four: air, fire, water, and earth, just like their counterparts in the elements.

But she was going to have to wait for the answer to her question, for when she returned to the bedroom, Grandma Faye was asleep, sitting upright. Lizzie tiptoed to the side of the bed, carefully placing the mugs of tea on the nightstand before snagging a crocheted afghan from the end of the bed to drape over the old woman's lap. She stood for a moment, watching both women, listening to their steady breathing, their features relaxed in restful repose. She knew they both needed to sleep, but that didn't stop the frustration from building. Bear was still lost inside the portal, and there was nothing she could do until both women were awake. Every muscle in her body ached, and another blasted headache was building behind her eyes. Retrieving one of the mugs from the nightstand, she retraced her steps to the living room, unsure of what to do while she waited.

She stumbled on the edge of the carpet as the chaos in the living room confronted her. The large bloodstain in the middle of the rug, already darkening to a sinister black, and the dust-coated debris encircling the room ripped Lizzie back to that terrible moment when she'd watched Madison's life slipping away, and she'd flailed around in helpless panic. Her legs buckled, and she sat down hard on the edge of the couch, spilling hot tea across the top of her hand. She hissed, quickly placing the mug down by her feet. She stared at the angry red blotch on her hand, welcoming the scalding pain. The sharp bite of the burn cut through the pressure building in her chest, clearing her thoughts. Giving in to her emotions wasn't going to help Bear, and it wasn't going to change what happened to Madison.

She turned her hand over, palm up, and before she could call up her magick, it was there, bright and clear and powerful. She inhaled sharply, surprised at how so very different it felt and looked. Before the bonding, her magick had felt separate from her, unpredictable, sometimes flowing through her as easily as drawing breath, and other times frightening and uncontrollable. But now, she and her magick were one.

In her hand, she held a brilliant white ball of power. As it pulsed, sparks of gold winked throughout its depths, dancing like fireflies. No, she realized, it wasn't just her magick she was one with. It was the Elemental. There was no mistaking its energetic signature. She hadn't consciously reached out to it, but it was there in the orb of light she held.

She looked over her shoulder towards the bedroom. The urge to wake Grandma Faye and share her discovery was strong, but just as quickly, she dismissed it. Nothing good ever came out of involving others, she reminded herself. Turning back to the orb in her hand, she pondered what to do.

It had said it was the one Elemental in which all others were born, and although she didn't know what that was, she could feel it held more power than all the individual Elementals that had come to her when she called a circle. How could she use this to get to Bear?

"Hello," she whispered to the orb. "Can you help me rescue Bear?" As she asked the question, she held a clear picture of Bear in her mind, her power rippling out in waves. The one Elemental, *her* Elemental, remained silent, but her pulse quickened when she felt a familiar energy. It was faint, the connection brief, but she felt it. She felt Bear.

"Okay, okay, okay," she chanted, "This is good. He's still alive like the pendulum had shown, and now I can pick up his energy." Her Elemental remained quiet. Maybe they could only communicate directly when she was in the void, that place that existed out of time and space. Lizzie stood up abruptly. It had taken her to a liminal space, like her in-between, like the liminal space of a portal. "That means I can find him once I open the portal."

She wanted to jump into Grandma Faye's truck and return to the circle immediately, but she knew she couldn't leave Grandma Faye without a vehicle in case Madison's condition changed for the worse. And if she woke the old woman and told her what she was planning to do, Grandma Faye would try to stop her. She had no other choice but to make it back to Rose Cottage on foot. She decided to leave Grandma Faye a note but hoped she'd be back with Bear at her side before they woke. There was just one problem. "How do I open the portal?" She asked, the Elemental still flowing into her hands.

Suddenly, her body began to hum with the same resonance she'd felt when she found the faerie stone. Startled, she scanned the room, keeping her magick drawn. Near the wall of windows where one of the candlesticks and a pile of ritual tools had come to rest, all of it still coated in a layer of grey dust, something pulsed green, like a beacon, beneath the detritus.

She moved swiftly, her body tingling with energy. The magnetic pull she'd felt when she'd first stepped into Grandma Faye's home was stronger, more urgent. She knelt down in front of the pulsing green dust and carefully brushed it away, revealing a dark green, roughly textured, vaguely round crystal. There was a strange rune or sigil carved on its face, and the energy coming off it in waves felt of something ancient and powerful. Without thinking, she closed her fingers tightly around the crystal, her mind already turning to the walk back to the cottage.

Suddenly, the world winked out, and a searing cold darkness cut off Lizzie's terrified scream.

In the bedroom, Madison stirred, shifted onto her side, and then nestled back down into sleep. Next to her, the old woman slumbered peacefully, her head tilted back against the pillows. In the living room, a flurry of grey dust filled the air again, then slowly, gently, it settled down to the floor, carpeting the empty room.

CHAPTER FIFTEEN

Lizzie's vision swam, and her mouth watered. She was on her hands and knees, and when she tried to stand up, the world spun, and she dry heaved onto the ground. Pressing her forehead against the cool earth, she squeezed her eyes shut until the vertigo subsided.

Ground? Not the hardwood floor of Grandma Faye's cabin.

Her eyes flew open, catching sight of the steady green glow shining between the fingers of her closed fist. She looked up, slowly taking in her surroundings. She was back at the stone circle, and something else was there with her. Scrambling backwards, desperate to put some distance between herself and the thing sitting in the middle of the circle, she bumped up against the stones around the perimeter. She quickly scanned the trees, checking the reaction of the hundreds of ravens still surrounding the circle, finally resting her gaze on Quinn. They hadn't moved or changed their behavior from when they first appeared. They were all calmly, silently focused on the portal that now stood open, not at the edges of the circle like the three women had theorized, but at the very center.

She'd imagined a portal would be circular, but it wasn't round at all, but egg-shaped, wider at the bottom, narrowing at the top. In the center of the egg, a white mist swirled and eddied, punctuated by bolts of blue lightning that sizzled and snapped. The air smelled of ozone. She heard a bark, faint but unmistakable. She scrambled to her feet, dropping the faerie stone to the ground, forgotten.

"Bear?" She called out, her heart in her throat. The sound

of his replying bark had her running straight for the portal. The thunder of two hundred ravens calling out in alarm erupted around her, stopping her in her tracks. Adrenaline rushed through her body, and she shook her head to dislodge the realization of what she'd almost done. If the ravens hadn't stopped her, she would have rushed headlong into a portal. There was no telling what would have happened to her, and no one would have known what had happened to her or where she'd gone. As she stepped back from the portal, the ravens fell silent.

"Bear, come! Follow my voice, come to me!"

Bear continued to bark in reply to her voice. It sounded like he was coming closer, but with his next bark, it seemed farther away, like it was echoing off an enormous cavern. She shouted over and over to him until her throat ached and her voice was hoarse. But still, she kept calling.

She wanted to scream in frustration. This wasn't working. For whatever reason, he couldn't get through or couldn't find the exit.

Think Lizzie. Think. Grandma Faye had mentioned using a Beacon spell to guide Bear home. She may not know the spell. But she could be the Beacon.

Just like she did when Madison was bleeding out on the carpet, she called up all of her power until she vibrated with the light. Before she sent it through the portal, a thought occurred to her, and she pushed her magick down through the soles of her feet, imagining her energy as an anchor hooking into the earth itself. She gasped when she felt Gaia herself grabbing hold of Lizzie's energy and assisting in holding her in place.

Then, raising her hands so her palms faced the portal, she sent out a stream of power. She searched for Bear's energetic signature and found it almost immediately. The relief was so intense she faltered, almost breaking the connection, then redoubled her efforts. As soon as she felt Bear's resonance latch on to hers, she started drawing her energy back, reeling Bear in with it towards the entrance of the portal. As Bear drew nearer, suddenly, her energy snagged on something. She couldn't pull Bear forward. They were stuck.

"No, no, no," she shouted. She tried to draw up more energy, but she'd no more to pull from. Looking up at the ravens, her arms trembling with effort, she cried out, "Please, help me. Do something instead of just sitting there watching. Help me!" But the ravens remained impassive, looking down at her with no more concern than watching the breeze blow through the trees.

She dug in her heels and focused back on the portal. To her surprise, the mist had thinned, and she could make out indistinct shapes moving towards her. The sapphire lightning bolts increased across the surface of the portal, coalescing in a spinning ball in the center of the opening. The hair on her arms and the back of her neck rose.

The spinning blue ball suddenly dilated open, the light pouring through so intense Lizzie squeezed her eyes shut, but not before an image burned in her retinas: the silhouette of a man and a large beast moving towards the opening. The man was tall and broad-shouldered. The beast had massive shoulders and a long snout, too long to be a dog's.

Her energy, loose of whatever it was snagged on, came racing back into her. She was hit with a force that felt like a tank, and she was hurtled backwards and pinned to the ground.

She tried to laugh as a wet tongue covered her face, but the wind had been knocked out of her, and it came out as a gasping huff instead. "Bear," she croaked, sinking her fingers into his thick ruff and pulling his head back so she could look at him and stop him from bathing her face in dog saliva. "Don't ever do that again. You scared the life out of me." It was then that she noticed he was covered in glistening water droplets. They winked and sparkled like diamonds in the overcast light.

Quinn flew down from his perch, landing on one of the stones near Lizzie and Bear, and let out several raucous Guwacks and happy shakes of his tail feathers. Upon hearing his friend, Bear leapt off Lizzie to say hello, touching his nose to the raven's beak.

Once freed, Lizzie rolled onto her side, still struggling to take a full breath. She sat up slowly, watching Bear and Quinn cavort raucously around the clearing. Bear moved with a powerful grace, leaping, sprinting, turning suddenly. His limp was gone. Her eyes misted as she watched how freely Bear now moved and how powerful he really was. She'd only known him since the accident, and although he'd come a long way in his recovery, he had, up until now, walked with a very pronounced hitch in his step.

As if remembering an important task, Bear left off greeting his bird friend and trotted over to where the green crystal lay on the ground, still glowing steadily. He nimbly picked it up in his mouth and returned to Lizzie, dropping the crystal on the ground near her. He sat down, looked pointedly at the stone, and then over his shoulder to the still-open portal.

"Oh, right," Lizzie said cautiously, picking up the stone. Looking over at the portal, she noticed the smaller opening was gone, replaced by a thick white mist and streaks of blue lightning. She stood up but didn't approach the portal. "I'm not sure how to do this?" She looked down at Bear, who gently nudged her hand, holding the crystal.

Before she attempted to close the portal, she called up her powers and surrounded both of them in a protective bubble, linking her energy with his. "I'm not taking any chances," she said, holding out the crystal.

"Close the portal now," she demanded, then added, "Please." In response, the crystal pulsed its light towards the mist. There was an intense pressure in her ears, and the portal seemed to fold in on itself. Lizzie's ears popped as the portal disappeared. She looked down at the crystal in her hand. It was no longer glowing.

Slipping the crystal into her pocket, she looked around the circle. She increased the strength of the magick surrounding them, entwining their energies. "Let's go home." She motioned to Bear, and he followed by her side. Holding her breath as Bear stepped across the stones, she let out an audible sigh when nothing happened. Just as Madison had done previously, she snatched a twig and threw it at the center of the circle, where it landed softly. Then she grabbed a pinecone and threw it in the circle, then a stone. They both landed where she'd aimed.

Satisfied, she motioned for Bear to follow her down the path to the cottage, but instead, he turned and trotted around the outside of the stone circle, touching his nose to the ground occasionally. Puzzled, she watched him complete the circle, then raised his head to the ravens. She was still connected to him, and she sensed he was somehow communicating with the birds, but she couldn't discern what he was telling them.

She let out a startled cry as all two hundred birds took flight. The thunder of their wings was impressive, and as they circled up into the sky, an unnatural night descended on the forest. Lizzie tilted her head back to watch, but she couldn't see much more than an undulating, shivering current of black. They spiraled higher and higher until they cleared the treetops, where they dispersed in all directions.

She glanced down from the now-empty sky when she felt a cold nose bump her hand. Smiling down at the dog, she gave him a scratch behind his velvety ear when he suddenly shook his head and shoulders, the rippling motion carrying through his whole body, the golden droplets flying through the air. But instead of falling to the ground, what she'd originally thought were water droplets slowly drifted up and around Lizzie, flashing like fireflies. As each spark of magick touched her skin, they dissolved like gentle kisses, spreading warmth throughout her body and releasing a cacophony of scent around her; warm skin bathed in moonlight, the mineral tang of rushing water over dark stones, and a sensual ambery musk that filled her heart with longing threatening to undo her. She remembered that smell.

And then—she remembered him.

CHAPTER SIXTEEN

Lizzie's eyes darted back and forth, but she no longer saw what was in front of her. She couldn't feel her limbs. Her breath came out in ragged gasps in counterpoint to the staccato rhythm of her heartbeat. She was lost in the avalanche of memories raining down on her. They rushed in not as a coherent linear stream but as shards in a kaleidoscope, the fragments shifting, turning until they fell into place to reveal a complete image, the memory slotting into place in her mind.

Suddenly, two beams of light pierced her eyes, and she threw her arm across her eyes against the penetrating brightness.

"Lizzie, what's happened?"

The beams of light winked out, the rumble of an engine died, and Lizzie slowly lowered her arm, squinting into the darkness.

Grandma Faye quickly called up an orb of apple-green light, pushing back the darkness surrounding them.

"Are you alright? Are you hurt?" She approached the bottom step of the porch where Lizzie sat. Bear was on the step behind her, sitting on all fours, looking over her shoulder, his tail thumping loudly.

"I'm fine," Lizzie croaked, leaning back into Bear's warm, solid bulk. She frowned, looking past the old woman into the night. She couldn't remember walking back to the cottage or sitting on the stoop. How long had she been sitting like this, lost in her memories?

"Bear!" Grandma Faye inhaled sharply. "You got him back."

Bear shifted behind Lizzie and scrambled nimbly down

the steps. Without his warmth at her back, the cool night air snaked across her neck and back. She shivered, grabbing hold of the wooden tread she sat on with both hands, focusing on the rough wood against her palms as the memories kept flooding in.

"What time is it?"

"A little after eight." Grandma Faye released her orb of magick to float gently above her head as she bent to pet Bear. "Madison woke up needing to use the bathroom. Otherwise, I'd probably still be asleep. You should've woken me before you left."

"How is she?"

"She's doing remarkably well, but she still needs to rest. I had to force her back to bed and threaten to hide her satchel of tools when we realized you'd gone. You gave us both quite a fright."

"Sorry, I didn't mean to disappear like that." She struggled to get her words out. The distraction of her returning memories made it difficult to keep her thoughts in order. She dug in her pocket and held out the crystal to Grandma Faye.

Grandma Faye plucked the stone from Lizzie's hand, examining it closely. "What is it, and what does it have to do with finding Bear?"

"I don't know. I think it came out of the Faerie stone when it exploded. I felt it calling me, and when I picked it up, it instantly transported me to the circle, and the portal was there. It was open." Her words rushed out in her haste to explain what happened as she struggled with the more pressing thoughts in her head. "I used my bond with the Elemental to guide Bear out of the portal, then closed it down. It's safe now, I think."

Grandma Faye turned the crystal over in her hand. "It must be like some kind of key, acting on your intentions." Her hand visibly shook as she handed it back.

Lizzie cradled the now inert stone in her cupped hands.

"But that's not all that happened." A wave of sorrow engulfed her, catching her off guard, so when she tried to explain, a heart-wrenching sob came out instead.

Both Grandma Faye and Bear rushed to her side. "Lizzie, what's wrong? Talk to me. What happened?" she asked, taking a seat next to her, rubbing Lizzie's arm as Bear leaned his weight into her legs.

Through hiccupping sobs, Lizzie stuttered, "I—I—I got my memories back. All of them."

Grandma Faye's hand stopped moving up and down Lizzie's arm.

"It wasn't stress making me forgetful or my emerging bond with the Elemental. It was a man who called himself Wren. I met him shortly after I moved here." Her words tumbled out in a torrent. "He'd come to the cottage several times. I thought he was my friend. I thought he was…" Her words trailed off as she curled her fist around the crystal in her hand. Looking off into the night towards Emma's tree, she tried to put the fragmented memories into a coherent order. "I had just planted Emma's tree, and he showed up and asked me to go for a hike in the woods." She glanced down at her feet. "That's why I was wearing hiking boots when Gideon and Madison showed up." Her gaze followed the path she'd taken with Wren when they'd come back from their hike. She inhaled sharply. "He—he cast a spell on me when we returned from our hike. He must be a warlock." Chills ran down her spine. "But how did he get through my wards?" She turned back to Grandma Faye as she tried to make sense of what he'd done to her. Why steal the memories she had of him? What would be the point?

Lizzie expected to see surprise or shock on Grandma Faye's face, but in the soft green glow of the orb, she caught the resignation flickering across the old woman's eyes. It sent an ice-cold wave of dread washing over her.

Another memory slammed into place: the night of Audley's death. "He was there that night when Audley was shot." She remembered begging Wren to save Audley. She remembered…. "Oh my god." Lizzie scrambled to grab the railing and pushed herself up so she stood towering over Grandma Faye, the shock reverberating through her. "That night, you saw him too. You called him Light Bringer."

Grandma Faye remained seated, her head bowed.

"Who is he? What is he?" she demanded when Grandma Faye remained silent. "Tell me!"

"I don't know his real name. He never told me," Grandma Faye said softly, raising her head to look up at Lizzie. "But his kind has been called by many names: Light Bringers, Fair Folk, Sidhe, Tuathna Dé Danann, Faeries."

Lizzie scrambled down the steps, putting distance between her and the old woman. "I don't know what you're playing at, but that's not funny."

Grandma Faye raised her head, looking over at Lizzie. "But they do exist. And you are right. It's not funny at all."

"So why did he seek me out in the first place?" she cried, pressing her hands to her chest where an unbearable ache grew.

"I don't know."

"Why didn't you ever bring up Wren after the night Audley died?" she spat out.

"Because he asked me not to tell anyone of his presence there that night. And I wasn't aware you and he had already met, otherwise I wouldn't have agreed to keep silent."

"How could you let him do that to me?"

Grandma Faye's shoulders sagged. "I only knew what he'd done once he'd cast the memory wipe. He came to me *after* he'd already taken your memories to ask me to watch over you, to make sure there weren't any side effects to the spell. He said it was the only way."

"The only way to what? To make me think I was going crazy?" Lizzie felt sick.

"No, to keep you alive. That's why Wren could cast the spell, and your wards didn't stop him. His intention wasn't to harm you. It was to protect you, to keep you safe."

"From what?"

"From the Fey Council. They wanted you dead to remove any evidence of their existence here, but Wren argued your case and won. So, along with banning him from ever trying to contact you again, he was ordered to remove any memory you had of him."

"And why me and not you too?"

"Because they didn't know about me. Wren, in his haste to help you the night you were shot, forgot to cover his tracks when he crossed the veil to our world. Just like us, the Fey can detect when magick is used. They sensed he'd used his magick in our world, and they felt your magick, too, through the veil."

"Who is this council, and where do they get off deciding whether I get to live or die?" She clenched her fists at her sides, the crystal she still held in one hand dug into her palm.

"They are the governing body of his world. They are the highest authority in his world. The Fey broke off contact with humans eons ago, and their High Council strictly enforces their no contact rule with us. You see, Wren did what he had to do to protect you. There was no other way. He cares deeply for you."

Lizzie barked out a harsh laugh. "Well, he has a funny way of showing it. He violated my trust. He stole something from me that wasn't his to take. And you knew and said nothing. Did nothing. I don't know what is worse, your silence or that you didn't think I was capable of handling a threat to my own safety or making my own decisions about my own fucking life!" she shouted, pounding her chest with her fist.

Bear whined and nudged Lizzie's leg with his nose. She

looked down at him. "It's okay," she said as hot tears slipped down her cheeks. She kept her head down, threading her fingers through Bear's fur. "Am I in any danger now that I've got my memories back?"

"No, I don't think so. Wren said the council had ordered the bridge between our worlds to be destroyed as soon as he returned to his home. So, there is no way for them to know you retrieved your memories. And there is no way for you to go after them even if you could find another place where the veil has thinned because only the Light Bringers, the Faye, can travel between our worlds."

Lizzie startled when the old woman voiced exactly what Lizzie had been thinking of doing.

"Lizzie, I am more sorry than you can ever imagine. When I realized you were having breakthrough memories and that the spell didn't work, I was trying to find a way to help without revealing Wren's existence. Until I could figure out how to help you, I thought staying silent was the right thing to do, but I was wrong."

Lizzie looked down at Grandma Faye, who still sat on the stoop, the lines of her face etched deeper in the green light of the orb, her shoulders rounded in exhaustion. Lizzie desperately wanted to understand why the old woman had kept silent. Her explanation was reasonable, but it didn't feel that way to Lizzie. It felt like a betrayal. It felt like a thousand knives shredding her heart.

"I thought you were my friend, but you kept me in the dark. You lied to me."

"What can I do to make things right between us?"

"Leave." Lizzie looked back down at Bear, her fingers restlessly kneading the fur on his neck as the hot tears continued to burn her cheeks. "You can leave. Now."

"Yes, of course," she replied, resignation thick in her voice.

She grabbed the handrail and slowly pulled herself up. "I hope in time you can come to forgive me. You are as precious to me, Lizzie, as precious as a daughter. I did what I thought was best to keep you safe."

Lizzie kept her head down, staring at her fingers threaded through Bear's fur as Grandma Faye walked over to her. "If you choose to cut me out of your life, I will accept that, but if you ever need me, you just need to call, and I'll be there."

Lizzie stood silent, unmoving, tasting the bitter salt of her tears as the green orb of light followed the old woman to her truck, leaving Lizzie in darkness.

She remained unmoving as the sound of the truck engine faded into the distance. Bear looked to where Grandma Faye had gone, then pointed his muzzle to the sky and let out an anguished howl.

CHAPTER SEVENTEEN

The power had come on in the early morning hours, and now the coffeemaker burbled and spluttered, wafting the rich scent of dark roast through the open door to where Lizzie sat on the porch. She looked up from the shopping list she was scribbling on the last scrap of paper left in the house to catch Bear leaping up to snag the stick Quinn had flung through the air. Goosebumps rose along her arms as she watched her dog gracefully pivot in the air, land on all fours, and then tear off in the opposite direction.

Although she was in desperate need of a hot shower, the thought of having Bear out of her sight for even a moment made her heart bang painfully in her chest. So, for now, she was content to watch her companions have a morning romp while she waited for her morning coffee to brew. No longer having a limp wasn't the only change she'd noticed since Bear had returned. Not once had he used his magick to dematerialize and materialize through closed doors or when playing as he was now, nor was he turning on the taps to tell Lizzie that he wanted fresh water in his bowl. She didn't know if being trapped in the liminal space of the portal had altered his magick or if the experience made him reluctant to use his power anytime soon.

When she'd first noticed this change in his behavior, her first thought was to call Grandma Faye, and she'd gone as far as picking up the phone before she stopped herself. She was still so angry with the old woman despite the niggling suspicion that, faced with the same situation, Lizzie probably would have acted just as Grandma Faye had.

But when her thoughts inevitably turned to Wren, she didn't harbor any doubts about how she felt about what he'd done. She alternated between wanting to curl up in a ball to block out the pain, to screaming at the top of her lungs, and relieving the tightness in her body by smashing things and pulling down the world around her.

Suddenly, the coffeemaker shrilly beeped three times, startling Lizzie, and she dropped the tiny nub of pencil she'd been using to write her list. She let out a sound of dismay as it bounced across the wooden planks and disappeared through the space between the boards. She didn't really need it anymore as she'd finished her list, and there wasn't really much left of the pencil but a two-inch stub. But the pang of sorrow she'd felt when it fell from her grasp had her calling up her magick, and with a flick of her wrist, the pencil popped up from between the gap in the planking and into her hand a second later. She curled her fingers around it protectively.

She knew it was stupid to care so much about something as inconsequential as a worn-down bit of pencil, but it was the only thing of Audley she had left. And without thinking, she'd used it all the way down to nothing. She held it tight to her chest, squeezing her eyes shut as she fought back tears. She'd promised him she would find out what had happened to his granddaughter, Cathy, and she hadn't kept her promise.

She heard the click of nails on wood as Bear clambered up the porch steps. When he nudged her leg, she opened her eyes and smiled down at him. "I'm okay, buddy. I just need my morning coffee, that's all." She gave him a scratch behind the ears. "And I bet you two would like some breakfast." Before she even had a chance to stand up, Quinn chortled enthusiastically and flew into the cottage. "I guess that would be a yes," she laughed and headed inside with Bear following behind.

After filling Bear's food dish with the last of the kibble, she scrounged around in the refrigerator for something to feed Quinn. Last night, when she fed them, she was alarmed at how low her food supply was, not to mention she was almost out of coffee, prompting the need to go shopping this morning. She managed to find a bit of cheese and a tiny piece of leftover pie for the raven. Placing Quinn's breakfast in a saucer on the table, she finally snagged a cup of coffee for herself. Leaning against the counter, she sipped her coffee, her gaze roaming around the mess she'd made in the living room last night.

After Grandma Faye had left the night before, Lizzie had retreated inside the cottage, distracting herself momentarily with lighting both fires in the fireplace and woodstove and filling up the woodstove's water reservoir so she'd have hot water. But those small tasks hadn't stopped her anger and hurt from building. As she'd watched the flames licking at the fresh wood, her mind kept circling around, replaying the moment her memories came flooding back and confronting Grandma Faye with her part in what Wren had done to her. She'd been desperate to stop her mind from going over and over the pain like a needle stuck in a record groove playing the same discordant notes, so when she had the idea of writing down all her newly restored memories, she ran with it. It was something tangible she could do with all her pain, to get it out of her body and slow down her thoughts.

She'd soon discovered she didn't actually have any writing paper or anything resembling the efficient steno pad and mechanical pencil Madison carried around with her. Lizzie hunted through every cupboard and drawer, searching for anything she could use, even dumping out the contents of her purse on the kitchen table.

She'd managed to scrounge together an odd assortment of paper bags, receipts, and even a half roll of parchment paper to write on, and in the kitchen junk drawer, she'd found a nub of a carpenter's pencil left behind by Audley.

Setting the bits of paper on the coffee table, she'd spent the night feverishly writing, spurred on by an irrational fear that somehow her memories would evaporate before she could get them out of her mind. By the time the darkness pressing against the window panes began to fade to grey, signaling the coming dawn, there was a motley pile of scribbled on bits and scraps of paper swamping the small coffee table. She weighed down the whole mess with the chunk of lightning glass that normally sat on the mantle to protect them from being disturbed by Bear's large tail, which had a habit of sweeping clean any surface it got near to.

Now, looking at the mountain of paper, she wasn't sure her nightlong journaling had helped much. She still had unanswered questions, and she was still angry. She also realized she needed to add some notebooks to her supply list. She gulped the rest of her coffee and then placed the empty mug in the sink.

"Enough," she reprimanded herself, her voice sounding too loud in the quiet cottage. She could do this on her own, whatever *this* was. She didn't need Grandma Faye or Gideon or the Order, for that matter, to learn all she could about Wren and his kind and fulfill her promise to Audley. It made sense to start with Cathy. Seeing as she had to go into the village to buy food, she could ask around, maybe starting with the grocery store clerk. Although Lizzie wasn't sure how she'd go about getting the villagers to tell her anything they might know about where Cathy might be. During her few forays into town, the villagers hadn't been very welcoming, and some had even been rude to the point of aggression. Then she remembered the young man at the coffee shop. He'd been pleasant enough. Perhaps she'd start with him.

Stretching her arms in the air to relieve the stiffness from spending the night hunched over the coffee table writing, she caught a whiff that made her nose wrinkle. She hesitated for a moment before heading to the bathroom, thinking to shut and lock the front door to keep Bear inside while she jumped in the shower. Instead, she marched into the bathroom and flicked on the light. She'd already done all that she could to secure the portal and ward her property. She had to accept there was no such thing as safety in this world, either for her or the ones she loved, no matter how much she wanted to protect them. And she couldn't, wouldn't be like Wren and take away her dog's freedom to make his own choices, no matter how much it scared her.

She did, however, have a brief moment of panic after she'd showered and dressed and come out to the kitchen to find the cottage empty. But as soon as she stepped out onto the porch, she found Bear and Quinn lounging under the large shading branches of the cedar trees that grew near the house. Bear had chosen to stretch out on the cool sand of the driveway, and Quinn picked a nearby low branch to roost on. Bear raised his head in her direction as she approached. Lizzie jingled her truck keys, and in one fluid movement, he rolled his substantial bulk onto his feet and trotted over to her side. The ease in which Bear moved still astonished her. She shook her head and smiled.

"Do I even need to ask if you want to come?"

Bear shook himself, spraying damp sand in every direction. Lizzie raised her arm to shield her eyes from the mini sandstorm. "While I appreciate you not tracking half the driveway in the truck, did you have to shake right next to me?" She admonished, but there was a smile in her voice. "Now you have to promise me no dematerializing while we are in the village, understood?"

In reply, he cocked his head to one side, one ear flopping over his eye. "I'll take that as a yes." Patting him on the head, she opened the passenger-side door of the truck. "In you go," she said, stepping aside as he vaulted up and onto the seat. "Quinn," she said, calling over the side of the vehicle, still holding the door open, "Did you want to come too?"

Quinn gave an odd vocalization somewhere between a caw and his happy guwah sound that she'd come to understand was his version of no. He slowly stretched out his wing and began to preen his feathers.

"Okay, we shouldn't be gone long. I've left the window open so you can head inside if it starts to rain," she said before hopping into the truck and firing up the engine. As they drove down the driveway, Bear stuck his head out the window and barked a goodbye to Quinn, who was still busily preening. She drove to the still open gate but stopped just outside it to close it and secure the lock. She knew it wasn't necessary with all the magickal protection surrounding her property, but it made her feel more secure in leaving the place and Quinn by themselves.

The whole way into town, Bear kept his head out the window, his paddle-shaped ears flapping frantically behind him, his jowls wobbling from the breeze as he tilted his nose up to catch every scent whizzing past him. Lizzie glanced over and burst out laughing. It felt good to laugh, and she reached over to scratch his broad back before focusing back on the curving mountain road.

Her mood continued to improve as she drove into the village, the sky clearing as if to match the change in her outlook. The June morning was everything one would want. The bright, clear sunlight bounced diamonds off the lake as a gentle breeze rocked the handful of pleasure boats tied up along the docks in the small harbor, the sky a bowl of cerulean blue. She was just approaching the grocery store when she spied a collection of colored canopies lined up on either side of the road that led down to the lake. The road had been cordoned off, and two large wooden sandwich boards announced the Beaton Farmer's Market.

She parked in the lot facing the market, and leaning over the steering wheel, she scanned the stalls. She had planned on leaving Bear in the truck with the windows rolled down while she went to the grocery store. But eyeing the stalls closest to her truck piled with fresh vegetables, neat displays of jars of jellies and preserves that sparkled like rubies and garnets in the morning light, and another with loaves of bread in wicker trays, she quickly made up her mind. The market had just opened, so it wasn't too crowded, and she'd already spotted a few people walking their dogs as they shopped the vendor's tables. Maybe this would be a better place to inquire about Cathy? She also knew she was taking a risk, even though Bear hadn't used his magick since he came back from the portal, but she was willing to take it.

"Change of plans. Did you want to come with me while I go shopping over there?" she said, pointing to the market. Bear tried to wag his tail, but the cab of the truck was too small, and he had to content himself with wiggling his bottom into the seat. "You need to be on your best behavior, no drooling on strangers, watch where your tail is wagging, and I would really appreciate it if you didn't use your magick," she said with mock sternness. He leaned into her and touched his wet nose to hers. Pulling her head back and laughing, she said, "Okay, let's go."

Holding Bear's leash loosely in her hand, she decided to start on the stalls on her right. The first vendor was selling canvas shopping bags, which was no doubt strategic in their choosing to be the first booth, as Lizzie quickly realized she'd forgotten to take a tote or bag of any kind with her when she left Rose Cottage.

The wiry young man behind the display table shot Lizzie a welcoming grin and then glanced down at Bear.

"Whoa, hey there, fella," he said, leaning over the table. "Aren't you the handsome boy?"

Much to Lizzie's amusement, Bear's response was to plonk his butt down in a perfect sit, with his back straight and his head erect. And she could have sworn he puffed up his chest. "And he knows it," Lizzie laughed, patting Bear's head affectionately.

She turned her attention to the tote bags spread out on the

table. "This is my first time at the market, and I forgot to bring any bags." She fingered the heavy canvas of a bag closest to her. "These are wonderfully made."

"Thank you. My granny taught me how to sew on her old Singer machine, and I took a course in silk screening and linocuts in college. I like the idea of making something practical but also beautiful."

"I'll take these two," she said, placing two large bags off to the side. One had a black and white image of a raven. The other she immediately recognized as a stylized image of the view of the lake from the promenade.

"Sure thing," he said as he waited while Lizzie dug out her wallet. "And depending on how long your vacation is, the pub has karaoke every Thursday night, and next weekend is the annual dragon boat races."

"Good to know. The dragon boat race sounds like fun, but I'm not a tourist. I live here. Well, not here in the village, but fifteen minutes out of town. I moved a few months back. How much do I owe you?" She looked up from her open wallet when he didn't reply. He was looking at her strangely.

"Are you the lady who bought Grey house?"

She was about to say no, then she remembered when Birdie had first shown her Rose cottage, she'd called it Grey house. "Umh, yes, I did."

"Well, it is sure good to finally meet you." He stuck out his hand. "I'm Hank."

"Lizzie," she replied, slowly offering her hand.

"Hi, Lizzie," he said vigorously, shaking her hand. "And put your money away. These are on the house," he said, handing over the bags.

"That's very generous of you, but I couldn't possibly."

"It's the least I can do."

While she appreciated the young man's generosity, his

words struck her as a bit odd. Why was giving her free bags the least he could do? It wasn't until she thanked him again and began wandering down the stalls with her list in hand that she realized she'd missed her first opportunity to gather information about Cathy.

She quickly filled the first bag and most of the second one with spring greens, a bunch of radishes, a small bag of new potatoes, pots of homemade strawberry and rhubarb jam, and even a large jar of freshly ground peanut butter. And with each stop she made, she noticed a pattern emerging. Each vendor greeted her warmly, and when Lizzie went to pay for her purchases, they all refused to take her money and instead gifted her with free products or produce. The strange behavior not only increased her unease but also stopped her from asking anything about Audley's granddaughter. Bear, on the other hand, was more than happy to taste his free samples of peanut butter, hear the endless praise of 'what a handsome boy,' and get scratches behind the ears. After the first few stops, people stopped asking if she was new in town, and instead, the greeting was a welcome to the village. If this continued, she would end up getting everything on her list for free.

On the surface, the vendors' behavior should have made her feel mildly amused or even surprisingly grateful for the unexpected welcoming gestures. Instead, as she made her way through the market, she began to feel uneasy, like there was something else motivating all the vendors' behavior that she wasn't privy to. And how did they know without asking that she was the woman who had bought Grey House, or new to town when she could have just as easily been a tourist? The only person she'd told was Hank, and as far as she'd noticed, he hadn't left his booth since she'd talked to him.

And was it just her growing unease making her paranoid, for she would swear there was a lot of whispering and furtive glances aimed her way. But when she turned towards anyone, they always met her gaze with an open, warm smile and polite words of good morning, and so nice to finally meet you.

She was contemplating cutting her wander through the market short and escaping back to the safety of her cottage when she approached a stall selling new and used books. One half of the table had neat piles of old leather-bound volumes with embossed titles. The other half displayed new clothbound books in bright, juicy colors. There was also a wooden tray of pens, and behind it were several bottles of ink stacked expertly in a pyramid.

As she stepped in closer, she realized the new books all had blank covers. She put her overflowing carrier bags down by her feet and reached out to the nearest book, one with a bright green of a ripe melon, and gently opened the cover. She discovered the thick cream-colored pages inside were blank, and on the inside cover was a hand-stamped logo that read Black Bird Bindery. A small flutter of excitement tickled her belly. The journal was exquisite. She'd originally thought her best bet at finding something to write in would be the new age shop where she'd bought the crystals she'd needed when she'd confronted the demon, as she remembered seeing some there. But the ones now displayed before her were not only beautifully made but just the right size for resting in your lap and offered ample space for writing.

As she perused the journals, Bear tugged at the leash and proceeded to wack her leg with his enthusiastic tail wags. Looking down, she saw Bear was standing up, staring across the market. A young girl, probably no more than seven or eight years old, was making a beeline for Bear. She wore a cotton sundress with smocking on the bodice and printed with bright red ladybugs. Her chestnut hair was tied back in two high pigtails that bounced merrily as she ran towards Bear, her arms thrown wide.

Bear sat down and waited. The little girl didn't slow her

pace as she ran straight into Bear's chest and wrapped her pudgy arms around him in greeting. Bear sat patiently while the little girl embraced him, his tail thumping the ground. Then, just as abruptly, she let go and, placing her hands on either side of his face, she leaned in and kissed him on the nose. Bear reciprocated with a slurp of his tongue on her cheek.

"You're so pretty," the little girl said, giggling. Her laughter was high and sweet. She fluffed up the hair on his head, twisting a length of it around her little fingers, getting it to stand up straight like a water spout. "There, now you look even prettier. Like a unicorn. A faerie dog unicorn," she said, clapping her hands. "Can faerie dogs be unicorns, too? I mean, I've never met one, but they could exist, couldn't they?"

"Hello there," Lizzie said, trying hard not to laugh at Bear's new hairstyle. "Are your parents nearby?" Lizzie was used to living in a big city, and it made her nervous to see someone so young not accompanied by an adult. She scanned the growing crowd but didn't see anyone coming over to collect the young girl.

The girl looked up, shading her eyes from the morning sun as she leaned one hip into Bear's side, one arm draped over his back. "Oh wow, you sparkle too."

Lizzie squatted down so she was at eye level with the girl. She looked vaguely familiar, but she couldn't place where she would have seen her before. "Are you here with your mom or dad?"

"My mom. When I saw the faerie dog, I asked her if I could come over and pet him. She said I could because you were a nice lady, but I had to be quick about it. I am supposed to be helping her today." She waved over in the direction of a white food truck that had The Milk Wagon painted across the side. A woman standing at the serving window of the truck waved back. The young girl twirled back to face Lizzie. "I didn't know that you were a faerie, too, but I guess that would make sense because who else would have a faerie dog than a faerie. My name's Allachka, what's yours?" Her words came out in a rush, leaving her a little breathless.

Lizzie inhaled sharply. Instantly, she was back at the women's shelter peeling carrots in the kitchen with Sweetie, the cook. Sweetie mentioned another little girl who was staying there with her mom had left her a gift. The gift had been a little faerie figurine she'd hand painted, which now sat on the mantelpiece in Lizzie's bedroom. That young child had been able to see the magick around Lizzie just like this little one could see it on both her and Bear. Lizzie pushed down the rest of the memories from that time, of the fear in that child's mother when she saw what Lizzie could do. How, after that, everyone at the shelter avoided her. A new frightening thought dawned on her. Although she lived out of town, the village was the closest place to buy food and supplies. The vet was here. How was she going to avoid the children seeing her magick and calling her a faerie or, worse, a witch?

Lizzie focused on keeping her voice light. "I'm Lizzie, and this is Bear," she said, motioning to Bear, who was still proudly sporting his new hairstyle.

"That's funny. You named your faerie dog after another animal. Are there bears where you come from? Are they faeries, too? Why don't you have wings? I thought faeries are supposed to have wings. Do you live in the forest? My mom says you live at Grey House, so I guess that's in the forest. But I thought faeries had their own magical world. Maybe you do. Do you? Is there a magickal tree in the forest with a magickal door? Is that how you come here to visit us? And can I go with you when you go back home? I would love to meet more faeries and maybe a unicorn. Do you have unicorns where you come from? I would really like to pet a unicorn and give him a hug."

Lizzie tried to follow the barrage of questions and wasn't sure where to start trying to answer them, but before she could open her mouth to reply, Allachka turned her attention back to Bear. "I have to go now, but I'll be back," she said and planted another kiss on Bear's nose. "It was nice to meet you."

"It's nice to meet you, too," Lizzie replied, but the young girl had already turned away from her and was skipping back towards her mother.

Lizzie stood up and watched the young girl climb up the steps at the back of the food truck before returning to look over the journals displayed on the table. To the green journal she still held in her hand, she added two more, a pale pink and a soft red one. She looked up to pay for them, but no one was manning the booth. She turned to her left to ask the lady, whom she'd just bought two jars of peanut butter from, if she knew where the vendor was, but she was busy with a customer. Turning to her right, she waited while the young woman manning the stall was putting away cash in a small metal box from her last sale. Her back was towards Lizzie.

"Excuse me," Lizzie said, intending to ask when the vendor of the journals would be back when the young woman turned to face her. "Birdie," Lizzie exclaimed at the same time Birdie called out in surprise. Birdie had undergone yet another transformation of her looks, but this time, Lizzie was pleased to see it was for the better. The last time she'd talked to Birdie had been when she'd been working at the Burger Hut, and she had looked defeated and wrung out. The young woman before her had cut her glossy black hair into a sleek, angled bob. Her eyes were bright, no longer rimmed in heavy kohl. And gone were the dark circles under her eyes. Instead, she looked vibrant.

"Hi," Birdie said and hesitated before stepping over to stand behind the table of journals. She wouldn't look at Lizzie, her hand fluttering up to her neck where a red flush bloomed.

"It's good to see you," Lizzie said earnestly, puzzled as to Birdie's less than enthusiastic greeting. "So, both these booths are yours?"

"This one with the handmade journals is my booth, but I also man my Aunt's antique stall. Since I quit the Burger Hut, I work part-time for my Aunt's antique shop again and the farmer's market over the summer."

Holding up the journals Lizzie had picked out, she asked, "You made these?"

The flush on Birdie's neck now spread to her cheeks as she toyed with the edge of a nearby journal, still avoiding Lizzie's eyes. "Yes. I know they aren't perfect. I'm still learning. I started making these first," she said, picking up what Lizzie had originally thought was a second-hand book. "My aunt buys lots from Estate sales, and she inevitably ends up with a pile of old books that we can't sell because the bindings are shot or the paper is so badly foxed or mildewed they aren't readable. I hated the idea of throwing them out, especially when some of the covers are so beautiful, so I upcycled the covers and made them into blank journals. I sold a few at the antique store, so I tried my hand at making new journals, too. I figured if I had to be here running my Aunt's booth anyway, I could try to sell some of my journals so I could make money to buy more supplies. I eventually want to get a website up and sell them online, too." As she spoke, Birdie's voice took on a more animated quality, but she still kept her gaze focused on the journals.

Lizzie put down the stack of new journals she'd picked out and selected an upcycled book in a deep teal color with a design of leaves and vines in navy. She smiled when she read the title. It was an early edition of The Secret Garden.

"I'll take this one, too," she said, adding the book journal to her growing stack. "And don't sell yourself short. These are beautifully made. If I may be so bold, you didn't look very happy when I last saw you at the Burger Hut. From what I can see, your talents were wasted serving up fast food."

"Umh, about that." She shifted uncomfortably. "I'm sorry I never got back to you about going antiquing with you like I promised. I was going to call you, but realized I didn't have your current phone number. Then I thought I would come out to Grey House, but I..." Birdie kept her eyes downcast as she spoke, her hands nervously fiddling with the pen display. "I kept putting it off, and then it got to the point where too much time had passed, and it felt awkward and overwhelming. And now, saying that out loud, I can hear how lame that all sounds."

Lizzie reached across the table to gently squeeze Birdie's hand. "It's okay, it really is. I was surprised when I didn't hear from you, but I was more concerned when I saw you at the Burger Hut and realized you weren't working at the realty office anymore. You don't have to explain why you didn't come out to see me because I understand what it is like to be in a dark place mentally. I know what it's like when just getting out of bed takes a monumental amount of energy."

"Really?" Birdie asked with relief, finally looking up at Lizzie.

"Really," Lizzie repeated. She realized not only was it good to see Birdie again, but Birdie might be able to help her to find Cathy. Maybe not help her find the missing girl, but give her some information to start her search. "And I insist you come out for a visit. We could have lunch, and I could show you what I've done to the cottage."

"I would love that."

"When are you free?'

"Is today too soon? I'll be done here at about one."

"Perfect. One it is." Lizzie smiled, handing over the small stack of journals she'd collected. "And I would like to take all of these." Sunlight glinting off the faceted glass bottles of ink caught her eye. Lizzie thought of Audley's pencil stub she'd been using. "And I need a pen. I was just going to pick up a disposable ballpoint, but those fountain pens are stunning."

"I get them from a small shop on Granville Island where I get my bookbinding supplies from. They formulate their own inks and get these pens custom-made using local artisans." Before Lizzie could point out a tortoiseshell one with brass fittings, Birdie's fingers plucked it from the tray and held it out. "I think this one would suit you perfectly. It's not real tortoiseshell, of course, just finely made Lucite. It has a medium nib, which is what I like for journal writing."

Lizzie took the pen. It had a pleasant weight as she turned it in the light to catch the depth and richness of the colors, ranging from amber to a deep mahogany.

"And," continued Birdie, delight filling her voice, "one always needs at least two colors of ink." As Lizzie looked over the ink samples Birdie had produced on swatches of paper, Bear pulled on the leash again. She glanced down at her dog, smiling at his new hairdo. "I'll be done in a few minutes, and then we will get moving." Turning back to Birdie, she said, "He's been given treats at almost every table we've stopped at, and now I'm afraid he's become a bit of a princess expecting attention and food."

Birdie smiled. "I can see why people dote on him. Even with Allachka's hair styling, he is a very handsome boy." Bear acknowledged the compliment with a tail wag.

Lizzie and Birdie turned their attention back to ink swatches. Lizzie had just decided on two bottles, one of a deep black and the other a sepia-toned brown, when Bear tugged again on the leash, and Lizzie heard the now familiar laughter of Allachka.

Lizzie looked over her shoulder. The young girl held out an ice cream cone. Bear, whom Lizzie had seen wolf down a whole bowl of kibble in seconds flat and gobble down a spoonful of peanut butter with one swipe of his tongue, now proceeded to delicately lick the vanilla ice cream. She watched his face as he tasted ice cream for the first time, his eyes growing wide. He scooted closer to the cone, and the little girl held it out for him to take another taste.

"I knew you'd like it. Ice cream is the best," she said, then took a few licks of her own. Lizzie was horrified. What if Allachka's mother saw her little girl sharing her ice cream with Lizzie's dog? She glanced over to Birdie to see what she should do, but Birdie just threw her head back and laughed.

"I'm so sorry," said a woman from the food truck as she scurried over to the young girl. She was the complete opposite of her daughter. Her blonde hair was styled in a bun with a few stray tendrils framing her high, round cheeks and brilliant blue eyes. She was petite with a curvaceous figure that the white cook's apron couldn't hide. She exchanged greetings with Birdie before turning her attention to her daughter. "Allachka, I told you to ask first if you could give the dog some ice cream."

"Sorry, Mom, I was going to ask Lizzie, but she was busy talking to Birdie, and you've always told me never to interrupt people when they are talking. I was just waiting my turn to ask, but Bear really wanted a taste, and he only took a very little lick."

"It is very generous of you to give Bear a treat, and I can see that he really likes it," Lizzie said. "And yes, it's okay if he has some."

Allachka's face was a picture of innocence as she held out the cone for Bear to take another lick, and then she proceeded to take a large lick of her own.

"I can tell by the look on your face that you're worried about her sharing her food with your dog. Don't be," said the woman. "We live on a farm, and trust me, dog germs are the least of what she's exposed to. No doubt that is why she never gets sick. Her immune system has been exposed to a variety of things.

She even used to make mud pies and eat them."

"Mom, that was ages ago when I was a baby. I'm not a baby anymore. Besides, I like to lick rocks now. They taste better, less gritty." Allachka turned her attention back to Bear and continued to share her ice cream treat with him, the adults now forgotten.

This time, it was Lizzie's turn to laugh out loud.

The woman shifted a large carrier bag she'd been holding in her right hand to her left and held out her hand. "I'm Anna. It's so lovely to finally meet you."

"Lizzie," she said automatically, even though she now understood everyone at the market knew who she was. "It's nice to meet you, too. So, you have a dairy farm?" She asked, pointing to the logo on the carrier bag.

"Yes, it's just south of town. Along with cows, we have a few laying hens. Oh, and this is for you," Anna said, holding out the bag. "Just a few goodies from our farm to welcome you to the village."

"That's awfully generous of you." Lizzie peered inside the bag. There was a wedge of cheese wrapped in white butcher paper, a carton of eggs, two glass bottles; one of milk, the other of cream, and, from the smell, a fresh loaf of bread. "You make bread too?" Lizzie realized she wanted to learn how to make bread and cook from scratch. She had relied on Grandma Faye to provide much of the home cooking Lizzie had enjoyed. Since she'd entered the market, she hadn't once thought of what Grandma Faye had done to her, how she had betrayed her. She blinked hard at the sorrow that pierced her heart and focused her attention on Anna as she spoke.

"When I first started coming to the market with the Milk Wagon, I just sold my dairy products and eggs, but I realized people would probably enjoy a breakfast sandwich, being that the market opens early, so I started selling those, then people started requesting loaves of bread to buy. And, of course, I sell coffee, juice, and water."

"And you run a farm?"

"Yes. I only operate the food truck during the summers when the market is open, and my husband and I run the farm, which is a full-time occupation."

"I help too," Allachka said, munching on the cone, the ice cream long since devoured by her and Bear. "I collect the eggs and read to the cows. They like stories about princesses and Dr. Seuss books because they like how things rhyme." She held out the last remnant of cone in the palm of her hand, and Bear carefully placed it in his mouth and crunched it down.

"You should come out to the farm sometime, and I can show you around. Our phone number is on the bag. Give me a call soon. But for now, young lady, we have to get back to the truck. We have customers waiting. And you need to wash that ice cream off your face."

"Okay," Allachka said, sounding less than enthusiastic. "Bye, Bear, I'm glad we're friends now, and maybe next weekend we can have another ice cream." She reached over, and just like she had when she'd first met him, she grabbed his face in her hands and kissed him soundly on the nose. And just like before, Bear reciprocated, but this time, instead of licking her cheek, he happily licked off the smears of vanilla ice cream around the little girl's mouth.

Anna smirked and took her daughter by the hand. "Don't forget to wash up before you help me serve. You might not mind dog slob, but our customers will. Come on, little miss." To Lizzie, she said, "Again, it was such a pleasure to meet you, and I look forward to having you come for a visit."

"I look forward to it too. Perhaps the both of you could come and visit Bear and me. And I have a few hens of my own you could read to, Allachka."

"Did you hear that, Bear? I can come for a play date. But I

should probably tell you, chickens don't really like to be read to. They prefer to have someone sing to them."

"I'll keep that in mind. See you soon," Lizzie said as Anna and her daughter headed back to the food truck. Turning to face Birdie, she said, "Okay, what the hell is going on? I have yet to pay for anything I've picked up at the market. Despite my attempts to pay, vendors keep giving me things for free." She held up the bag full of goodies Anna had just given her. "I've lived here for months now and have come in town to shop, and if anything, the villagers were far from friendly. Why this sudden change of heart and this over the top generosity?"

Birdie eyed Lizzie with an assessing look. "You really don't know, do you?" she asked incredulously.

"No, I don't. Enlighten me."

Birdie chuckled. "It's because you single handily brought down Jon's drug cartel. We've been living under his thumb for years, and his father before him. You've freed us, Lizzie. And as you can tell, we just want to thank you for giving this place back to us, giving our lives back to us. You're a hero."

Lizzie blinked hard. "The whole village knows what happened? How is that possible? I haven't told anyone." Lizzie felt oddly exposed. What did the villagers know about that night? Surely, they didn't know about the Order, or that magick was involved?

"I keep forgetting you've never lived in a small town. There are no secrets in small towns. News travels fast along the gossip telegraph. The police who were called in to help that night, the ones not on Jon's payroll, aren't immune to gossiping. They've grown up here, too. Of course, they told the rest of us, and it was in the papers too."

"What?" Lizzie was now truly alarmed.

"I kept the article if you wanted to read it, or you can go online as the paper publishes there, too. Although the article didn't mention you by name and, of course, there wasn't a picture of you. If they had asked me, I could have told them who you were, but I was out of town when the whole thing went down."

"So, if my picture wasn't in the paper, how does everyone here know who I am?

Instead of answering right away, Birdie reached into her back pocket and pulled out her cell phone. She poked and swiped the screen, then held it out for Lizzie to see. Leaning across the table, Lizzie peered at the screen. The display showed a series of text messages, the first one from Hank, the young man at the first booth Lizzie had stopped at. She looked up at Birdie for an explanation.

"You were the one who told Hank you bought Grey House. And all of us vendors are part of a chat group set up by the organizing committee. It is supposed to be for keeping us informed of any changes or issues involving the market, but we mostly use it for sending funny memes and gossip, of course. As soon as Hank found out who you were, he sent a text to the group," Birdie said matter-of-factly before putting her phone down on the table and wrapping Lizzie's journals in brown paper.

"Oh," Lizzie said in alarm. She turned to scan the market stalls. A few vendors waved hello when she looked their way. Just then, Birdie's phone started to vibrate, making the nearby pen display rattle. Lizzie saw Birdie glance down to check her phone, her eyes growing wide.

"Um, Lizzie—" Birdie said, looking up from her phone. "You might want to finish up your shopping and head for home as soon as possible if you don't want to be swarmed by more attention."

"Why?" she asked instinctively, looking over her shoulder, then turning back to Birdie, "What's going on?"

"Hank just texted the group that Ginny and her Welcome

Wagon troop are on their way down to see you. If you're uncomfortable with the vendors showing their gratitude, you're not going to like what's heading your way. Ginny and her underlings are not only going to shower you with gifts and praise, but they will do their best to rope you into volunteering for as many committees as they can. Ginny also heads up several community organizations for *the betterment and beautification of the village*," Birdie said, using air quotes. "You won't have a second of free time or privacy. She will wear you down until you willingly volunteer for every organization just to get her to stop pestering you."

"You can't be serious."

"Oh, I am. I'm deadly serious." Birdie proceeded to place Lizzie's journals, pens, and ink in a small craft paper carrier bag and handed it over to Lizzie. "If I were you, I would skedaddle."

A small bubble of panic started to form in Lizzie's chest. Reminding herself yet again what obstacles she'd overcome recently, not the least of which was opening a portal to another dimension and rescuing her dog, she took a deep breath before replying. "I will head for home, but not until I pay you for my purchases, and I still need to pick up Bear's kibble from the grocery store." Lizzie pulled out her wallet and then raised a hand to stop Birdie from refusing payment. "While I am, like the rest of the villagers, relieved to be rid of Jon and his henchmen, I didn't do it alone. I am no hero. Now is not the time or place to get into the details of what actually happened and who was involved, but you need to understand the significant role you played in all of this."

"Me? I didn't do anything."

"Yes, you did. If you hadn't gone above and beyond your duties as a realtor's assistant and found the paperwork for Grey House and then facilitated the sale, none of the following events would have occurred, and I would have never met Bear or Quinn." She was about to add Grandma Faye to the list, but stopped herself. "And you lost your job as a result. So, allow me my turn to show you my gratitude by paying for these beautifully crafted journals and honoring the courage it took to start your own business." Noticing the stubborn look on Birdie's face, she added, "And if you still feel the need to show your appreciation, you can bring a bottle of wine for lunch. Deal?" She held out several bills.

"Deal," replied Birdie softly. Unshed tears glistened in Birdie's eyes as she took the proffered money and placed it in a metal cashbox hidden under the table. Lizzie wondered if the young woman before her had ever been praised for her talents and skills before. "I just had a thought," Birdie said, her emotions now under control, "Seeing as Ginny's probably mere minutes away from arriving. Not only will I bring the wine for this afternoon, but I will also pick up Bear's kibble so you can get going."

"That sounds like a plan," Lizzie easily agreed. She dug out a few more bills from her wallet. "This should cover his food. And I will see you at one. Just honk your horn when you arrive, and I will come down and open the gate," she said, and after telling her the brand of Bear's food, she looped Bear's leash on her wrist, gathered up all her shopping bags, and headed for her truck.

As she drove out of town, she spared a glance at Bear, who was curled up in a ball, fast asleep on the passenger seat, the fur on the top of his head still styled in his unicorn horn. His gentle snoring filled the cab, a soft putt-putt sound emitting as his jowls vibrated on his exhale, had Lizzie smiling from ear to ear. Someone enjoyed his outing and all the treats and praise he received. And much to Lizzie's relief, he hadn't once dematerialized. "You're my good boy," she whispered, gently twisting his unicorn horn before turning her attention back to the road home.

CHAPTER EIGHTEEN

Bear followed at Lizzie's heels as she swung the gate wide and signaled Birdie to drive up to the house. Quinn was nowhere in sight. She'd given the raven a butter tart as soon as she got home, and after devouring it, he and Bear played in the yard for a bit before he flew off into the forest to do whatever ravens did in the forest. She knew he wouldn't be gone long, especially when it was so close to another mealtime.

As Birdie drove in, Bear followed her car, his tail helicoptering with excitement. Lizzie took a moment to swing the gate closed, locking it securely, before joining them at the cottage. Birdie stood outside the car with the driver's side door open, talking to Bear, who was sitting politely, his tail making large sand angels in the driveway.

"Hello, sweet boy," Birdie said, stroking his ears. "I didn't give you a treat when you came to visit my booth, so I brought you something special." She ducked into the car and pulled a small brown bag from the passenger seat. "Is it okay if I give him a treat?" she asked Lizzie. "You didn't get to Lindsey's booth at the market, and she makes these homemade dog treats. I got him one with peanut butter." She pulled out a large bone-shaped cookie and held it up for Lizzie to see.

"Of course, and peanut butter happens to be his favorite." To Bear, she said, "You've been rather spoiled today, Mister, so don't expect a treat every time you meet someone new." Bear ignored her, focused entirely on the large cookie Birdie held out before him. Remaining in a sit position, he scooted forward on his rump, his nose almost touching the cookie.

Laughing, Birdie handed Bear his cookie, which he gently

took in his mouth, then trotted onto the porch to devour it. "I have a few treats for you, too," Birdie said to Lizzie before reaching into the car to pull out a bottle of white wine, a bag of dog food, and a small box wrapped in old book pages. "These are from me. The wine and kibble as promised, and the box is, I guess you'd call it, a housewarming present." She handed the items over to Lizzie before heading to the back of the car and opening the hatchback to reveal an enormous gift hamper wrapped in clear cellophane, secured by a ridiculously large pink satin bow. "And this is from the Welcome Wagon."

Lizzie peered into the back of the car. "It's — it's rather large. Is this how the Welcome Wagon greets all new residents?" Lizzie flipped over the gift tag attached to the bow. It read, "*We welcome you to our community and are honored to call you one of our own,*" signed *Ginny, president of the Welcome Wagon.* The handwriting was a round, extravagant script, so unlike the writing on the card of the first basket she'd thought was from the Welcome Wagon that had been left on her front porch a few weeks back. That one had been left by Audley on Jon's instructions, the 'gifts' inside being liberally laced with a sedative that was supposed to keep Lizzie out of the way while Jon's underlings did a drug run from Lizzie's barn.

"No, that's not the standard. Not that many people move out here, but the baskets usually contain a book of coupons, a box of chocolates, a bag of coffee, and a mug. This one's a bit over the top, but knowing Ginny, she wanted to make a good impression after all you did for the village. You were lucky you left when you did. You missed bumping into Ginny and her crew by mere seconds. I intercepted her, and when she'd found you already left, she was planning on heading here to deliver the hamper herself. It took a bit of convincing, but I managed to get her to let me deliver it as I was already coming out here on your invitation."

Lizzie stared at the basket; a sliver of panic slicing through her calm. Although Lizzie surprised herself when, in a span of a few minutes, she'd invited Anna and her daughter and then Birdie out for a visit. But inviting them out had felt right, and she genuinely felt the urge to spend time with Birdie, not just to get information about Cathy. But that didn't mean she wanted a steady stream of visitors trying to come onto the property. She wondered about putting up a similar illusion ward like the one Grandma Faye used on her place to keep people away.

"It's alright, Lizzie, Ginny isn't hiding in there, I promise. Although I don't guarantee your safety when you come into town, as Ginny is sure to ambush you sooner or later. But I am pretty sure she won't be dropping by unannounced. I told her you needed your privacy as you were busy writing your memoirs, including moving to the cottage and what happened here. And I may have hinted if she wanted to be written up in a positive light, it wouldn't do to just come by uninvited, as writers can be very protective of their time."

"Birdie, tell me you didn't say that. I'm not writing my memoirs or anything for that matter. What's she going to do when she finds out there's no book being published?"

Birdie made a dismissive gesture with her hand. "Not to worry, writers sometimes take months and even years to complete their books." She smiled broadly. "By then, hopefully, someone else new will have moved into town, and she will have a new target to focus on. In the meantime, you may as well enjoy the Wagon's generosity because, by what I can see through that cellophane, you scored some great goodies."

Lizzie forced herself to smile. "You're right. It was very thoughtful. It's just that I am not used to being the focus of so much attention."

"I get it. I am a bit of an introvert myself. I prefer one-on-one interactions and am not a fan of big crowds," Birdie said, encircling the hamper with both arms, the cellophane crackling as she lifted it out of the back of the car.

Lizzie smiled in agreement. "So, which do you want first, a tour or lunch?

"Definitely lunch, I'm starving."

"Lunch it is. Everything's prepared. I just need to bring it out to the porch. I thought we could eat there, seeing as it is such a lovely afternoon."

"Sounds perfect." Birdie shifted the large hamper as she struggled to close the hatchback.

Lizzie bent to put the bag of dog food down so she could help Birdie when she felt her powers gently unfurl, heading towards the car. She didn't have time to pull it back before it gave the hatchback a firm push. Startled, Birdie stepped back to watch the door close with a solid click.

"The wind must have caught it. It's constantly catching my truck door when I least expect it. Now, how about that lunch?" She said hastily, ushering Birdie into the cottage before she could notice there was no wind blowing through the tree.

The cookie long since devoured, Bear attached himself to the visitor as they headed up the porch steps, a hopeful look in his eyes. Lizzie deposited the wine and gift on the corner of the kitchen table next to a tray set for lunch. Putting the bag of kibble away, she called over her shoulder, "You can just put the hamper on the counter by the sink over there."

Birdie remained standing on the threshold, peering inside.

"Don't tell me you are still spooked by the house. I promise you there are no ghosts here." She opened the fridge and began pulling out the lunch things. "Anymore," she added.

"Anymore?" Birdie gulped, taking a half step back.

"I'm joking. The only negative forces at play in my cottage were Jon and his thugs. The house is spirit-free, I promise," she said, glancing out the window to the apple tree marking Emma

Hawksworth's grave.

Squaring her shoulders, Birdie took a tentative step inside. When her eyes adjusted to the gloom, they widened in surprise. She turned in a slow circle. "This is amazing. I can't believe the changes you've made in such a short time, especially considering everything else that was going on." Moving into the kitchen, she placed the hamper on the counter. "It's so homey in here, and it doesn't feel spooky at all. You picked up some great second-hand pieces, too." Birdie cleared her throat, her eyes dropping to her feet.

"Thank you. I quite like how it's turned out, too. Although now that I've had a chance to get to know the cottage, I'm rethinking the modern kitchen cabinets I put in. It seems a waste to rip out perfectly good cabinets, but I think what this space really needs is more of an unfitted kitchen. What do you think?"

Birdie's head snapped up, and her eyes narrowed as she surveyed the kitchen. "I can see what you're saying. The modern aesthetic is all wrong for the vibe of the cottage." She stepped further into the room. "But, not a rustic kitchen, either, but one that is inspired by an 1800s British cottage with a kitchen. And as far as the new cabinets, you could donate them. My aunt just got in a kitchen dresser that would be perfect on the wall next to the fridge."

Lizzie gave her a quizzical look. "A dresser in a kitchen?"

"A kitchen dresser. It's a piece of furniture that is half sideboard on the bottom to store large things or dry goods, and the upper part is half shelves to store and display plates, bowls, and cups," she explained. "It's both practical and pretty to look at."

"Oh, I like the sound of that. And the idea of donating the new cabinets is a great idea." Lizzie picked up the wine and corkscrew. "Now, how about a glass of wine?"

"Yes, please," Birdie smiled. "But I'll open the wine, and

you can open your gift basket. I'm dying to know what's all in there."

Lizzie handed over the bottle and corkscrew, then turned her attention to the gift basket. They sipped their wine while Lizzie pulled out the items one by one, showing them to Birdie before putting them off to the side. There were tins of tea and bags of coffee, chocolate truffles that Lizzie decided to add to their luncheon, and a lovely bottle of champagne, which Lizzie handed over to Birdie to place in the freezer. "Now, don't let me forget that is in there, I don't want to waste good champagne." There was even a salami, and when Birdie saw it, she exclaimed in excitement. "I take it from your reaction that this is good salami, and seeing as we are a little light in the meat department for lunch, why don't we cut into this."

"I'll do that while you open this," Birdie said, taking the sausage out of Lizzie's hand and replacing it with the small wrapped box. "Where are your knives?" She asked, putting down her wine glass and washing her hands at the kitchen sink.

"Second drawer to the left of the sink, and you can use that cutting board there," Lizzie said, pointing to its place on the counter before carefully peeling back the paper, which turned out to be old book pages to reveal a faded pink velvet box.

Birdie stopped slicing the meat to watch Lizzie as she opened the box and pulled out a gold locket on a chain. "I wanted to give you a housewarming gift, but I couldn't think of what to bring. But when I was packing up my aunt's booth, I saw the locket, and I knew it was for you. I know it sounds odd, but sometimes I get a feeling when an item needs to go to a particular person. I remember seeing you wearing that necklace with the cross, so I wasn't sure you would want another one, but the feeling was quite insistent, and so far, I've never been wrong. I hope you like it."

Lizzie held up the chain so the locket spun lazily in the

air. The burnished gold seemed to glow in the softer light of the cottage. "This is absolutely stunning." She caught the locket in her hand to take a closer look. It was round instead of oval and thicker than any locket Lizzie had ever seen. She carefully pried it open, and instead of finding a place to put a photo, the top opened to reveal a deep cavity lined in velvet similar to the box, but the lining was still a deep, rich red. "Is it a keepsake locket? She snapped the lid closed and ran her thumb over the chasing on the front, caressing the metal until it warmed under her skin.

"Yeah, at first I thought it was a piece of mourning jewelry, but it's the wrong time period. In fact, even my Aunt was stumped, and she's the expert on antique jewelry. The age and design would suggest farther back than Victorian, but she's never seen that design before. Even after researching, she couldn't find a comparison, and there's no maker's mark, so no way of narrowing down a date."

Lizzie could tell just by looking at it, it was very old and very finely made, but there was something else about it that made her eyes mist over and a lump form in her throat. She curled her fingers around the locket and held it to her chest. There was a faint echo, a subtle resonance. Both familiar and strange, a longing for home. She took a deep breath to steady herself before speaking. "I did have a necklace. It was my mother's, but I lost it recently. And quite frankly, I feel a little naked without it." She opened her palm to look at the locket again. "You were right. This is the perfect gift." Although the locket was nothing like the cross she used to wear, even holding it in her hand was comforting.

"Here, let me," Birdie said, coming to stand behind Lizzie. She reached over and plucked the chain from Lizzie's hand and secured it around her neck. The locket rested comfortably against the skin of her chest, the weight a reassuring presence. "Yup," Birdie said with a nod of her head as she came around to look at Lizzie. "Just as I thought. It was meant for you."

Lizzie's fingers sought out the locket, then she reached over and gave Birdie a tight hug. "I'm just going to pop into the bathroom and see how it looks on. I'll be right back."

Lizzie left Birdie to finish cutting up the salami as she ducked into the bathroom. Instead of standing in front of the mirror, she dug into the front pocket of her jeans and pulled out what she now thought of as the key stone. It was cool to the touch and looked like an insubstantial piece of glass in her hand.

She'd returned to the stone circle before Birdie arrived just to double check the portal was closed and all her wards were firmly in place. But she still felt compelled to keep the key on her person. And now, if she was right, Birdie had just gifted her not only an exquisite piece of jewelry but also a convenient way to carry the crystal with her. Using her thumbnail, she released the catch on the locket, revealing the compartment again. She dropped the stone inside, and it nestled perfectly in its new bed of velvet as if it was always meant to be there. Closing the locket with a satisfying click, she let it rest back on her skin and went to join Birdie in the kitchen.

***

"That was delicious," Birdie said, leaning back in her chair. "If this was my place, I would eat all my meals out on the porch in the summer. The view is spectacular, and it is so peaceful out here."

"Mmm," Lizzie murmured. The peace Birdie spoke of, at least for Lizzie, had been an elusive, fleeting thing, overshadowed by darkness, violence, and murder. Anyone else would have put the cottage on the market and found a safer place to live with no drug cartels, trapped spirits, or strange portals in the forest. She couldn't explain it even to herself why she stayed. But she couldn't imagine living anywhere else. "Do you want to have dessert now, or would you like a short tour of the property first?"

Birdie stretched her arms above her head. "I think a walk

would be perfect. I'm stuffed, and if I don't move, I think I may fall asleep. And more importantly, I need to make room for that strawberry tart and whipped cream you mentioned."

Lizzie gathered up the dishes on the tray and put them in the kitchen sink to wash up later. Coming back out to the porch, she carefully stepped over Bear, who was fast asleep now that he'd had his fill of goodies that Birdie kept sneaking to him during lunch and which Lizzie had made a point of not noticing.

"I thought we could head out to the west side first. There is a sweet little creek running through there, although it's a bit of a hike to get to." She instantly regretted the suggestion as the memory of her first hike to the creek with Wren flashed vividly in her mind.

"Over there," she pointed to her right as they walked up the property, "is my sad excuse for a garden, which you no doubt saw as you drove up. I have big plans for it, but lately, I just haven't seemed to find the time to get to it."

Lizzie led Birdie to the chicken coop, where her hens were happily scratching around their enclosed yard. She started to point them out by name, but instead of joining Lizzie at the chicken wire fence, Birdie stood several feet behind her. Lizzie looked over her shoulder, "Sorry, I forgot birds make you nervous. Let's skip the introductions and head over to the forest."

"No, I'm fine, really," Birdie said, inching a little closer to the wire enclosure. "I'm working on getting more comfortable around birds. It's one of the things I promised myself I would do after I got fired. I vowed to stop being so scared of everything and everyone around me. I've been afraid of birds for the longest, so I thought I would start there. It's one of the reasons I called my journal business Black Bird Bindery. Every time I finish a journal and put the stamp with that logo on it, it's a reminder," she said, stepping right up to the chicken wire.

Lizzie smiled and continued pointing out each hen. Birdie

laughed out loud when Lizzie told her the story of how Ginger Chicken got her moniker. By the time she'd finished with her tale, Birdie had laced her fingers through the chicken wire and was gazing at the birds with interest.

"Your banty hens are quite beautiful. And they seem quite friendly."

"They are on both accounts. Remind me to send you home with some eggs. I have more than enough to spare," she said as she guided Birdie across the yard and towards the fence bordering the cleared land and the western woods. They ambled in quiet companionship through the forest, with Birdie occasionally pointing out with delight when they came across familiar plants or fungi that grew along the forest floor. They didn't make it all the way to the creek before curving around back to the fenced area at the far end of the property. As they climbed over the fence back into the yard, Lizzie gazed up to the tree tops, scanning for any sign of Quinn. Although it wasn't unusual for him to take off into the forest for a few hours, it wasn't like him to miss mealtime.

Birdie followed Lizzie's gaze. "What are you looking at?"

"I'm looking for Quinn. It's not like him to miss out on a meal," Lizzie said, turning her attention back to Birdie.

Birdie raised her eyebrows, scanning the treetops again, "And you expect to find this Quinn up a tree?"

Lizzie shook her head, smiling, realizing her mistake. "Sorry, I forgot you've never met Quinn. He's not a person but a raven."

"You have a pet raven?" Birdie asked, looking back into the forest one more time.

"No, he's not a pet any more than I think of Bear as one. He's a friend." Lizzie caught the nervous twitch of Birdie's fingers as she rubbed her hands on her thighs.

"How exactly does one befriend a raven?"

"Actually, it was the other way around. He found me just

before I discovered Rose Cottage, and he followed me out here. Although he spends the majority of his time with us, he is free to come and go as he pleases."

They walked in comfortable silence as they made their way across the meadow. Birdie broke the silence first. "You're not at all what I expected when we first met."

"How so?"

"You seem more—confident, maybe. I was surprised that, even after seeing the state of Grey House, you bought it and moved in by yourself, but I didn't think you'd stay long. And now, not only are you still here living in a haunted house, but you also brought down Jon's drug ring by yourself. That was pretty brave."

"Not haunted anymore, remember," Lizzie interjected. "And it wasn't brave at all. I was looking for some peace and quiet."

"That may be why you moved out here, but from everything you told me, you haven't really hidden from adventure." Birdie countered. "You renovated the place, got chickens, befriended a raven named Quinn, got a dog, and last but not least, not only uncovered a drug operation on your property but single-handedly broke up the cartel."

And released a trapped spirit in her cottage, discovered a portal to another dimension, performed a surgery on Madison using magick, and saved her dog from said portal. Not to mention defeating a demon that was hunting her, which brought her to Rose Cottage in the first place. Perhaps Birdie was right; she may not have gone looking for adventure, but it kept seeking her out.

A weariness crept into Lizzie's bones. It had been an exhausting couple of days. Although she enjoyed the bright activity of the farmer's market, the villagers' over-enthusiastic gratitude, and the unexpected easy company of Birdie, she suddenly just wanted to be alone for a bit.

"Shall we have that tart now?" She asked, hoping to send Birdie on her way shortly.

"Oh," Birdie replied, a hint of disappointment in her voice. "I was kind of hoping to see the barn," she said, pointing towards it. "Ever since I showed you the property and we couldn't get in, I've been dying to see inside. And now that I know it was where Jon's crew was running the drug operation, I really want to see." Birdie stopped abruptly, a blush staining her cheeks. "Sorry, my Aunt's told me numerous times when I get obsessed with an idea, I have a tendency to get a bit pushy."

"You're not pushy," Lizzie said reassuringly, "just curious. And there is nothing wrong with that. Come on," she said, leading the way to the barn. "Besides, I'd rather it be you telling the villagers what really happened that night, and maybe it'll stop them gossiping about me."

Birdie followed Lizzie up to the barn, laughing. "I can try to set the record straight, but if you think it's going to stop the gossip and interest in you, you're going to be disappointed. It's like I said earlier, this town's favorite occupation is gossip."

Lizzie scowled as she opened the side door to the barn and stepped inside. She really didn't want any more attention on her or Rose Cottage. "Well, I'd appreciate it if you could at least try to set the record straight. I really would like to keep my private life private," she said, flipping on the bank of light switches just inside the door. It was still quite gloomy, the shadows still thick in the far corners of the building, and when Lizzie looked up, she noticed several lightbulbs needed replacing.

"Wait here, and I'll open the barn doors to let in more light." She walked with confidence through the gloom, stirring up dust as she went. The bolts securing the barn doors slid easily open as Jon's men had made sure to keep everything well-oiled and in working order. The afternoon sunlight flooded into the barn, illuminating the dust motes dancing thickly in the air.

"It looked so much smaller from the outside when I first showed you around," Birdie said, stepping further into the barn. She walked over to the first stall and peered inside.

"Yes, it's deceiving," Lizzie said, following her. She didn't add that it looked smaller because of the layers of magick Jon had placed on the barn.

Birdie continued down the barn, peering into each stall as she went. "And it is in better shape than I recalled. It looks almost newly built, although it could use a bit of a cleaning up," she said, wiping the dust off her hands. "So, is this where they shot you?"

Lizzie stopped dead in her tracks, her hands suddenly slick with sweat. "No, it was out in the forest." Lizzie glanced up into the rafters and caught sight of an orb spider systematically dismantling her tattered web. She watched as the spider then set about with methodical precision to spin a new one. Lizzie focused on the movements of the spider and the gleam and shimmer of her silk as the web took shape.

Taking a deep breath, Lizzie began spinning a tale of what happened that night. A story leaving out any reference to how magick played a part in the events of that night, nor did she mention the Order or Wren. She downplayed her role in all of it and emphasized Audley's sacrifice to save her and the part Bear played in protecting her. She glossed over her own injury, describing it as a mere graze rather than what it really was. There was no way to explain how she recovered so completely and so quickly from a bullet wound that went clear through her shoulder. She finished her tale just as the spider finished her new web and crouched in the center, waiting for her next meal. Her elegant web shimmered in the late afternoon light pouring in through the barn doors.

"I'm sorry," Birdie whispered. "I had no idea." She took a step towards Lizzie and reached out her hand to touch Lizzie's arm, but stopped short of making contact. "How Audley died wasn't reported in the paper. It just said he was killed in the takedown, and we all assumed the cops had killed him. Reading about it kind of made it feel unreal, like it happened to characters in a story or a movie. But it wasn't make believe, was it? Audley was murdered, saving you. He really was a hero," she said softly.

"That's one of the rumors I'd like you to set straight," Lizzie said, finally lowering her gaze to look at Birdie. "Audley was a good man placed in an untenable situation, and he tried to do the right thing, and it cost him his life. The only reason he was part of all the drug running was because Jon was holding someone named Cathy hostage to keep Audley trapped into being his errand boy." Lizzie's throat tightened.

"Jon was holding his granddaughter hostage? We all thought Cathy had gone to a relative when her mother died."

"Her mother died? Did Jon have anything to do with it?" Lizzie balled her fists at her side. She knew Jon had been capable of murder, but he wouldn't have sullied his own hands. He would have had one of his henchmen do the deed just as he'd ordered Audley to kill her.

"I guess in a way. She was a heroin addict, and she'd OD'd. She got her drugs from Jon's crew."

"Jon trafficked in heroin, too?"

"Yeah, in a lot of other illegal substances. You name it, he either had a grow-op, meth or heroin lab, and things like ecstasy and molly. His business was diversified, you could say. And you know the government was getting set to make personal use of weed legal. That's more than likely the reason he was shifting his inventory in such a rush. He wanted it out in the market before the customer base dried up," Birdie said, wandering further down the aisle and glancing into each stall as she went. When she came to the second to last stall, she turned to Lizzie, who was still standing in the middle of the aisle. "So, what are you going to do with the barn? I wouldn't blame you for tearing it down after all that happened to you here."

Lizzie glanced up at the spider, now settled calmly in the center of her web, waiting for her next meal. A small tingle tickled the back of her head and neck, and she raked her hands through her hair. In the vision she'd had, Birdie had been there, in this barn that had been transformed into something other than a barn, filled with light and happy people.

"No," she said, joining Birdie at the last stall. "I won't be tearing it down. That's Jon's M.O. He destroyed things and people to gain power and control. I want to do the opposite, although I don't know what that looks like just yet. Something that brings life to the area, brings the community together." She had no idea where that thought came from because the last thing she wanted was to have Rose Cottage swarming with people. She tried to clarify her thoughts. "I want to build more good, not less. Make this place more alive if that makes sense."

"You could get a few goats and a donkey. I love donkeys, and goats are cool. I took care of Grandma Faye's animals while she was helping you recover from your injuries.

"Perhaps, although for now, my chickens are enough responsibility. And I still have a lot of work to do in the garden."

Birdie wandered to the end of the aisle when she exclaimed, "So that's where it is." She turned right and disappeared into what Lizzie thought was the last stall.

"Where what is?" she asked, following Birdie. But instead of stepping into yet another stall, she narrowly missed colliding with Birdie, who was standing just a few feet into the space where it ended in what appeared to be a freight elevator.

"If you are thinking that is a freight elevator, I would say you are right, and the metal door to the right of it probably leads to a stairwell, both of which would take you down to where the grow room was." As she spoke, she took a few steps over to a grey metal door and tried the handle. It was unlocked, and it pushed open easily. Instantly, the smell of pot hit Lizzie, and she stepped back quickly, waving a hand in front of her face. "Birdie, close the door before I get sick."

Birdie did as she was asked, the door closing with a heavy thump. "Not a fan of pot, I take it."

"No, apparently not. How does anyone smoke that stuff?"

"Beats me," Birdie shrugged. "I prefer the wine we had at lunch or chocolate, for that matter. But aren't you curious about what's down there?

"Not really. There shouldn't be anything left down there but an empty room. The authorities removed all the plants. But I am curious as to why go through the hassle, not to mention the cost, of putting the grow-op under the barn when Jon already used his powers to—" Lizzie caught herself before she finished saying 'cast a glamour spell and a ward on the barn.' "—to keep the villagers under his thumb," she finished awkwardly.

"Oh, that's easy to answer," Birdie said. "He may have had the villagers under his control, but he couldn't do the same to the RCMP. They regularly run reconnaissance flights over wooded areas like this where illegal grow-ops are a problem. They look for structures out in the forest where there shouldn't be any, but they also use infrared cameras to detect heat signatures. Did you know that pot plants have a very specific signature, and the cameras they use can detect it even through walls?

"Um, no, I didn't. How do you know so much about it?"

Birdie gave a sardonic laugh. "When you live in a village controlled by a drug boss, it's just common knowledge. And I know what you're thinking. Why did we put up with a drug lord taking over the village? Why not just move away?"

Lizzie hadn't been thinking that at all, but it was a good question. "So, why didn't you?"

"I'm not sure. It's complicated and hard to describe. When

you grow up in a small town, you have connections, family, friends. Out here, many never leave. They are born, get married, raise a family, and die here. It's not easy to leave all that behind and start again out there." She gestured with her hand. "For some, it was because it was lucrative to be paid off by Jon to look the other way, and others benefited from having steady work, illegal as it was. The economy has not been kind to areas like ours. We depend on tourism, and when the economy tanks, tourism goes down. As far as myself," Birdie huffed in frustration. "Oh, I don't know, maybe it is because I'm a coward or just lazy. The idea of moving away, by myself, out into the big, wide world scared me. Hell, the idea still scares me. Sometimes the familiar feels safe, even if that familiar comes in the form of an asshole like Jon. And for good or bad, this is my home, you know what I mean?"

"I didn't up until moving here. I don't have any family, and this parcel of land, this cottage, is the first place that's ever felt like home."

"I didn't know, I'm sorry."

"Don't be, I was orphaned at birth, so I can't miss what I've never had. When I found Rose Cottage, I could see myself putting down roots and making this my home. Despite what has happened here, or maybe because of it, I feel even more determined to make this place mine." As Lizzie spoke, she realized this was true. The only fly in the ointment to the idyllic picture forming in her mind was her fight with Grandma Faye.

And maybe it was a combination of the wine, the sunshine, and the company, but throughout lunch, as she had chatted away with Birdie, she let herself admit she understood why Grandma Faye hadn't told Lizzie what Wren had done to her. She probably would have done the same if she'd been put in that position. She was still angry, but Grandma Faye was family. She owed it to the old woman not to just throw away their friendship. She decided she'd call her in the morning.

"The vendors' generosity and kindness this morning were overwhelming at first, but I have to confess it felt good to find strangers opening their arms to me even if they wrongly think I am the one that saved them from Jon."

"I think you will find the people here, including me, will still call you one of ours even when I tell them about Audley's role in all this. You may not have a biological family, but I hope you will consider me, if not family, at least a friend." Birdie squeezed Lizzie's arm gently.

Much to her surprise, Lizzie felt the hot prick of tears welling up. "I'd like that. I'd like that very much." Rubbing her hands together, she said in a bright voice, "Now, shall we finish up the tour of the barn? I think I hear dessert calling me, and I'm sure Bear is probably awake and ready for his next round of treats."

"That sounds like a great idea. Could we start with a quick peek downstairs? I'm dying to find out what's down there."

"Fine. You can take a quick look, but I'm not going with you." She shivered involuntarily as she remembered what it felt like to be trapped in the dark below ground when Audley had shoved her down in the cellar of her own home.

Birdie fairly hopped with excitement as she swung open the metal door. Again, the pungent odor of pot wafted up through the staircase. Lizzie joined her, pinching her nose to try to block out the smell. Leaning into the darkened doorway, Birdie patted the wall until she found the light switch and flicked it on. There was a faint buzz, and then the stairwell and room below flooded with the cold blue light of fluorescent tubes. The metal stairs led to a landing halfway down, the stairs turning ninety degrees to the left so that the bottom few steps were hidden from the view at the top.

"I'll be right back, I promise," Birdie said, making her way down the stairs, her footsteps clanging loudly on the metal treads, echoing into the cavernous space below.

Lizzie braced the door open with her back and leaned sideways to follow Birdie's progress, keeping one foot on the barn side of the door. She lost sight of her as Birdie headed off the landing down the last flight. "Don't go too far," Lizzie called out, her voice sounding hollow.

"I won't," Birdie called back. "Wow, it's humungous down here."

It felt like an eternity waiting for Birdie to come back. Lizzie cocked her head, straining to pick up Birdie's footfalls on the concrete floor below. "Okay, you've had your look come back upstairs. I can't take this smell any longer." Lizzie let out a long sigh of relief when Birdie's head and shoulders popped into view as she approached the landing. Lizzie stepped back into the aisle, and Birdie let the door swing closed with a satisfying clunk.

The miasma of pot clung to Birdie's hair and clothes, and Lizzie waved her hands in front of her, trying to dissipate the smell. "I know, I reek of pot, but it was so worth it. You're right, the plants are gone, but they left the grow tables and all the hydroponic and processing equipment. There must be hundreds of thousands of dollars of equipment down there. And there are several rooms I didn't have time to look into, but I am guessing the HVAC equipment would be in one of the rooms. I bet if you turned on the air exchange, that smell would be gone in a few minutes."

"I'll keep that in mind, but for now, it can wait. Although it does seem a waste to leave all that down there," Lizzie said, leading Birdie to the front of the barn to finish the tour.

"Can I take a peek at the hayloft? Birdie asked, already heading for the ladder.

"Sure, there's nothing up there, but you're welcome to take a look." She glanced warily up at the loft.

"I'll be quick," Birdie replied, grasping the ladder and

preparing to climb up. "Don't you just love old wood ladders and railings when they get like this," she said, rubbing her hands up and down the sides of the ladder. "The wood becomes worn from all those hands having held on to it, and now it is all polished and silky." She started to quickly ascend, then stopped abruptly. "This ladder is older than the barn, and now that I think about it, it's probably the one that is original to the house, the one they would have used to access the loft, or I guess I should say bedroom that's now on the second floor." She started climbing again.

Lizzie went over to the ladder and trailed her hand down the satiny wood. She liked the idea that the ladder to her house was still here. She was thinking about putting it back in the house and maybe using it to hold her extra blankets on when Birdie stopped on the ladder again.

With her chest level with the hayloft floor, she looked into the space. "Wow, this is another great space. I've always loved lofts. They feel like secret hideaways, like a tree fort. The barn door faces south, doesn't it?" Birdie called down.

"Yes," Lizzie replied. She squinted up at Birdie, the contrast between the sunlight slanting through the barn doors and the shadows in the hayloft playing tricks with her eyes. She caught a flash of pink haloing Birdie's head, but when she looked again, it was gone.

"So, the hayloft door faces north?"

"Why do you ask?" The hairs on the back of Lizzie's neck prickled.

"Well, if you plan on converting the barn into something other than housing animals, replacing the hayloft door with a stained-glass window would be so cool. It would let in north-facing light and really brighten up the space. Oh, and my aunt just got in a whole swack of stained glass from a house that was recently demolished. I think she has the perfect one that I'm almost certain would fit. It's art nouveau and has these sinuous branches on either side with leaves and — "

"Apple blossoms," Lizzie whispered in unison with Birdie.

"Sorry, what did you say?" Birdie called down.

"I said that would be a great idea, depending on what I do with the space," Lizzie said, gripping the side of the ladder to steady herself.

"Don't you think it would make an amazing writing room? You could write your memoirs up here," she giggled. "But seriously, I could totally see a desk on the west wall and bookshelves. Lots and lots of bookshelves." Birdie started to climb down but stopped again. "Oh, I just got another great idea," she said, looking down at Lizzie. "Not about the loft but the grow-op. You could lease the space to the local growers. It's already set up and ready to go. Not only could you help them out, but you would have a bit of money coming in from the lease." Birdie's voice rose in excitement.

Lizzie scrambled to catch up with Birdie's non-sequitur before vehemently replying, "Absolutely not. I don't care if the government is making it legal and they have permits to grow the stuff. After what Jon's drug ring did to the villagers and myself, I won't have any of that on my property. I'm surprised you, of all people, would even suggest it."

Birdie threw back her head and laughed. Then, placing her hands on either side of the ladder, she hopped off the tread, bracing her feet along the sides, and slid down the rest of the way, landing lightly on her feet. "Man, I forgot how much fun that is. I haven't done that since I was a kid." She dusted off her hands and turned to Lizzie, "No, not pot growers. I'm in complete agreement with you on that one. No, I was thinking about the small farmers like Anna. If they could use that space to grow their vegetables over the winter, it would extend their growing season and provide year-round fresh veggies to the locals. Everyone would benefit."

"Why would the farmers want to do that? Don't they have their own greenhouses to grow things over the winter?"

"Do you have any idea how much a greenhouse facility would cost to build that could withstand the amount of snowfall we get in the winter. Not to mention, these are small family-run farms, and the cost just to run a farm is high."

"Um, Birdie, just how much snow does this area get?"

"Well, we are considered a rainforest, but our rainy season starts in the late fall and ends in the spring. So, when the temperature drops, that rain turns to snow, so on average, we get about two to three meters."

One of the odd quirks about being raised in a cloistered convent is that the nuns did everything in imperial measures, and that's what she'd been taught. Even now, Lizzie still had trouble visualizing things like amounts in metric. "What would that be in feet?" Lizzie asked, feeling a cold lump of dread growing in her stomach.

"I think—it would be," Birdie looked up as she made the conversions in her head, "about four to five feet."

Lizzie's mouth fell open as she tried to imagine what living at Rose Cottage would be like with that much snow.

"Oh, sorry, I got the math wrong. Just a sec," she said, squeezing her eyes shut in concentration. Lizzie's shoulders relax.

"In feet, that would be six to about ten feet."

Lizzie's breath left her body, and she leaned up against the wall. "Six to ten feet?" She wheezed out.

"Didn't I mention that when you came to view the cottage? I'm sure I mentioned it."

"No, you didn't, I would have remembered that little detail."

"Are you sure? I know I at least told you to get a heat tape on the pipes so they don't freeze in the winter. In any case, I'm sure Del at the hardware store could hook you up with a snow blower for a good deal. You're definitely going to need it to keep your driveway and a path to the chicken coop clear."

Lizzie glanced out the open barn doors. Everything was lush and green, the late afternoon sun bathing the property with a golden tint. She couldn't imagine what it would look like with that much snow blanketing the ground. She couldn't, wouldn't leave Rose Cottage. This was her home, and if she could handle a portal in her backyard and a drug lord, surely she could handle a few feet of snow. She'd have to just deal with winter when it came. For right now, she had a more pressing question she needed an answer to. How did Birdie describe exactly what Lizzie had seen in her vision of the hayloft?

"Birdie, I've noticed you have a talent for seeing the potential of this empty space. You've come up with two great ideas for my barn so far. Before we go have our dessert, I'd love to see what you dream up for the tack room," she said, pointing in the direction of the room. "Go on, take a look. The light switch is to your left."

Lizzie leaned against the door jamb as Birdie flipped on the light and stepped into the room. She watched as Birdie turned a slow circle, tapping her index finger against her bottom lip. She stopped, facing the front wall, her face breaking into a huge smile.

"Well, don't keep it a secret. What do you see?"

Birdie pointed to the blank wall. "There is a lovely big window here. It's north-facing, so it will bathe the studio in indirect clear light, perfect for working in. Just below the window is a work table, and over here is a peg board with tools hanging for it and those little containers filled with brushes, scissors, bone folders, rulers, spools of linen thread, my needles." She turned again. "Over here," she said, pointing to the back wall, "is the antique architect drawers I picked up last month that's just perfect for all the sheets of paper I use. And there are shelves above it holding bottles of glue, brush cleaner."

Lizzie felt a smile creep over her face as she heard the joy bubbling up in Birdie's voice. And then she saw it again. It hadn't been a trick of the light. The air around Birdie began to shimmer. Lizzie quickly schooled her expression as she watched Birdie's magic expand outward from her body, filling the empty tack room with little sparks of pink light. Birdie seemed unaware of her magick as she continued to describe the room: "And over here are several lovely dark shelves, and they're all filled with my journals. They look so beautiful all lined up and ready to go, and over there are all the shipping materials I need to send out."

Birdie had powers and was seemingly unaware of it. Lizzie wasn't sure what to call what Birdie could do. Was she looking into the future or somehow connecting to objects and places and picking up on the energetic potential around them? In Lizzie's vision of the future, she'd seen Birdie coming out of this exact room carrying not journals but newly bound books, so this room had definitely been converted into a book bindery.

Lizzie called up her own magick and gently sent out a tendril of white light towards Birdie. She directed her magick to touch one of the rose-colored orbs swirling around the young woman, and the second it made contact, Lizzie smiled and then pulled back her powers. Birdie's magick was weak, but it was there, and Lizzie felt a definite alignment with fire. She would let Grandma Faye know what she discovered, as she was the best person to know how to approach Birdie with the information that she was a young witch and was already amongst women of her kind.

"Oh," Birdie suddenly exclaimed, slapping her hand over her mouth. Instantly, the swirling pink motes winked out, leaving the space just an empty, dust-filled room.

"What's wrong?" Lizzie asked, straightening up from

the door frame, noticing a deep crimson blush staining Birdie's cheeks.

"You asked me what you could use the tack room for, and I got carried away imagining what I would use it for. I'm sure now I sound like a self-serving narcissist."

Lizzie smiled gently, "There's no need to feel embarrassed, and I would never describe you as self-serving. Talented, creative, courageous, yes. And from what I've seen of you so far, definitely not a narcissist."

Birdie raised her hand to shut off the light, but Lizzie stopped her. "No, wait, I've got a question before we go. Installing a window on that wall," she said. "Would that be a difficult reno to do?"

"No, not at all. The walls in here aren't finished, so it would be just cutting an opening the size of the window, framing around it, and installing the window. I could do that in my sleep."

"That's good to know. What about electrical outlets?" Lizzie continued. "I noticed there are a couple in here, but would that be enough for, say, a book bindery studio? Or is there special equipment that needs more power?"

"No, there's more than enough outlets in here. A clamp light for task lighting and to use as a raking light is really all you need." Looking up, she said, "And for overall lighting, you could just change out that bare bulb with a proper light fixture."

"And would you happen to know of a second-hand light fixture I could get my hands on and a used window that would work?" Lizzie asked, feeling the rightness of the decision she'd just made.

Birdie eyed her warily, "Lizzie, you aren't suggesting what I think you are suggesting?"

"I most definitely am, and you haven't answered my question," she said, unable to stop herself from smiling.

Birdie blinked hard, her eyes shiny with tears. "I know

the perfect window for the wall, and we just got in a collection of pendant lights from an old library that would work. But...I couldn't possibly impose on you like this. I know you value your privacy."

Lizzie waved a dismissive hand. "You wouldn't be imposing on me. It's true; I do like my privacy, but I also don't want to end up a recluse. And it's not like you'd be in my back pocket the whole time you are here. You'd be in your studio while I'd be puttering in the garden, or feeding the chickens, or in the house." The more she thought about having Birdie working on her property, the more she warmed up to the idea. "And I think it would be lovely to have you come down to the house and share lunch with me and the boys. It would be a refreshing change to have a conversation with someone over a meal who would reply back. And it would be the perfect opportunity for you to get more comfortable around birds." As she spoke, she couldn't help but glance out the barn door and up to the treeline, hoping for a glimpse of Quinn returning home.

"I would really, really like that too, but—" Birdie looked down at the ground. "I just don't have the money right now to pay for a space, no matter how reasonable the rent is, or even to buy the window and light fixture. So, I still really want the space as my studio if you could give me time to save some money first."

"Nope, that's something I can't do." When she saw Birdie's face fall, she spoke quickly, "But this is what I can do instead. I would like to invest in Black Bird Bindery. I want to be a, what do they call that, an angel investor?"

"More like a fairy godmother," Birdie whispered.

"No, not even close," she smiled. "I will provide the funds to purchase what you need to renovate the studio and to hire tradesmen and such, but in return, until your company makes a profit, you will have to add your own sweat equity by cleaning out the space and organizing the purchase and installation of the window and light. And when you are making enough money to cover your business and living expenses, then we will talk about what a reasonable rent would be for the space. Until then, in exchange, you will make me one new blank journal a month." A deep calmness rose up in Lizzie. She knew with unwavering certainty the rightness of what she was proposing. "Oh, I just had another thought. You mentioned over lunch that your aunt has an old printing press sitting in her shop she wants to get rid of because it takes up too much space. How would you feel about that printing press being housed here? You said your aunt wouldn't charge you for it as long as you moved it. So, why not move it here? There's no lack of space.

"Yes, yes, and yes. OMG, yes to all of it." Birdie ran over and threw her arms around Lizzie in a tight hug. When she let go, she said, "I promise I will not let you down."

"I know you won't. So, when would you like to get started?"

"Is tomorrow too soon? Birdie asked with a sheepish grin. "I get Sundays and Mondays off, and I could start on the cleaning and taking measurements for the window opening right away."

"Tomorrow it is. Why don't we head back to the cottage and toast our new venture with champagne and dessert? Lizzie turned to look out the barn doors as Bear trotted up the dirt path and into the barn. "And a couple of peanut butter cookies for our friend here?" He waved his tail in ecstatic circles and let out two hearty woofs.

"I think that is a yes," Birdie laughed, scrubbing Bear's ear and making his tail spin even faster.

CHAPTER NINETEEN

The shadows had lengthened across the property by the time Lizzie had waved goodbye to Birdie at the gate, with a promise from Birdie to return first thing in the morning. Before heading inside, Lizzie checked on the stone circle with Bear at her side. She made sure to tether herself and her dog to the earth with her magick before approaching the stones. Satisfied the wards were holding and the portal had not reappeared, she wandered back to the cottage, scanning the trees for Quinn. She tried to reassure herself that Quinn had just gone off to do whatever it was that ravens did during the day, but the unease tickling under her ribs made her stop in the driveway and call up her magick again. She didn't think the delight and awe she felt as the Elemental instantly entwined with her own power would ever get old. Centering herself, she placed the image of Quinn in her mind and then released her power into the forest and beyond. She didn't really think contacting Quinn with her magick would work, as they didn't share a magickal bond like she did with Bear, so when she felt something familiar nudging back, a tingle of excitement fluttered down her fingertips.

"Quinn, are you okay?" she spoke into the quiet air. She wasn't sure the raven understood English, so she sent her sense of concern for him trailing through the filaments of her power. The almost instant response sent a wave of relief washing over her. Then, to her astonishment, Quinn flashed her images of himself flying with a large flock of his fellow kind. She couldn't bring herself to even think of a flock of ravens as an unkindness. The word felt like an insult. The impression she got from Quinn was that he and his flock were searching for something and that he would return home when he was done.

She, in reply, sent her love and, at the last minute, added the image of a tart topped with whipped cream. She laughed out loud when Quinn sent back a picture of two tarts covered with mountains of whipped cream before he broke their connection.

Just as Lizzie stepped inside her home, the phone rang. She dashed across the room to answer it. When she saw Grandma Faye's number on the call display, her thoughts immediately went to Madison. Her hand shook as she punched the talk button.

"Hello," she said breathlessly, her free hand seeking out the cameo resting in the hollow of her throat.

"Hi, Lizzie."

"Madison?" Lizzie sank down in the nearest chair. "You're awake. Is everything okay?"

"Yeah, I'm fine. I've been awake for a while, but Grandma Faye insisted I stay in bed and rest. But frankly, I'm getting a bit antsy. And when she told me you got Bear out of the portal all by yourself, I couldn't believe it. I had to find out right away how you did it."

"Well, at least she let you out of bed to call me."

Madison chuckled. "She didn't. She went out to check on her animals because I guess another storm is coming through, so I snuck out of bed. Come on, Lizzie, the suspense is killing me. How did you get him out?"

"I'm not really sure exactly how I did it. When the faerie stone exploded, it released a crystal housed inside it. When I took the crystal inside the stone circle, it worked like a sort of key, opening the portal. Then I simply used my bond with the Elemental to locate Bear and pull him out."

"You bonded with an Elemental? Wow. When did that happen? Man, I need to be writing this down, but I don't know where Grandma Faye put my satchel or my notebook."

"You were still unconscious when the bonding occurred."

"Darn, it sounds like I slept through all the good stuff. And Bear, he's okay?"

"I'd say he's more than okay. I'm not sure exactly how it happened, but it seems the time he spent in the liminal space healed his injuries from his accident. He doesn't have a limp anymore. And right now," she said, looking over at Bear, "he's lounging on the sofa after eating his body weight in dog treats."

"If only he could talk. I'm dying to find out what he saw, what it felt like, what was in there."

"Yes, it would be fascinating to know." Lizzie thought back to what she thought she'd seen when the portal had first opened. She was almost certain someone had been standing next to Bear. "And how are *you* doing?"

"I'm fine. Great actually. I'm not sure why Grandma Faye is so adamant about me resting. The wound couldn't have been that deep, as I barely have a scar. I take it the fast healing was due to your magick. Thanks for that."

"You're welcome." Lizzie hesitated before continuing. "Do you remember anything that happened to you?"

"No, I wouldn't have even known I'd been stabbed if Grandma Faye hadn't told me. The last thing I remember was the stone started to spin, and there was a horrible whining sound that hurt my ears, and it was hard to breathe. What did I miss?"

Lizzie shivered as she recalled the blood-stained carpet, the deathly pallor on Madison's face as her life ebbed out of her body, and the one particular moment when Lizzie had felt Madison's soul resisting Lizzie's efforts to bring her back. Was Madison telling the truth? Did she really not remember anything? "What did Grandma Faye tell you?"

"Just that the stone exploded, and the power of the explosion caused the athame to fly off the table and stab me. And that you used your magick to heal the wound, and then both of you brought me to her bed. Where I have apparently been asleep for almost 24 hours."

"Yeah, that's pretty much it."

"And there's nothing else? I didn't say or do something to Grandma Faye before I passed out?"

"Why do you ask?"

"It's just that, since I've been awake, she's acting differently from how she was when I first met her. Granted, I haven't known her for very long, but she seems distant and withdrawn. So, I thought maybe I did or said something to offend her."

"No, Madison, you didn't do anything wrong." Lizzie couldn't bring herself to share what had actually dampened Grandma Faye's mood. "She's probably just tired. It's been a rather exhausting couple of days for everyone, myself included."

Madison sighed. "You're probably right. And she's been so incredibly kind to me. She's fed me an amazing lunch, washed all my clothes, and even fixed my cardigan. And I can tell by the delicious smells coming from the large pot on the stove she's got a stew or something on the go."

Lizzie heard something in the young woman's voice. "But?"

Madison blew out a breath. "I don't feel right spending another night sleeping in her bed. I've already offered to take the sofa, but she wouldn't hear of it. Like you said, she's exhausted, and it's not right for me to make someone old enough to be my grandmother sleep on a couch. Do you think maybe…."

"Did you want me to come get you?"

"Would you mind?"

"Not at all." Butterflies erupted in her stomach at the thought of seeing Grandma Faye again. "I'll be right over."

"Ooh, I have a great idea. We could all have dinner together here, and you could bring Bear, too. Then we could drive back to your place afterwards. I know Grandma Faye would agree."

Lizzie leaned her head back against the chair and closed

her eyes. Could she sit down to dinner with Grandma Faye? Did she want to? Grandma Faye had said she was trying to protect Lizzie by keeping secret what Wren had done. To Lizzie, that secret, once revealed, felt like a betrayal. But hadn't she just done something similar to Madison just now? She hadn't told Madison how severe her injury had really been because Lizzie hadn't wanted to upset her. So, wasn't Lizzie keeping something secret that Madison had a right to know?

But, in telling her she'd almost bled out because of the stab wound, was Lizzie then bound, if not by friendship, but by simple human decency, to tell her the rest of it? To tell Madison what she'd done without Madison's permission? Because when Lizzie had gone to work on healing her, she knew with utter certainty that, in that moment, Madison had *wanted* to die and had welcomed it, in fact. That was the resistance Lizzie had felt when she'd been trying to retrieve and anchor Madison's soul back into her body; Madison had wanted to die so she could be with her father again. And Lizzie had ignored her desire and forced her spirit back into her body. Lizzie knew first-hand how the pain of living could make someone choose death, but in Lizzie's own life, she'd realized only after the attempt had failed that she had never really wanted to kill herself. It was the pain that she wanted to stop, not her life. Although Madison hadn't tried to kill herself, she hadn't fought to stay alive even when Lizzie had literally thrown her a lifeline.

So how could she be angry at Grandma Faye if Lizzie was now struggling with telling Madison something far worse? She'd overrode Madison's right to choose her own destiny, and if she had to do it all over again, Lizzie knew she wouldn't change what she'd done. She'd do everything in her power to save Madison, whether she wanted to be saved or not.

"Lizzie, are you still there?"

"Yes, I'm here. I'd love to join you two for dinner, and

I'll bring Bear. I just need about forty-five minutes to tidy up, and I should probably see to my chickens if Grandma Faye says another storm is coming. Tell her I'll bring the dessert."

"That sounds great. I should get going," Madison said in a rush. "I just spotted Grandma Faye heading for the house, and I don't want her to find me out of bed. See you in a bit," Madison chirped, then ended the call.

Lizzie smiled as she replaced the receiver and stepped outside to deal with her chickens. She wasn't sure how Madison was going to explain how she called Lizzie and invited her for dinner from the bed when the phone was in the kitchen.

She quickly gave the chickens their feed and fresh water before locking the coop. The hens sensed the change in the weather and had already taken themselves inside, making the job easier for Lizzie. She dashed inside the cottage as the wind whipped up, signaling the coming storm, and made her way to the back bedroom, where she changed the sheets Madison had earlier soiled with her dirty feet when they'd returned from the circle.

With that done, she'd have just enough time to wash up the wine and champagne glasses from lunch before grabbing the carton of chocolate ice cream Anna from the market had gifted her to take to Grandma Faye's.

As she stood at the kitchen sink, her attention kept drifting out the window towards the section of forest that led to the stone circle. Although the bulk of her stolen memories had returned, some of the details were still a bit foggy, and there was a persistent nagging sensation that there was something important she needed to remember. Instead of trying to force the memory to return, she redirected her attention to the sensation as she plunged her hands into the hot, soapy water and began washing the glasses. She carefully rinsed a wine glass under the faucet and gently placed it on the dishrack to dry, then grabbed a wine coupe next. Before she could place it in the water, her hold on it loosened as the memory she'd been chasing came back.

She snatched the glass just before it tumbled into the sink. She grasped the stem tightly in her hand as she looked out the window. Grandma Faye had said the portal in the circle couldn't be the same one as the one Wren had used because his people had destroyed it the day before Bear had disappeared. But she was wrong. She had to be. Because Lizzie remembered the moment when the cop had chased her to the circle when he'd sighted his gun at her. Wren had come through that very portal and had stood behind her. Had lent her his power to stop her would-be murderer. And she'd first met Wren inside the circle that night under the full moon. She was certain it was the same portal she dragged Bear through. She knew it beyond a doubt. That would mean the portal hadn't been destroyed. That would mean Wren—

Suddenly, a terrified scream came from outside. Bear let out a guttural growl, making the hairs on the back of her neck stand up, and she whirled around in time to see Bear launch himself off the couch and dematerialize through the front door. The glass slipped out of her hand unnoticed and shattered on the floor as she flew out the door after her dog.

Before she was halfway down the driveway, her feet spraying sand as she sprinted to catch up with Bear, she threw her hands out in front of her, releasing two orbs of light that soared past her dog to hover above the gate, the white light illuminating the area.

What she saw had her skidding to a halt.

On the road, just outside the gate, was a child. She looked to be about the same age as Anna's daughter, but unlike the bright and well cared for Allachka, this child was thin, her tear-filled eyes looked too large in her gaunt face, and her hair appeared tangled and matted on one side of her head. She wore a faded cotton T-shirt, at least a couple of sizes too small, and shorts that were ragged at the hem. She was holding one arm close to her chest, the shoulder hanging at an odd angle. On her uninjured arm, she wore a cumbersome black stone around her frail wrist, the leather cord wrapped several times around it, suggesting that it wasn't meant to be worn by a child, let alone one so thin.

Quinn swooped in and circled above the child, screaming angrily. Whenever she tried to take a step forward towards the gate, he dove at her, driving her back to the middle of the road. Bear continued to growl, his hackles raised. He paced along the gate, his lips raised in a snarl, his canines flashing white in the light of Lizzie's orbs.

"Bear, Quinn, stop that at once," Lizzie ordered, raising her voice above the cacophony, but both animals ignored her. Quickly realizing the futility of trying to calm the animals down, she focused on the little girl. She raised her voice again but intentionally kept her tone calm. "It's okay. They won't hurt you, I promise. They just aren't used to strangers, and they're scared, probably like you are right now. But everything is going to be okay. Stay where you are, and I will come and get you," she called out. Quinn continued to circle a few feet above the girl, and Bear hadn't ceased pacing or growling.

They were frightening the child, and she needed to do something fast. Infusing her words with her power, she called out in an authoritative voice. "Bear, Quinn, enough. Bear, stop growling. And Quinn, stop flying around her this instant." Bear stopped, but his lips remained pulled back in a snarl, his head lowered, and his eyes locked onto the girl. Quinn flew to the top of the stone fence, his head darting back and forth between Lizzie and the girl. Lizzie took a deep breath in an attempt to slow down her racing heart. "My name is Lizzie," she said, approaching the gate with a calmness she didn't feel. "What's your name?"

"C-C-Cathy," she stuttered out between sobs. "I want my

poppa. I want Poppa Audley," she wailed.

Shock jolted through Lizzie's body. "I bet you do," she said, gathering her thoughts. "How about we get you inside, and we'll see what we can do about that?" Lizzie felt sick as she lied to the frail, scared little girl, but she just couldn't speak the truth. Lizzie suspected by the odd angle her shoulder was hanging that Cathy's shoulder was dislocated. She pushed away thoughts of how that had happened or who would have done that to an innocent child. "Does that sound like a good idea?" Lizzie placed her hand on the gate to open it when suddenly Bear leapt up and, in one swift motion, clamped his mouth down on her arm. Then everything went black. She only had a split-second to sense shock before Bear released her arm, causing her to stumble back as she tried to regain her footing. She was standing not by the gate but in the kitchen of Rose Cottage.

She reached out to grab the back of a chair to steady herself. "Bear?" She blinked hard, trying to stop the room from spinning. He was blocking the open doorway, his hackles still raised, but his eyes held Lizzie's with what looked like frustration. She didn't have time to process what he'd just done. She needed to get to Cathy. "Bear, move," she said as she strode to the front door. Instead of moving, Bear planted his feet and refused to budge.

Lizzie stood for a moment, dumbfounded. Bear had used his magick on her and somehow managed to jump both of them from the gate to the cottage. She had no doubt that if she tried to move past him, he would just do it again. Raising her hands, she called up her powers. As the air around her crackled with magick, Bear raised his head, a look of fierce determination in his eyes. She quickly spoke the words of warding and, with a slashing motion, brought down her hands. She could never bring herself to use her magick on Bear, so she did the only thing she could think of. As soon as she felt the energetic shield take hold, she charged for the door, intending to dash around her dog. Bear simply stepped forward, pushing his massive head against her torso, and pushed her steadily back across the floor until she bumped up against the kitchen table. Then he took a step back and sat down. Gripping the edge of the table, too astonished to speak, she looked down at Bear. He shook his head and huffed.

"I'm scared?" came the terrified cry from the road. "I don't like the dark. Please help me, I want Poppa Audley."

At the sound of Cathy's cries, Bear turned his head towards the open front door, and Lizzie took advantage of the distraction. She side-stepped her dog, spun on her heels, and raced to the back door. She flew down the back porch and raced around the side of the house, where she collided with a massive wall of muscle and fur. Before she hit the ground outside, the world blinked out of existence. When it blinked back, she landed with force on the wooden planks inside her cottage with Bear laying on top of her. With his nose, he gave her cheek a sharp prod, then rose, lifting his legs carefully over her. As soon as she was free of his bulk, she rolled onto her side. Gathering her strength, she grabbed hold of the edge of the table with one hand and pushed herself onto her feet.

"Help me, Lizzie, help me. I'm scared," Cathy sobbed, her voice carrying in the silence.

The young girl's terror pierced her heart. She took a step forward, and Bear countered her movement, blocking her path again. "I get it," she croaked, feeling winded. "You don't want me near her. And I'm not leaving the cottage. I'm just going over to the phone, okay?" She reached over and patted his head. He held her gaze for a moment, then took a step back, clearing Lizzie's path. Grabbing the receiver, she quickly punched in Grandma Faye's number and felt relief wash over her as she heard the old woman's voice on the other end of the line.

"Grandma Faye, Audley's granddaughter, Cathy, is outside my gate. She appears to be injured. A dislocated shoulder, from what I could tell. And Bear won't let me near her. He keeps using his magick to block me from opening the gate. I can't get near enough to her to check if Jon used some kind of dark magick on her or if Bear is picking up on the scent of where Cathy was being kept. I need your help, but you need to be careful. Both Bear and Quinn are sensing something's not right."

"Got it. We'll be prepared. We're on our way," Grandma Faye said without hesitation.

Lizzie replaced the receiver and turned to Bear. "I'm just going out on the porch to wait for Grandma Faye and Madison, so there is no need to try and stop me." She strode purposefully towards the open door. Bear followed by her side, his nails clicking loudly on the hardwood floor, but he didn't try to block her. As she stepped on the front porch, she noticed the sun had set, and it was properly dark, but she could see the steady glow from the orbs of light still hovering on the road. She leaned over the railing and peered down the driveway to the gate. She could make out the huddled form of the little girl on the gravel road.

"Cathy," she shouted out into the still night air. "Help is on the way. Two nice ladies are coming to take care of you. It's going to be okay." Silence greeted her. Lizzie pushed down the swell of panic rising in her chest. "Cathy, honey, can you hear me? Answer me if you can hear me. Help is on the way." She watched helplessly from her vantage point on the porch as Cathy remained hunched over on the road, her head bowed, her knees pulled tight to her chest, and her good arm wrapped around her legs. Then, slowly, Cathy raised her head, slowly turning it until she was looking in the direction of the cottage. Lizzie felt a cold stab of fear hit her chest before Cathy spoke.

"You lied," she spat. "You're a liar, liar pants on fire. You know what they do to liars, don't you? Liars get punished." The little girl's voice was shrill and filled with hate. Lizzie took an involuntary step back as Bear issued a low growl, his hackles rising again.

Lizzie's attention shifted from Cathy's strange words to the sound of Grandma Faye's truck slicing through the night air, followed by the yellow beams of the headlights piercing through the dark. The beams got wider as the truck accelerated at breakneck speed down the road, only slowing down as the light bathed Cathy, still crouched on the gravel.

"Bear, I need to go down there, she said, pointing down the driveway where Grandma Faye's truck had come to a stop several feet from the girl. "I won't open the gate, but I need to be there if Grandma Faye and Madison need my help." She stepped off the porch, half expecting to feel Bear's teeth on her arm, but instead, he followed her down. Picking up her pace, she trotted the rest of the way with Bear at her side, stopping a few feet from the gate just as Madison and Grandma Faye leapt from the truck.

Grandma Faye nodded in Lizzie's direction before cautiously stepping towards the little girl, with Madison following two paces behind. Bear rushed at the gate, barking furiously while Quinn, who had been hunched on the stone wall, erupted into the air in a flurry of black feathers, his caws matching Bear's in ferocity.

"Bear, Quinn," Lizzie pleaded, "please stop. Grandma Faye needs to help Cathy." But just like before, both her companions ignored her.

"Bear," Madison said from around Grandma Faye's shoulder. "You need to stop barking." At the sound of her voice, Bear swiveled his head in her direction but continued his volley of baying. "I understand, but your barking is making things worse."

Much to Lizzie's amazement, both of them obeyed Madison, Quinn taking up his post again on the top of the wall. Bear, his hackles still raised, positioned his body so as to block Lizzie from getting any closer to the gate. Lizzie placed her hand on his head to reassure him. He let out a low whine. "It's alright."

Grandma Faye brushed down her skirt and stepped forward. "Hello, Cathy," she said in a soothing voice. "My name is Grandma Faye, and this here is Madison," she said, pointing over her shoulder. "We're here to help. That arm looks like it probably hurts a lot. Would you like me to fix it?"

Cathy slowly raised her head, blinking against the glare of the headlights. "Lizzie said she was going to help me, but she lied. Are you lying too?" She asked, her voice tremulous as a tear slipped down her grimy cheek.

"No, sweetheart, I'm not lying. I promise to take you to a safe place and stop your arm from hurting."

"Will Poppa Audley be there too? I want my Poppa." Her lip trembled, and more tears streamed down her face.

Grandma Faye looked quickly over at Lizzie, understanding registering in her eyes before turning back to Cathy. "I know you do, hun, but let me take care of your arm first, okay?"

"Okay," she sniffled, swiping her nose with the back of her hand. When she struggled to rise on her feet, Grandma Faye held out her hands but didn't approach the girl.

"No, stay where you are, and I'll come and get you. We don't want you hurting yourself more. Now, I just need to check something out," Grandma Faye said, slowly raising her arms.

Cathy let out an ear-splitting scream and covered her head with her good arm. "I'll be good, I promise. I won't try to run away. I'll be good. Please don't hurt me. No more dark sparkles, please. They hurt."

Lizzie could feel the absolute terror rolling off the little girl in waves. Grandma Faye quickly lowered her arms and crouched down on the ground. "Cathy, I'm not going to hurt you. I know you've been hurt by some very bad people, but they're gone, and they're not coming back. And see, my sparkles are a pretty green. They don't hurt people. They help them feel better." Grandma

Faye held out her hand as several green sparks of light danced above it.

Cathy lowered her arm and looked at the dancing glitter of magick, then up at Grandma Faye. "Your sparkles are pretty. And they don't hurt people?"

"No, only help. Will you let my green sparkles help you now?"

Cathy nodded her head.

Grandma Faye took her time in standing and then very slowly raised her arms again. "I'm just going to make sure the bad men didn't leave anything behind. And I promise this won't hurt."

Right as the old woman was drawing up her magick, Cathy suddenly slumped forward on the ground. Madison inhaled sharply, and it was all Lizzie could do to stop herself from running to the little girl.

"Madison, Lizzie, stay where you are; don't move until I've checked her out," Grandma Faye ordered as she swiftly called forth her magick and sent it swirling around Cathy's limp body. The old woman drew several symbols in the air as she walked closer to the little circle and then circled around, all the while her hands dancing in the air, drawing spell after spell.

"She's clean. No enchantments, no wards, no traces of dark magick anywhere on or around her," she said as she knelt down and gently gathered the motionless child in her arms. Immediately, Grandma Faye sent out healing to the little girl cradled in her arms. Cathy stirred, then her eyes fluttered open, and she looked up into the old woman's face.

"Where am I?"

"You are just outside the village, close to my home. Do you remember how you got here?"

Cathy's face scrunched up in concentration. "No."

"That's okay. Where's the last place you remember being?"

Cathy blinked slowly before saying, "I—I was in the room without windows."

"How long were you in the room without windows?"

"A long time."

"Were there any other people with you in the room?"

"No, but the mean man would come in to give me food and a cup of water, but something must have happened to him because he stopped coming."

"Do you remember how you got out of the room?"

The little girl's forehead furrowed. "No."

"What is the last thing you do remember?"

There was a long pause before she replied. "The shadow came back." She blinked slowly several times before her eyelids remained closed. Then she whispered, "I'm hungry. Could I have some food, please? I promise to be good, I prom…" Her voice trailed off, and she appeared to have fallen asleep.

Grandma Faye shifted the little girl in her arms before standing up. "I've taken her pain away, but you were right. Her shoulder is dislocated, and I have to pop it back in manually. It's probably best if I take her to my place," she said, nodding her head in the direction of where Bear stood at the gate. "Madison, could you get the door?" Turning back to Lizzie, she said, "And I'll call Vivienne as soon as we get home. We might need her to retrieve Cathy's memories about the dark man and where she was held. We have to be sure there aren't any more like her being held somewhere. Also, this poor, innocent soul has been through a trauma, and she will need more resources than I can give her."

"Yes, of course." Lizzie looked down at the sleeping child in Grandma Faye's arms. With the combined illumination of the headlights and Lizzie's magick orbs, Cathy's true state of emaciation was apparent. She felt a rage building in her, and if Jon had still been alive, she would have hunted him down and made him suffer before she ended him.

Grandma Faye gently placed the sleeping Cathy on the bench seat of the old truck and moved out of the way to let Madison climb in. Before the old woman got in the driver's seat, she called to Lizzie, "I'll call you as soon as I check her over."

"Thank you." Lizzie looked directly into Grandma Faye's eyes. Thank you—for everything."

Grandma Faye nodded and got in the truck. She executed a quick U-turn, and as the truck disappeared down the road, Bear looked up at Quinn and barked in what sounded like a command. Immediately, the raven flew off, following the taillights into the night. Bear led the way back to the cottage. His head lowered in what to Lizzie looked strangely like defeat.

CHAPTER TWENTY

Lizzie wandered around the living room, rearranging her meager stash of books on the bookshelves according to height, then repositioning a pair of candlesticks on the mantle, only to put them back in their original position. She made a circuit around the coffee table, refolding the previously neatly folded afghan, draping it on the back of the sofa, and plumping up the already plumped seat cushion on the chair, her gaze constantly pulled to where the telephone sat sullenly silent on the end table.

She'd called Vivienne as soon as Grandma Fay and Madison drove off with Cathy, but the call went straight to voicemail. She left a brief message updating her about Bear's return and Cathy's appearance at her gate and asking her to call back as soon as possible, but the phone remained stubbornly quiet. Between waiting for both Vivienne to return her call and Grandma Faye to update her on Cathy's condition, Lizzie was going stir-crazy.

Her restless meandering eventually led her to the open front door. Stepping outside, she absently rubbed her forearm where Bear's mouth had clamped down on it, the skin smooth and unmarked despite the vise-like grip she'd felt when his teeth had trapped her arm. She joined Bear on the front porch where he'd stationed himself since Grandma Faye had driven away, ignoring Lizzie's continued attempts to bribe him inside with his favorite cookies. He sat looking out towards the driveway, his ears forward, his back rigid.

Had he always had the ability to take someone with him when he dematerialized, or was this something new, something that happened when he'd been trapped inside the liminal space of the portal? Was it the same as when Vivienne came to Lizzie's *in-between*? And what about Bear's odd behavior with Cathy? Had he merely sensed the fear on the little girl, or was it the lingering scent of dark magick that had provoked him?

She blew out a frustrated breath and then headed back inside to get a glass of water when she spotted the broken crystal strewn across the kitchen floor. Here was a problem she could easily fix, something she could put right. Quickly snagging a broom, she swept up the shards, then meticulously went over the area with a damp paper towel to pick up any remaining small bits of glass.

She felt a temporary relief as she surveyed the clean floor, but the phone still hadn't rung. Bear still refused to come inside, and she still had more questions than answers. The smell of rain billowed in through the open door, thunder echoing off the mountains in the distance, but Bear remained at his station on the porch, the wind rippling through his fur.

When the pressure began to build inside her again, Lizzie drifted from room to room, turning on lights as she went, eventually ending back in the living room. The cottage lit up the night like a bright beacon in the storm.

Even with all the lights blazing, it wasn't enough to chase away the dread nestling beneath her ribcage, so she stacked log after log into the fireplace, and with the flick of her fingertips, eager flames shot up in the hearth. Finding no other distraction to occupy herself, she rejoined Bear on the porch. He didn't glance up as she gently stroked the top of his head, his eyes trained on the front gate. Instead, he leaned his comforting weight against her leg.

With an ease now familiar to her, she rolled out her energy to touch the edges of her property. She could feel the strength of the wards and even the one she'd placed on the portal. All was secure; no danger or dark magick had infiltrated the protective barriers, but the knowledge did nothing to ease her mind. Where had Cathy come from? How had she ended up outside Lizzie's gate, injured and alone? On the surface, it didn't appear that Bear's trip through the portal and his subsequent return were tied to Cathy's appearance, but every fiber of Lizzie's being told her otherwise.

Instead of powering down her magick, she strengthened her connection to her Elemental, calling forth the golden white orb. As it floated before her, she focused her attention towards it.

"Elemental, can you show me how the events of the past two days are connected?" The orb flashed gold, the energy spinning faster. "Show me now, please," she whispered into the night.

The vision came on suddenly, just like the one she'd had in the barn; one moment, she was standing on her porch with Bear at her side. The next, she was in the middle of the stone circle, surrounded by four women, each one shimmering with the color of their bonded element. They stood, arms raised, their power flowing out of their palms and into each other. And from their hearts, more light flowed into the center of the circle, like spokes in a wheel, to where Lizzie stood frozen.

She gasped as a searing cold enveloped her and, along with it, a terror so penetrating, so vast, it overwhelmed her senses. She opened her mouth to scream when a dark, oily smoke slithered down her throat, cutting off the sound of her fear. Just before the piercing darkness touched her heart, the clatter of a bell shattered the vision, leaving Lizzie gasping for breath as she leaned into Bear for support. He nudged her gently with his cold nose as the phone continued to ring. Lizzie had forgotten to switch over the phones when the power had come back on, and the old rotary's ring clanged metallically in the empty cottage.

She dashed inside, snatching up the heavy receiver and holding it to her ear with both hands. "Vivienne?" she gulped.

"Is everything okay? You sound out of breath?"

"Madison?" Lizzie sat down hard on the overstuffed chair by the phone, her mind scrambling to refocus her thoughts back to the present moment. "I'm fine. It's just the phone startled me."

"You haven't talked to Vivienne yet?"

"No, I tried earlier, but my call went straight to voicemail. Is Cathy okay?"

"Better than expected, considering what she's been through, but she hasn't spoken a word since we brought her here. Except when Grandma Faye tried to remove that bracelet with the black stone she's wearing. She got hysterical and kept screaming something about her Grandfather and keeping safe, so Grandma Faye just left it on." Madison said, her voice sounding tinny and far away through the old receiver. "We managed to pop Cathy's shoulder back into place, and before you ask, we used our magick so Cathy didn't feel a thing. She's tucked up in bed right now, and Grandma Faye is feeding her some broth. She seems to have latched onto Grandma Faye, and hopefully, she'll feel safe enough to start talking again."

Lizzie blew out a breath and leaned back in the chair. Cathy had been found, and she was safe. Audley's dying wish had been fulfilled, not through anything Lizzie had done, but by someone bringing her to Lizzie's gate. But why? Lizzie shifted the receiver to her other ear. "I hope she opens up soon. We need to find out who brought her here."

"Grandma Faye mentioned to me that Cathy's the granddaughter of the guy who was your handyman, the one who got shot."

"Yes, Jon kept Cathy hostage to keep Audley in line."

"Could the Order have missed rounding up all of the goons who worked for Jon, and one of them is after revenge for what you did, using Cathy to get you outside the protection of your wards? That would explain why Bear wouldn't let you open the gate. And maybe, when Grandma Faye and I showed up, we scared him off."

Lizzie thought about sharing with Madison the premonition she'd just had. Without getting some insight from Grandma Faye or Vivienne to find out what it meant, she didn't see what good it would do to worry Madison, especially when it had been less than a day ago that she'd almost lost her life. "I honestly don't know. If it was someone wanting revenge, they could have attacked me anytime I left Rose Cottage over the last few weeks. They could have done it yesterday, as a matter of fact, when I was at the farmers' market."

"Unless whoever brought Cathy only just discovered where she was being held, or maybe that person was lying low until the Order left and things died down before going after you?"

"You're making some good points, but until Cathy can tell us who brought her here, we're just shooting in the dark," Lizzie said. "Could you get Grandma Faye to call me when she's free?"

"Sure thing."

"In the meantime, it wouldn't hurt to be extra vigilant and stay put until we know exactly who we are dealing with."

"I agree, but..." Madison hesitated, "I don't like the idea of you being there all by yourself."

"Don't worry about me. You forget I've handled a demon on my own and lived to tell about it. And that's before I bonded to my Elemental. Besides, I'm not alone. Bear's with me, and you've seen first-hand the lengths he'll go to, to protect me." She looked out the open door at her dog, who was still standing guard on the porch. Quinn still hadn't returned, and *that* did worry her. "Promise me you'll keep Cathy safe, and call me if anything changes with her. I'll try calling Vivienne again."

"I will," Madison promised before hanging up.

Lizzie immediately dialed Vivienne's cell and yet again got her voicemail.

Determined to do something useful while she waited for the phone to ring, she angled the armchair she was sitting in so she had a clear view of Bear through the open doorway, filled her fountain pen, and grabbed one of the new journals she'd left on the coffee table.

She intended to jot down everything she'd seen in her vision and all that had happened from the time Bear had leapt off the couch to when Grandma Faye and Madison had driven off with the sleeping Cathy in an attempt to see where the connections lay, but when she touched the pen to the crisp white page what flowed from her hand was not Cathy's appearance on the road but the last moments she'd shared with Wren.

As her hand raced across the page, filling it with her looping script, she remembered how his touch felt as it traced across her cheek and the way her body had responded. The way her heart swelled when he said he loved her and the confusion that followed when he'd spoken the last words she'd ever hear from him; *I'm so sorry, Lizzie. I wished we'd had more time.*

With Ian and Gideon, her connection to them hadn't been one of love but of desperation. She could see that now. She'd been seeking a lifeline when she'd found herself in a world she didn't understand, where her fear of being alone was the only driving force to her actions. But what she felt and still felt for Wren was something new, something unexpected. Something she had no reference to draw upon. It went beyond just the physical attraction she'd felt, the way their bodies fit together, the pleasure and release she'd experienced the night they'd made love under the full moon. It still astonished her that she'd done that, but it had felt so right, so natural. When she'd seen him standing there bathed in the silvery light of the goddess — it had felt like coming home.

She kept writing even when her eyelids got heavy, and her head began to nod. But at some point in the night, while Bear remained sentry on the porch and the storm gathered strength outside, sleep took her gently in its arms. Lizzie's hand relaxed, falling open in her lap. A jagged black line trailed down the page as the pen fell to the floor unnoticed.

CHAPTER TWENTY-ONE

Lizzie walked briskly up the driveway. She couldn't help but notice her new bond with the Elemental had altered the previous version of the *in-between*. The colors here had always had an intense vibrancy that didn't exist in the real world, but now the air was filled with lines of color that hummed and vibrated with life, each light line connecting to the in-between's version of the plants in the garden, the trees, the earth and even the stone walls of the cottage. She tried not to gawk at her vegetable garden, which in this new iteration was lush and full of leafy green lettuce the height of shrubs, corn stalks that stood six feet tall, tomato plants as large as saplings, and a row of dill that looked more like a stand of bamboo than a delicate lacy row of herbs. Even Emma's tree stood tall and proud, a mature tree covered in both pale pink blossoms and fully ripened apples, their deep red skins glossy in the ethereal light.

As she approached the cottage, she spied Vivienne seated on the porch steps. She was dressed in her version of casual wear: black, wide-legged trousers topped with a white silk blouse, the sleeves rolled up to her elbows, and thick-soled sneakers on her feet. She wore oversized sunglasses.

She joined Vivienne on the steps. Facing her, their knees almost touching.

"Are you in any immediate danger?" Vivienne asked, reaching out to touch Lizzie gently on the arm.

"No, I'm perfectly safe inside my cottage, and Bear is guarding me. What's going on? I've been trying to reach you all night. Has something happened to the others?"

"No, everyone's fine. I'm at Grandma Faye's right now.

I arrived a few minutes ago. I was out in the field where there was no cell service, but as soon as I could check my messages and saw you'd called, I immediately called you back, but you didn't answer. Then I called Grandma Faye. When she told me about Cathy appearing at your gate, I drove out here and asked Grandma Faye to keep trying your number until I arrived, but you never picked up."

Lizzie looked at her, puzzled. "Sorry, I must have fallen asleep. It's been a wild couple of days, and I didn't get much sleep last night." Worry churned in her guts, a large part of her not wanting to know the truth, but she asked the question anyway. "What *is* going on?"

"In the last couple of weeks, there has been a marked increase in dark magick across the world. And yesterday, there were organized attacks on us by the warlocks all along the western section of the continent. These attacks happened at the same time as Cathy showed up at your gate. Along with the strange behavior of the vortex on your property and Bear's reaction to Cathy, I knew it was tied to the attacks. When I arrived and you still hadn't called. I couldn't risk sending any of us to check on you until we know for sure if anyone is lying in wait in the surrounding area, waiting for another chance to get at you. My only other option was to pull you into your in-between."

"Attacks?"

"Before I continue, do you think you could dim your light? Even with these on," she gestured to the sunglasses, "I'm having trouble seeing you."

Puzzled, Lizzie looked around.

"No, not out there. You," she said, pointing at Lizzie. "Your light."

Lizzie looked down at herself, instantly realizing what Vivienne meant. Her magick combined with the Element, in the in-between, created a light so bright Lizzie could barely make out the shape of her own arms beneath the pulsing sparkle of golden white light. She pulled back her magick until she could see her hands and arms clearly. "Sorry, is that better?"

"Much," Vivienne said, waving her hand in front of her eyes, the sunglasses immediately disappearing. She looked directly at Lizzie. "I wish we had time to talk about your bonding, but time is of the essence. I've gathered a team to assist us, and they should be here within the hour. They will meet here at Grandma Faye's, and I'll connect with you to give you the plan." She raised her hand to stop Lizzie from talking. "I know you have questions, so I'll try to be as brief as possible.

"At approximately six o'clock your time, a team of warlocks attacked several locations from California up to Alaska. They hit locations where there are known vortices. Any witch, shaman, or healer who lived by or near a vortex was killed. All except two, a shaman who managed to escape the attack. And the other..."

Lizzie's stomach dropped as a chill ran through her. "Is me," Lizzie said, finishing Vivienne's sentence. "Madison was right. They were using Cathy as a lure to get me outside the protection of my wards."

Vivienne nodded.

"But why?"

"Because they are searching for a particular kind of individual. The shaman who survived the attack confirmed what we'd suspected by the evidence we found at the other crime scenes. He told us when he was captured by the warlocks, they slashed his forearm with an iron blade, but it wasn't a fatal wound. It was only when he didn't react to the iron that they tried to kill him, and that's when he managed to break free and get to safety."

"What are they testing for?"

"There is only one kind of being that would react to iron.

They are looking for a fey."

Lizzie gasped.

"I know it sounds far-fetched, as the Fey haven't been seen in our realm for eons, but it is the only thing that makes sense. We just need to find out why they are searching for a fey now, and for what purpose?"

Lizzie gazed out across her property, the lines of energy connecting everything like a giant shimmering spider web. "I know who they're searching for. He calls himself Wren, and the portal to his realm is on my property."

CHAPTER TWENTY-TWO

"Stop!"

Lizzie wheeled around, her heart in her throat. "What are you doing here?" she asked, looking at Madison in confusion.

"Saving you from getting trapped in the portal, apparently," Madison said breathlessly. She stood just on the edge of the clearing with Quinn perched on her shoulder. Brilliant yellow orbs pulsed in each of her upheld palms, her chest heaving as if she'd been running hard. She quickly powered down her magick, the yellow lights winking out instantly. Bear trotted over to greet Madison, and she absently patted his head.

"I'm not in any danger. I was just checking the wards." Stepping away from the stone circle, she looked over Madison's shoulder into the forest, wondering why she hadn't heard any car engines. "Are the others here too? I thought Vivienne was going to contact me when the reinforcements had arrived." Wind whipped her hair into her eyes, and she pushed the annoying tendrils behind her ears with an impatient hand.

"No—" Madison gulped, placing her hand on her chest as she tried to catch her breath, "They don't even know I'm here. Quinn showed up at the cabin. He told me I had to come here right away, that it was urgent."

Lizzie shook her head. "I'm sorry, did you just say—" She glanced over at Quinn and then back at Madison. "Quinn *told* you to come here?" A fat drop of rain plopped on her nose, and she swiped at it with her sleeve.

"Yes. Wait, let me start at the beginning. After Vivienne came back from the meeting with you in the *in-between*, she'd just started to tell us what's going on with the warlocks and that you met a fey. And she told us the portal to his world is right there," Madison pointed to the stone circle. "I was right. It was a portal." Her eyes went wide with excitement. "I have so many questions, like what does he look like, does he have wings, does he speak English, how did you meet him?"

"I'll answer your questions in a moment, but first, finish telling me why you risked your life to come here?"

"Right. Okay, where was I?"

"Vivienne had just told you about Wren and that the warlocks are hunting for him."

"Yeah, Vivienne was telling us about what was going on when Cathy woke up screaming. I think she was having a flashback or something. Anyway, Vivienne and Grandma Faye ran into the bedroom to try to calm her down, and that's when Quinn and his buddies showed up. They started beating and pecking on the living room window. Grandma Faye and Vivienne had their hands full, so I went to see what was up.

"I opened the door to find out what was going on, and that's when Quinn told me I had to get here now. He was frantic. He told me if I didn't leave that very instant, all would be lost. So, I snagged Grandma Faye's truck keys from the hook by the door and drove straight here. I freaked out when you weren't in the cottage, but Quinn said you were at the circle, so I ran here as fast as I could. And here I am." She craned her neck to stare at the raven on her shoulder. "I thought you said she was in danger?"

Quinn cocked his head and chortled deep in his throat.

"Well, you can't blame me for thinking she was hurt when you said 'all would be lost.' In fact, I'm still not clear on what you meant by that."

"Whoa," Lizzie said, her hands raised in front of her to stop Madison. "I know I'm not dreaming, even though this feels like one. Are you telling me you drove here without letting anyone know where you were going when there is more than likely a deranged warlock or two lurking outside my gate, willing to use a child as a lure and wouldn't hesitate to use you, too? And you did all this and put yourself in danger because Quinn told you to?"

"Yes," Madison said, her face lit in delight, a huge smile spreading across her face. "It seems that along with the healing you gave me, you also supercharged my magick. Kinda like what you did with Bear. My powers are not only much stronger now, but the best part is I can talk to birds, which makes sense since my bonded element is air, which is also the realm of communication."

Bear cocked his head and looked up at Madison. "Oh," she exclaimed. "I can talk to dogs, too. This is super cool." She looked over at Lizzie, "Although I am still getting the hang of it, otherwise, I wouldn't have thought you'd been hurt and rushed over here like a crazy person."

Quinn cawed loudly and bobbed his head. Lizzie looked at Quinn and then back at Madison again. "He says it's not his fault I didn't understand what he was saying, and he still insists that I had to come now."

"He said all that in one caw?"

"Yes and no. It's more like telepathy than actual speaking. I get a combination of images, thoughts, and words in my mind, not complete sentences. I think the vocalizations are just for emphasis. I wish I had my notebook to jot this all down, but I left my satchel back at Grandma Faye's."

"Speaking of which, we should call and let them know where you are. And that you're safe. The last thing we need is the two of them thinking the warlocks got to you." She covered the short distance to join Madison at the edge of the clearing. "And I don't know about you, but I haven't gotten much sleep over the last couple of days, and I need a cup of coffee."

"I wouldn't say no to a cup or to a quick shower and change of clothes, for that matter," Madison said as the four of them trouped back through the forest towards the cottage with Bear leading the way and Quinn still perched on her shoulder. "So, you've met a fey?"

"Yes, I'll fill you in on the details over coffee."

"You better believe you will. I want to know everything," Madison said over her shoulder, "And I mean everything. I can't believe you didn't tell me you'd met a fey."

They were just reaching the edge of the forest when Bear stopped dead in his tracks. He raised his head, scenting the air just as the sound of a car engine reached them. Before either woman could react, Bear tore through the trees and bounded towards the driveway, his tail helicoptering in a happy greeting.

"That must be Vivienne, or maybe the backup team has arrived." Lizzie felt her body relax as they reached the edge of the forest.

"No, Bear said it was the Bird Girl. Who's that?" Madison asked just as the little hatchback pulled up to the cottage.

"Oh shit," Lizzie said, jogging towards the car, "It's Birdie. I completely forgot she was coming to work on the barn today. She's early? We said nine o'clock, and it can't be much past six in the morning."

Birdie jumped out of the car just as the skies opened up. Grabbing a large satchel from the front seat, she slipped the strap over her head and dashed onto the porch. She raised her hand to knock on the door but stopped and turned as Lizzie called out to her.

"I came as soon as I could. I hope I'm not too late," Birdie said, as Lizzie and the rest of her friends scrambled up the steps and out of the rain.

Lizzie took a moment to gather her thoughts. This seemed to be her day to be confused by people showing up and saying the most bizarre things. All she knew was that she needed to get Birdie away as quickly as possible. "I'm really sorry to do this to you after you've driven out here, but something's come up, and we need to reschedule the barn renovation for another day." She tried to guide Birdie gently by the shoulders down the porch, but the young woman shrugged off Lizzie's hands and stood her ground.

"I'm not here to work on the barn." Birdie began rummaging through her satchel. "I just sat down to breakfast when I had a feeling that I needed to come here." She stopped rooting around in her bag and looked up at the two women. "I guess now that I know for sure what you are," she said to Lizzie, "and you, too," she said to Madison, and then continued to search inside her bag, "I can tell you the truth. I didn't have a feeling or a knowing. I had a vision. I've had them all my life, but I was always afraid if I told the truth, people would think I was crazy.

"I'm here because I'm one of the Daughters of the Earth. I'm here to help defeat that dark thing." She pulled out a long-handled bread knife and a salt shaker, holding them up for the others to see. "I wasn't sure what to bring to a battle of good against evil, and I was in a hurry to get here, so I just grabbed whatever was handy." Her hands shook slightly. "Will these do?"

Madison and Lizzie exchanged puzzled glances.

"Birdie," Lizzie turned towards the young woman, trying desperately to keep her voice calm, "despite what your vision showed you, need to leave *now*. It isn't safe for you to be here. There are trained people who have magick like us," she gestured to herself and Madison "who are on their way here to help, as we speak. So, I need you to get back in your car and go home."

Birdie lowered her hands and glanced from Lizzie to Madison. "No," she said, jutting out her chin. "I have to be here. All four Daughters of the Earth have to be here so we can join with the One Who Walks Between the Worlds. That's you," she said, pointing the bread knife at Lizzie, "in order for us to release the phoenix and restore the balance. To keep the worlds beyond ours safe. And those other people, I don't think they're coming. I didn't see them in my vision. It was just us, the daughters, and you. I trust my visions, and they have never been wrong." Bear let out an authoritative bark, and Quinn chortled as if in agreement.

Lizzie didn't like the idea of using her magick to force someone to obey her, but she needed to get Birdie to safety. She had started to call up her power when Madison grabbed her arm to stop her.

"She's right."

Lizzie swung around to gape at Madison.

"Well, she is," Madison said, letting go of Lizzie's arm. "Both Bear and Quinn said as much." She reached past a stunned Lizzie, her hand extended. "Hi, I'm Madison. Great bag, by the way."

Birdie quickly shoved the knife and shaker back in her satchel and shook Madison's hand. "Bernadette, but everyone calls me Birdie. And thanks, it just came into my Aunt's shop the other day."

"So, Birdie, I don't suppose your vision showed you who won this battle?" Madison continued, "Because I'd really like to have the opportunity to check out your Aunt's shop." She smiled, half-joking.

"No, it came and went fast like a thunderbolt. All I saw was me, you, Grandma Faye," she looked towards Grandma Faye's truck, "is she here already?"

"No, I borrowed her truck. Who was the fourth daughter?"

"I've never seen her before. She's tall and has dark hair cut into a bob. She looked very elegant, but also like she's used to being in charge, if that makes sense."

"Vivienne," Madison whispered.

"And you, of course," Birdie finished, indicating Lizzie.

"And what did you see in your vision?" Madison asked.

"Like I said before, we, the Daughters of the Earth, were

channeling air, fire, water, and earth energy in a circle of colored light, and Lizzie, the One Who Walks Between the Worlds, was in the middle, and this dark, horrible thing was trying to take Lizzie somewhere. We were sending our energy to her, into the center of the circle, and it looked like—"

"Spokes in a wheel," Lizzie finished the sentence.

"Yeah, just like that. A colored wheel of light with the spokes of white light radiating into the middle where you were standing."

Lizzie scrubbed her face with her hands as she tried to collect her thoughts.

"You keep calling Lizzie the one who walks between the worlds, but what does that mean?"

"I'm not sure."

The hair on the back of Lizzie's neck rose, and she pushed down a wave of dread that washed over her. She needed to take control of the situation, to do what she could to keep Madison and Birdie safe from what was coming. "Okay, I want everyone inside," she said, throwing open the door to the cottage. "Madison, you can put on a pot of coffee while I call Vivienne and update her on the situation. Birdie, I'll need you to—"

Before Lizzie could finish her sentence, Bear let out a deep, threatening growl and leapt off the porch, his hackles raised. At the same time, Quinn launched himself into the air, following Bear down the driveway. All three women turned to look towards the front gate just as the sky darkened, the air exploding with the angry caws of hundreds of ravens and the squeal of tires on the wet gravel. A lone SUV swerved up the road, almost landing in the ditch before the driver swung the vehicle hard in the other direction, skidding to a halt in front of the gate.

"Bear says it's too late. It's already begun," Madison said, her eyes wide with fear.

CHAPTER TWENTY-THREE

The sound of grinding of metal on metal could be heard even over the cacophony of ravens' caws, and Bear's threatening barks as the SUV's driver's side door flung open with such force it was ripped off one of its hinges and hung askew from the remaining one. The three women scrambled to the edge of the porch as someone stepped out of the vehicle.

Gripping the broken door for balance, Vivienne staggered out onto the road. Absent was the tailored blazer she always wore; the front of her white silk blouse was stained with something dark, and the knees of her stockings were shredded as if she'd been forced to kneel or crawl. She moved stiffly towards the gate, her limbs jerking as if pulled by invisible strings. She stopped inches away and raised her hand in greeting with that same jerking motion.

"Vivienne's hurt," Madison exclaimed, and she would have run down the steps had Lizzie not shot her arm out to block her. Birdie stood on Lizzie's other side and clutched the back of Lizzie's shirt.

"Wait," Lizzie ordered, "You remember what she said about the warlocks? This is a trap."

"Lizzie darling, be a good girl and let me in," Vivienne called out from the other side of the gate. Her voice was flat and lifeless, but underneath it was another one, its deep, lazy rumble, strangely hypnotic. "I have come such a long way to see you. Don't you know it's rude to keep a guest waiting?"

"What's wrong with her?" Birdie asked, tightening her grip on Lizzie's shirt.

"Lizzie, I can see you up there, my little pet. Be a good

girl and come down here and give me a hug," the Vivienne-thing said, opening its arms wide in a grotesque parody of a welcoming gesture, its fingers splayed, the wrists cocked at an unnatural angle.

"They must've enthralled her," Madison gasped. "And…" She craned her neck forward, squinting through the rain as she stared down the driveway at the SUV, "Oh dear goddess, I think that's Grandma Faye in the passenger seat, and she's got Cathy with her."

"Lizzie!" growled the oily voice. "Get down here at once. I'm losing my patience."

She turned to look at Lizzie, her voice rising, "We've got to do something." The fear in Madison's voice snapped Lizzie out of the strange trance-like power of the thing's voice.

"Right," she said, blinking hard, "the warlocks are using Vivienne just like they did Cathy to get me outside the wards and force me to take them down so they can get to the portal. We need to find where they're hiding and take them out first."

"They would have to be close by to maintain their control over Vivienne."

"How close?"

"Six feet. Ten at the most."

"So most likely they're hiding in the trees on the other side of the road," Lizzie said as her mind raced, her heart thundered in her chest. "We'll have to move fast so they don't have a chance to react." She raised her palms as Madison did likewise. As their magick flared in orbs of blinding white and yellow, Birdie gasped and took a step back, releasing her hold on Lizzie's shirt.

"Ready?" Lizzie said.

"Ready," Madison replied. Both women flung out their hands, sending their power rocketing down the drive through the wards. When their magick swept over Vivienne, she stiffened, her arms at her sides, her head thrown back. Lightning sliced through the air, scattering the ravens circling above. The boom of thunder shook the ground. And then Vivienne screamed.

"Pull back," Lizzie shouted, "pull back."

Both women reeled in their magick as Vivienne crumpled to the ground.

"Did you feel that?" Madison swayed on her feet, gasping. "That wasn't a spell. Vivienne is possessed by —"

"The Dark One," Birdie said, her voice sounding small and scared. "It's the thing from my vision." She stepped forward, holding the bread knife in her hand again, joining the others at the edge of the porch as they watched the Vivienne-thing pull itself to its feet.

"Bitches," the thing inside Vivienne screamed as it raised its head, "If you can't play nice, I won't either." It flung out its hand, and the passenger side of the SUV swung open. "Perhaps watching the old woman die will get your attention, or shall I start with the child first?"

Grandma Faye emerged from the passenger's side, cradling an unconscious Cathy in her arms. There was a large, angry bruise on Grandma Faye's cheek and what appeared to be more bruises around her throat. She shuffled forward on unsteady feet as if pushed from behind, her normally braided hair hanging loose over her face. She made it as far as the hood of the vehicle when she stumbled, leaning against the SUV to break her fall.

"Alright, I'm coming. Don't harm them," Lizzie said, taking the first step off the porch. Suddenly, she stopped and turned to face Birdie. "Is there anything I can say or do that would convince you to go into the cottage and stay behind the safety of the wards until this is over?"

"No," Birdie said with conviction. "I need to be a part of this." She gripped the bread knife tighter in her hand.

"That's what I thought you'd say." Lizzie again called up

her magick into the palm of her hand, "Then I'm going to give you a fighting chance to survive this." And with that, she plunged her magick deep into Birdie's chest, connecting with the spark of magic she felt there. She poured her magick into the spark until the spark grew to embers. She pushed deeper until the embers ignited into flames.

CHAPTER TWENTY-FOUR

"Let them go, and I'll give you what you want." Lizzie stood six feet inside the gate with Madison and Birdie flanking her, Bear, hackles still raised, standing point. "I know how to open the portal," Lizzie said, hoping her only bargaining chip was enough to save the people she cared about.

"Do you now?" The thing inside Vivienne purred as it stutter-stepped within a foot of the gate, its dark eyes focused intently on Lizzie.

"I do, and I'm also the only one who can take down the wards here and at the portal. If you want access to the Fey realm, the only way you are getting it is by releasing these people unharmed."

"Lizzie," Madison said, leaning in to whisper fiercely in her ear. "The stone. Bear said that thing is in the stone on Vivienne's wrist. That's what's controlling her. It's just like the one Cathy has."

Lizzie's eyes narrowed. The thing holding Vivienne in its grip was standing too close to the gate for Lizzie to get a clear view of Vivienne's wrist.

"And how exactly are you going to do that without a fey?" It chuckled. The deep rumble of its voice reverberated in Lizzie's breastbone. "We'll give you points for trying, but you are not clever enough to match wits with us. Remove these wards, take us to the Fey one and the portal, and we'll consider letting the witches go."

"You're wrong on both counts. I opened the portal once before, and I can do it again. And there is no fey here. He's gone back to his realm, so the only way you are getting that portal open is if I do it."

The Vivienne thing blinked its eyes slowly as if contemplating Lizzie's words.

"Do we have a deal?" Lizzie gestured with her hand, and the gate swung open. Birdie inhaled sharply. Now, Lizzie had a clear view of the dark stone held in place with a leather cord around Vivienne's left wrist. Before the thing had a chance to reply, Lizzie shot a bolt of energy, directing it into the stone. The stone didn't just explode. It vaporized into dust. Immediately, Vivienne crumpled loose-limbed to the ground.

"You did it," Madison exclaimed, fist-pumping the air as Birdie jumped up and down.

All three women surged forward to help Vivienne and Grandma Faye, but before they stepped over the wards, Vivienne raised her head and screamed, "Don't come any closer." Reaching out, she placed a hand on the SUV's bumper and pulled herself upright. "You didn't destroy it." She leaned heavily against the vehicle. "You just released it."

The stench of rotten eggs suddenly filled the air. Something shifted behind Vivienne as she moved towards Grandma Faye, using the hood of the vehicle for support. At first, Lizzie thought it was a shadow until it moved on its own accord.

Lizzie stared in horror as the shadow thing stepped towards the gate. It was roughly the shape of a human, but its limbs were too long, and there were no discernible features on its elongated head. Its whole body appeared to be covered in quills. It was a black thing that didn't belong to this world. It wasn't so much a shadow thing than a darkness that absorbed all the light around it, so it appeared as a matte humanoid shape punched out of the fabric of the air. A velvet cut-out of a vaguely human shape. The Dark One.

Lizzie rocketed a steady stream of magick at the monster just as Madison did the same. When a flash of heat seared the side of her face, and a deep red stream of magick joined the two streams already hitting the Dark One in the chest, Lizzie risked a quick sideways glance to see, to her amazement, Birdie wielding not a bread knife but a sword of fire and flame.

As their combined power struck the shadow thing, instead of being destroyed or forced back by their magick, it appeared to absorb the blasts and, in a sinuous movement, causing the quills to ripple, it arched its back and grew larger.

"It's feeding off our energy," Madison exclaimed. "What do we do now?"

Instead of answering, Lizzie drew up every drop of power she could and threw it at the SUV. The vehicle shot across the road directly in the path of the dark thing, but instead of slamming into it, the SUV passed through it, landing on its side in the opposite ditch.

"Stop, everyone, stop," Lizzie shouted, flinging her hands to her sides and powering down her magick. The other two followed suit, Birdie struggling for a moment before the sword disappeared, and she was again holding just a serrated kitchen knife.

"Lizzie, do *not* take down the wards. No matter what happens," ordered Vivienne. She now stood protectively over Grandma Faye and Cathy, swaying slightly in the effort to remain upright. She called up her magick, and it flared weakly, flickering in and out in her hand.

The Dark One shook itself like a dog and then stretched to its full height. The things Lizzie had first mistaken as quills covering its body were, in actuality, stiff, narrow tubes that made a dry rasping sound as the thing moved. It turned its blank face in Lizzie's direction. "Well, well, well," It purred from the flatness of its face. "What do we have here?" It cocked its head regarding Lizzie. There were no eyes she could see in the velvety blackness of its face, but she could feel its gaze on her, making her skin crawl.

"Now that we are free from the confines of the stones, let us turn to the business at hand. Time is running short, and we are running out of patience. Remove these wards and let us in, and we will let the witches go. Now!" it roared.

"No, Lizzie, don't do this," Vivienne shouted, "It can't be allowed to go through the portal and infect the other realm."

The Dark thing moved so fast that Lizzie couldn't track it. It was no longer standing in front of the open gate, but now loomed over Vivienne. It bent its neck at an unnatural angle, a gaping red maw opening up in its face, several rows of white needle-sharp teeth appearing.

"Stop," Lizzie screamed. "Leave her alone. I'll make the deal. I'll take down the wards and let you in if you promise to leave everyone here alone. Give your word that no harm will come to them."

In response to her words, the Darkness straightened up, backing away from Vivienne, its red mouth disappearing into the matte black of its face.

"Lizzie, no," Madison pleaded, grabbing Lizzie by the arm, "Don't do this. There has to be another way."

Lizzie turned to her, her back facing the evil at the gate, "Do you have any other ideas?"

"No, but—" Tears shimmered in her eyes.

"Listen to me. We need to buy time until the backup team arrives. As soon as the wards are down, you and Birdie get everyone inside the cottage. He won't be able to touch you behind the wards. I'm counting on you to keep them safe. And you, too, Birdie." She nodded in the young woman's direction.

"And what are you going to do alone with that thing?"

"Stall until help arrives." She moved away from the two young women to put as much distance between herself and them. "As soon as the wards are down, run as fast as you can to them, call up your magick to protect yourself like a shield."

Both women nodded, the tears in their eyes mingled with the rain.

"Do we have a deal?" Lizzie demanded.

"I agree to your terms. Now take down the wards," the thing said.

Lizzie stepped forward and raised her hands, drawing the sigils to remove the wards around the property. And as the last of the protections fell away, the Darkness surged forward. Madison and Birdie scrambled past her down to the others. Madison glanced back over her shoulder and skidded to a halt. "Bear, no!" she screamed as he leaped through the air and disappeared.

Lizzie felt her own scream rip through her throat as he reappeared, teeth barred inches away from the head of the dark being, and was flung through the air by a flick of the being's hand. She was still screaming when she felt the sickening thud as Bear collided with a tree trunk, sending his lifeless body plummeting to the ground.

Grandma Faye had been right all along. Lizzie knew without a doubt the moment of Bear's death. She howled as the pain of it shattered her soul.

CHAPTER TWENTY-FIVE

Her knees buckled, but before she hit the ground, a searing cold vise clamped around her wrist and hauled her to her feet. Waves of frigid air surrounded her, the suffocating stench of sulfur catching in the back of her throat.

"You lied," she spat at the thing, "You said you wouldn't harm them." Calling up her powers, she pulled and twisted against its hold on her, but instead of breaking free, its grip tightened on her wrist, its cold burning her flesh. She screamed in frustration.

"We have kept our part of the bargain. See," it said, spinning her around by her arm.

Through the rain and her tears, she saw the women had almost reached the safety of the cottage. Vivienne was carrying Cathy in her arms as Birdie and Madison supported Grandma Faye between them. They slowed their progress as they passed by Bear's still body as it lay at the base of a tree. He appeared to be merely sleeping, the low arching branches of the tree protecting him from the downpour. Madison broke free from the group to kneel down by the dog, running a gentle hand over his head. She rejoined Birdie and Grandma Faye, taking up the old woman's arm again as her eyes locked with Lizzie's. She shook her head, grief contorting her features.

"You said nothing about the dog, just the humans, and, besides, we were merely defending ourselves," the thing stated matter-of-factly. "But if you do not keep the second part of the bargain, they will forfeit their lives. The choice is yours." It casually raised its free hand, an obsidian orb forming in its palm.

"The portal is this way, through the forest," she said flatly, finally wrenching her hand free of its grip. As she led the way, she performed an old trick, one she'd used so many times in the past when the pain became too big, one that required no magick to cast. She merely allowed herself to slip away from the present moment. She went deep inside herself to that center that had always offered a safe haven. Somewhere beneath her heart, she made herself small where she fit snugly in the dark, where it was quiet and still, where nothing could reach her; not fear, not rage, not grief. And in that unreachable place, as her feet kept moving her forward, she plotted her revenge.

When they arrived at the stone circle, the dark thing sighed in what sounded like pleasure, the tube-like structures covering its body shivering, filling the clearing with a dry clicking sound.

Lizzie quickly sent out a flash of her magick and almost let out a sigh of her own when she sensed the women were safely behind the wards. Her hand twitched, and she stopped herself from curling her fingers around the locket at her throat, balling her hands into fists instead. Planting her feet wide, she prepared to fight tooth and nail until help arrived, so she wasn't expecting the thing to wrap its arms around her and pull her into an embrace.

She arched her back reflexively, trying to escape as the thing put its blank face up to her cheek. It had no nose, and its red mouth hadn't reappeared, but Lizzie felt its fetid hot breath on her cheek and heard it snuffling like a pig rooting around in the mud.

"What do we have here?" The thing moved lightning fast, and she was only aware it had grasped the locket when the chain snapped, the sting of it biting into the back of her neck. It continued to hold her tightly in a one-armed hug as he held the locket up to its face, turning it over nimbly in its skeletal fingers. It found the catch and opened the locket.

Before the thing could pull the stone out of its velvet nest,

Lizzie shot her magick from her free hand and destroyed both the stone and locket in a shower of golden sparks. The thing's head swiveled to look at her again. "You say there are no fey here, yet you had in your possession a Dowsing glass. How did you come by it?" It demanded.

When Lizzie remained silent, it jerked her closer. "What are you? You command the Aether and had a Dowsing glass on your person, but you do not smell like fey." He sniffed along her neck, and Lizzie clamped her teeth to stop from screaming. "Nor do you smell like human either."

It let go of her, so suddenly she stumbled back, but before she could draw in a breath to clear the stinging sulfur from her senses, it grabbed her hand, crushing the bones. She bit her lip when the sharp pain of it slipped through the walls of numbness she'd surrounded herself with.

Raising its free hand, it pointed one elongated finger, and a razor-sharp claw sprouted from its tip. With one swift motion, it pricked her finger and then squeezed her hand harder until a bead of blood glistened on her finger like a ruby. The wide gaping wound of a mouth split the void of its face, then a wet ribbon shot out, and with the tip of its tongue, it delicately licked up the blood.

"Oh, Elizabeth, my dear," its mellifluous voice caressed the air, "it appears the Fates have turned the wheel in our favor. It is time for us to conclude our bargain. Let us in."

Lizzie shook her head to clear her thoughts from the drug-like trance its voice had pulled her into. "I destroyed the Key stone. There is no way for you to open the portal now. You've lost. You can do what you want with me, but my friends are safe, and so are the Fey."

The thing threw back its head and laughed. "Elizabeth, you are so very mistaken. The stone you destroyed isn't a key. It's a Dowsing glass; it merely shows the location of the doorways to the Fey. And we have no need of it. The key we seek is standing before us. There are only two kinds of beings who can open those doorways: a fey or a World Walker. And imagine our delight that we have found the latter."

The One Who Walks Between the Worlds, Birdie had called her. "I won't do it. I won't take down the wards, and I won't open the portal."

"You are not required to open the doorway. All you have to do is complete our bargain. You agreed to let us in." It poked a bony finger on her chest. "We can take you without your permission, but that way can prove rather messy. We think Vivienne would agree with us. And you are such a rare find. It would be such a shame to damage you first."

"I'd rather die."

"We do admire your courage, dear one. But we grow tired of your obstinacy." It called up another orb of dark magick in its palm. This time, it looked like a glob of lava. It hurled the orb over its shoulder in the opposite direction of the cottage. It tore through the forest, ripping through the thick tree trunks as if they were paper. Something exploded in the distance, and the ground shook beneath Lizzie's feet. Her free arm flew out instinctively to keep her balance, even though the dark thing still gripped her hand tightly. Above the sound of the constant downpour, Lizzie suddenly heard the roaring rush of water.

"What did you do?" Lizzie screamed. Her magick flared and pulsed around her as she struggled to break free. "What did you do?"

"Just giving you a little encouragement. Now, now, now, Elizabeth, we see that look of protest in your eye. We gave you our word; the witches are still safely behind your wards. We simply destroyed the water line leading to the cottage. How long do you think they will last in there without water? Dying of thirst can be quite painful, or so we have heard." It looked around as if just noticing the rain, and with a graceful flourish of its too-long arms, the rain instantly stopped, replaced by the sound of rushing water from the broken water line, sounding like a waterfall in the sudden silence. And for the first time since the nightmare began, Lizzie felt the cold. She shivered uncontrollably, her drenched clothes clinging to her body, her teeth chattering.

"Even with their magick, how long do you think it will take before they die? Three days? A week? Longer? Or perhaps one of them will get brave and venture out to the lake to fetch water for the others. If that happens, we will simply kill them as soon as they step outside the cottage." The thing stretched its neck, its face now mere inches from Lizzie's. "And how long do you think you will last out here with us?" It whispered.

"As long as it takes," she spat back.

"As long as it takes for what? For the cavalry to arrive? Let us disabuse you of that notion. You see, when we took possession of the dark-haired one you call Vivienne, we became privy to all her thoughts and feelings. We knew she had ordered a team of Guardians here, and it was such a simple thing to call the Mother House and, using her security codes, we canceled their assignment. And if we are not mistaken, the warlocks have already started their siege on the witches' strongholds. So even if Vivienne could call in help, there is no one to call. There is no one coming to your rescue, Elizabeth. There is no one who will save you. We ask you for the last time. Will you let us in, or will we have to take you by force?

So, this is how it ends, Lizzie thought, looking up into the endless blackness of the thing standing before her. She'd thought she was saving her friends by sending them behind the protection of the cottage, but all she'd done was damn them to the same fate as Emma Hawksworth. She hadn't saved Wren's world either when she destroyed what she thought was the key to open the portal. And if she ended her own life, here and now, would it stop the thing before her from going after the women in the cottage, from finding another way into Wren's world?

Utter despair pierced her heart when suddenly her magick did something so unexpected that she inhaled sharply. It unfurled itself inside her without her bidding, sending a comforting warmth deep within her bones, its calming presence clearing her thoughts. She was unclear whether the idea came from herself or from the Aether moving inside her, but in a flash, she realized she needed to trap the thing somehow. No, she thought, not somehow, but somewhere. Somewhere where only she could go.

"You win. I will let you in," Lizzie whispered, infusing her voice with as much defeat as possible, all the while pulling her energy deeper within herself and wrapping the Aether around her like a cocoon.

The Dark One placed a bony hand on her chin, tilting her face up to look into its blank face. "This will only take a moment. It will be easier if you don't fight it." With that, it drew in closer, blotting out the grey sky above as Lizzie was engulfed in the darkness.

CHAPTER TWENTY-SIX

She looked down at the thing sprawled in the sand. She'd done it, she'd actually done it. She shuddered at how close she'd come to failing. When the idea had first come to her, she wasn't even sure it was possible, but she knew she had to at least try. She also knew she would only get one chance to do it. So, she had waited.

She had waited, hiding deep within herself, protected by her magick even when the Dark One had slithered into her thoughts and had taken control of her body, manipulating her hands to shape the sigils in the air, dissolving the wards around the circle. She continued to wait, crouched inside herself as it riffled deeper into her consciousness, looking to strengthen its connection to the Aether so it could open the portal to the Fey. And when it succeeded, and the doorway to Wren's world snapped open, the fear of what would happen if she failed made her freeze. It was only when the thing had lifted Lizzie's foot to step through the doorway that she surged forward and sprung her trap and sent them both here, in the in-between. Her friends were safe, Wren's world was safe, as long as she kept the Dark One trapped in this world, *her* world.

The dark thing sat up, and Lizzie advanced on it. Its body appeared more solid than it had been on the earthly plane. The black of its skin was faded to greyish patches in places, the stink of rotten eggs barely detectable. Instead of using her magick to strike out at it, she swung back her leg and kicked it with a force fueled by her rage.

"This is for Bear," she screamed. Suddenly, she was wearing thick-soled army boots, and when the steel toe connected with the thing's midsection, Lizzie heard a satisfying snap. It howled in pain, curling in on itself. The sound it made only enraged her more, and she struck out again and again, letting out several guttural screams of her own. Even as the thing scrabbled and clawed at the sandy driveway to escape the kicks, she continued to rain down on its body. She stomped on its hand as it grabbed for purchase in the sand, grinding her heel until she felt the pop of bones breaking.

It looked up at her as she raised her foot and smashed the heavy tread of her boot down on its blank face. When she raised her foot to do it again, its body rippled, the tube-like structures rearranging themselves. And before she could bring her foot down, it was Audley's face looking up at her, blood gushing from his broken nose as he cradled his misshapen, pulpy hand close to his chest.

"Please, Miss Lizzie, don't hurt me. I'm sorry about all the things I'd done. I was just trying to keep my little Cathy safe from Jon. I didn't mean you no harm." He looked up at her with pleading eyes.

"Go to hell," Lizzie snarled and drove her foot down on its face. She raised her foot again, intent on obliterating the thing below her when the illusion of Audley rippled, and in his place, she was staring down at Cathy. The blood streaming from her nose painted the lower half of her face in crimson.

"I want Papa Audley," the child wailed, "Papa Audley!"

She stumbled back from the illusion, tasting bile in the back of her throat. Even though she knew it wasn't really Cathy huddled before her, she couldn't continue. Instead, she crossed her arms, trying not to flinch as the thing wearing Cathy's image reached out her mangled hand, the fingers sticking out at unnatural angles.

"Please don't hurt me," the tiny voice begged.

"Really, is that the best you can do? Using an old man and a helpless child to try to protect yourself?"

Cathy's features wavered.

"If you are going to choose Gideon next, don't bother. He doesn't have a hold over me." As the thing morphed again, Lizzie narrowed her eyes. The thing was now the color of ashes, the tubes reduced to nubs, and she thought she'd seen the outline of a mouth.

"I know," said Jon. The piercing blue of Jon's eyes and the scar running down the right side of his face was frighteningly accurate. Although his nose was still broken and gushing blood, his hand was still crushed and unusable. Then Jon dug his good hand into the sand and, much to Lizzie's alarm, began drawing up the energy of the in-between, *her* in-between. Jon's nose immediately stopped bleeding, the cartilage straightening out.

"Why are you helping that thing?" Lizzie silently demanded of the Aether. In response, the air shimmered, and the golden threads connecting everything vibrated as if strummed by an unseen hand.

Jon wiggled his now graceful, intact fingers, and satisfied, he leaned back on his hands, stretching out his legs in front of him and crossing his ankles in a leisurely pose.

The Aether's reply came as a whisper in the breeze that danced lightly through the in-between. *Look to see the truth, listen to hear the truth, feel to know the truth.*

"You're a clever girl, Lizzie, I'll give you that, thinking to trap me here. It's been so long since I've matched wits with someone almost my equal, so it pains me slightly to tell you your attempt failed."

"Has it? I seemed to have removed you from my world and stopped you from entering the Fey one. That looks like a win to me." She noticed even with the Aether healing its injuries, the thing remained sitting on the ground. *Look to see the truth.* Why hadn't it stood up and tried to overpower her like it had back on Earth?

Jon leaned back on his forearms, uncrossing and re-crossing his ankles. "That's where you're wrong. It's only a matter of time before I find the weakness in your construct and escape. And the one thing I have is an abundance of time. Can you say the same? How long can you remain here while your empty vessel is back in the physical realm? How long will its heart continue to beat without your life force fully inhabiting it?"

She kept silent. Was he speaking the truth? Could he really find a way out of the in-between? Was it possible to leave him here while she returned to her body? Did the in-between even exist when she wasn't here? And if it didn't, where would the dark thing end up? A movement at the edge of the forest in the direction of where the stone circle would be in the real world caught the corner of her eye. She scanned the trees, but there was nothing there.

Look, the Aether had said, and so she did, turning her attention back to the thing wearing Jon's face and body. When she'd accidentally released the Dark One from the stone, it was more energy than solid matter, but here in her in-between, it was more solid. And perhaps the reason it remained on the ground was because it wasn't strong enough to stand up. She suddenly remembered something it had said earlier.

"Who trapped you inside the stone?"

"What does it matter? I am free now."

"It matters to me. You were imprisoned against your will, a slave to do the bidding of whoever trapped you there."

"I was *never* a slave to the Warlocks. I commanded armies, governments, CEOs of multimillion-dollar companies." Jon's eyes flared with anger as he sat forward. "I controlled the events and outcomes of your world. I am all-powerful. The Warlocks did my bidding, not the other way around."

"I don't think that's true."

"You know nothing. I was surrounded by humans ready

and willing to follow my orders."

"But they were only following your orders because of what you could give them or what you could do for them. They were using you just like the Warlocks." Something stirred in her chest, and without thinking, she sat down cross-legged directly across from Jon. "That sounds like a pretty lonely existence to me."

Jon eyed her warily. "If you are so concerned about my loneliness, then join forces with me. Together, we can conquer worlds. Think of the power you would wield. Anything you desire would be yours for the taking."

"I already have everything I desire. I have people who care about me and whom I care about, too."

"You think those women cowering behind the wards around the cottage care about you? They could have stood by you, but instead, they abandoned you the second they had a chance to save their own skins." The image of Jon waivered, and in his place, Madison appeared the way she looked on that terrible day. But in that brief moment, before the image of Madison took hold, the thing's body appeared as the palest grey, almost white, like the color of the sky before the breaking of dawn. Gone were the tiny bumps that covered its body, its arms and legs more in proportion to its torso.

Lizzie instinctively reached out to the naked, battered image of Madison, her heart lurching in her chest, but the rage on Madison's face stopped her.

"Don't touch me," the thing wearing Madison's face screamed, drawing its knees up to its chest. "Don't come near me. I was there. I saw what you did to Richard. You enjoyed causing him pain. You are no better than he was. That's why I didn't want to see you. You are a monster."

Shame and guilt washed over Lizzie, her vision blurring as Madison's words hit home. Fighting down tears, she struggled to push the feelings down when a gentle breeze caressed her cheeks. *Feel to know the truth.* And then she stopped struggling. She stopped fighting with her tears. She stopped fighting with her emotions and just let go. Tears rolled down her cheeks as she looked into Madison's eyes. "No, you're wrong. Madison never thought I was a monster for what I did to Richard. That was me. I was the one who felt that way. And she didn't abandon me, she wasn't ashamed of me, she was ashamed of herself."

For the first time in her life, Lizzie didn't resist the painful memories of her marriage, allowing the emotions to rise to the surface. In a blinding flash, she saw the parallels between her life and Madison's. She saw where their choices intersected and why they picked the men they did. It all came down to a lie. Somewhere, early on, each one of them believed they were unlovable, and when Ian and Richard had given them an ounce of attention, she, along with Madison, had mistaken it for love.

"Madison was ashamed because she wasn't strong enough to leave Richard earlier and put me in the position to have to come to her rescue, to carry the burden of stopping him. And she stayed with him as long as she did because she didn't think she deserved better."

The golden lines of energy surrounding her, and the thing began to hum. Inside her, the Aether stirred again on its own accord. She felt it as it flowed back down through her light line, still connected to her body. "It was too painful for her to be around me afterwards because she felt she wasn't worth saving. She didn't think she mattered, not even to herself."

The thing shrank back from Lizzie's words and began to shift again. Before it took on a new shape, Lizzie caught a glimpse of its face because now it had one, with a defined nose, a slit for a mouth, and eyes that flashed gold before they were replaced with the old woman's gaze.

"You believe that I care about you, that I consider you

family. But I was just using you to get close to the Fey."

Before Lizzie could reply, the image of Grandma Faye blurred, her features melting away. The thing struggled as it tried to reinstate Grandma Faye's image, flickering back and forth between the old woman's body and its true form.

If Lizzie had any hope of destroying the thing, she had to do it now. Calling up her magick, drawing the power from her in-between and the Aether surrounding her, she flung out her arms, palms facing out. Two streams of white-hot power hit the dark thing in the chest. It writhed and twisted, trying to escape, but Lizzie's magick held it in place.

Then the thing screamed. The sound of its agony shot straight into her heart, but she didn't let up, pinning the demon to the ground. The dark thing shuddered, and she felt it through her magick as all its illusions fell away, replaced by a small wraith-like being. Its large, child-like eyes held pain and fear.

It was a child, only a child.

Lizzie flung her arms to her sides, powering down her magick. She suddenly felt sick as the thing pulled its legs up, hugging its knees to its chest, its arms and legs now in proportion with its childlike body, its iridescent skin glowing like mother-of-pearl. Its golden eyes were large, in a face marked with high cheekbones and a delicately pointed chin.

"We yield to your power," it said, "and will serve and obey." It lowered its forehead to rest on its knees. "But please don't put us back in the stones," it pleaded.

She should have been wary of the thing. This was probably another illusion to catch her off guard, to lower her defenses so it could strike out at her, but every instinct in her told her she needed to help the thing huddled before her, not destroy it. *Feel to know the truth.*

Holding out her hands, she conjured up a blanket of the softest weave and infused it with feelings of comfort and safety.

She leaned forward and gently draped the blanket over the thing's narrow shoulders, then sat back and waited.

The being slowly raised its head, drawing the blanket tightly around its body. In a cat-like gesture, it squeezed its eyes shut in pleasure and rubbed its cheek against the blanket. A deep, contented rumble emanated from its chest.

"I don't want you to serve me, and I won't imprison you in the stones. I just wanted to stop you from hurting the people I care about."

The thing opened its eyes and pinned her with its golden gaze. "We don't understand. Although you are not fully human, you live amongst them. They have shaped who you are, and they are violent by their very nature. You are supposed to want to subjugate others, to amass power and accumulate resources, to cause pain, destruction, and chaos."

"That's not what it means to be human."

"But you used violence against us. You hurt us."

"I did. I allowed my anger to rule my actions." Lizzie sighed, gathering her thoughts. "But there is a difference between using violence to defend against an attack and perpetrating violence to gain power over others." The grief over Bear's death welled up, tightening her throat, the pain of it piercing her heart. "You killed my best friend, and I wanted to stop you from hurting the rest of my loved ones. His name was Bear, and he was a beautiful, courageous, gentle soul, and you murdered him. I can't imagine my life without him, and now, because of you, I have to."

The being cocked its head and looked off into the distance. "We understand the logic of your statement, but we do not comprehend the emotion you are currently emanating." It returned its gaze to her. "We have not seen nor felt this one before. With the warlocks, we have felt anger, pleasure, insatiable desire, satisfaction, and even fear. But not this. What is it?"

"Let me show you," Lizzie said, holding out her hand.

When the being reached across the space between them and placed its hand in hers, she held it gently and poured all of her memories of Bear into it, right up until the moment of his death."

"Oh," the being said as Lizzie released its hand. "We understand now what grief is." It paused, looking deeply into Lizzie's eyes. "And we remember another emotion you revealed to us." A smile spread across its face. "It is what you call joy, and you felt it when Bear was in his physical form, but now that he has returned to energy, you feel only the grief. Now that he no longer resides in the material world, you miss feeling connected to him. You miss his physical presence."

Lizzie nodded, not able to speak around the sorrow clogging her throat.

"You are not like the humans who imprisoned us."

"No. I'm not, and neither are the majority of humans. We are nothing like the warlocks who used you for their own twisted desires."

Her power suddenly surged as the Aether returned, bringing with it the energy signatures of Vivienne, Madison, Grandma Faye, and Birdie, her family. The Aether whispered to her, *Look to see the truth, listen to hear the truth, feel to know the truth,* and so Lizzie did. She saw and heard and knew everything the five women had been through in their lives, the joys and the sorrows, the triumphs and disappointments, the secret wishes and dashed hopes.

"And right now, five humans, the women you said chose their own safety over mine, are at this very moment standing around my body back on the earthly plane, trying their hardest to save me. They are risking their own lives for me," she said more to herself as her own words hit home. "And I'm not saying humans are perfect because we're not. We make mistakes, we give in to petty jealousies, we sometimes do the wrong things, say hurtful words, but more often than not, we try to do better, we try to be better."

She looked down at her hands and then cupped them, conjuring a small earthenware bowl filled with the hot chocolate Sister Collette used to make her when Lizzie was feeling particularly lonely or sad. Looking into the rich, velvety drink, as the fragrant steam rose, scenting the air, she poured in the memories of the five women she was now deeply connected to. The liquid in the bowl swirled as sparks of light mixed with the bittersweet chocolate until Lizzie held in her hand a galaxy of stars suspended in a rich brown sky. She raised the bowl and held it up, but before passing it to the being, she added a dollop of whipped cream, just like Sister Collette used to do.

"This is just a small taste of what it means to be human."

The being took the offering from Lizzie's outstretched hands and, without hesitation, brought the bowl to its lips and drank.

CHAPTER TWENTY-SEVEN

The Daughters of the Earth gathered around She Who Walks Between the Worlds and called forth their magick. With arms outstretched, the wheel of life they formed; air igniting fire, fire beckoning water, water calling to earth, earth summoning air. Round and round, their magick spun, kept in motion by the women's courage, strength, and love, mixing, blending until all became one. Then, from each woman's heart, a ray of golden light shot out, like spokes in a wheel, to infuse Lizzie's body, which stood frozen at its hub. Outside the circle of ancient stones, they were joined by four others, lending their magick and their protection to the Daughters of the Earth.

And deep within Gaia, another wheel spun an ancient and invisible one. As the women continued to flow their magick round, the wheel of fate and fortune slowed its widdershins rotation, finally stopping and then slowly, ever so slowly, began to turn towards the light.

***

Lizzie's body twitched, straightening up.

"Hey guys, are you seeing what I'm seeing?" Madison shouted over the hum of magick. Suddenly, Lizzie's eyes snapped open. "I think she's back."

"What do we do now?" Birdie's voice sounded tremulous as she strained under her newfound powers. "How are we supposed to attack the demon when it's still inside her?"

"Hold the circle and wait for my —" Vivienne was cut off by a burst of light that pulsed from Lizzie's chest. Birdie instinctively covered her eyes against the flare, breaking the circle.

"No, wait," Lizzie cried, spinning around to face Vivienne,

shielding the light being with her body and her magick, "They aren't a threat anymore. They won't harm you. They remember who they are now."

Vivienne looked from Lizzie to the being behind her, then with a quick nod to the rest of the women, she powered down her magick. The rest followed suit. Lizzie also drew back her magick as she looked around the circle at her friends and startled when she noticed their appearance. Madison stood to her right, Vivienne to her left, and Grandma Faye directly in front of her, but none of the women were looking at her. They were all gazing up at the light being towering behind her.

"Oh," came Birdie's voice from behind Lizzie. "Are you an angel?" Lizzie turned towards Birdie, looking through the luminous body of the being and the open portal that was sparking blue lightning. Before she could explain, the being spoke, turning to Birdie, whose face was lit with wonder and astonishment.

"No, my child, we are known as The Emissary, although in the past, we have been mistaken for the angels of which you speak. We were summoned here by Gaia at the start of her quickening to watch over all her children, to keep the balance between the light and dark," the seven-foot being of light spoke.

The women drew in closer, Birdie skirting around the open portal to join the others. And much to Lizzie's surprise, Gideon, whom she had just noticed standing just beyond the stone circle, strode over to Vivienne to stand protectively next to her. The being placed a gentle hand on Lizzie's shoulder as they stepped forward. She felt the comforting weight of their touch even though the being had returned to a state that was more energy than solid matter. Instead of the biting cold she'd experienced when they had first touched her, as the Dark One, this time, a gentle warmth enveloped her shoulder and, with it, a feeling of profound peace.

"We are deeply grateful to you, Daughters of the Earth, for

allowing us to experience what it truly means to be human. And for assisting She Who Walks Between the Worlds in releasing us from the Warlocks' prison and helping us to remember our sacred duty."

The Emissary glanced up, their golden eyes unfocused as if checking in with some unseen force. "Be assured the Warlocks no longer control nor have access to our power," they said, returning their attention to the group. "The strikes against your people have ended, the Warlocks scattering as we speak, and any being who benefited from the use of my power will now find themselves at the mercy of the light."

Then the Emissary approached Vivienne, holding out their hands in invitation. Without hesitation, Vivienne placed her hands in theirs. "Daughter of Water, you have the heart of a lion, your courage unmatched. We humbly ask for forgiveness for the hurt we have inflicted upon your person."

"I forgive you," Vivienne whispered. The Emissary beamed as it leaned down to place its forehead gently to hers. "May the blessing of an open heart be yours." They slowly straightened up and turned to Grandma Faye.

"And to you, Daughter of the Earth, we ask the same of you."

"You are forgiven," Grandma Faye replied, her voice faltering, tears shining in her eyes.

"Wisdom Keeper, may you continue to share your gift of nurturing for many years to come, and may the children gather around you as you share your knowledge and grace," they said tenderly, touching their forehead with hers. When the Emissary moved back, Lizzie noticed the bruises on the old woman's neck had disappeared.

"Daughters of Air and Fire." The Emissary took up both Madison's and Birdie's hands in theirs. "We are blessed to know you both." To Madison, they said, "We understand the depth of your grief for the one you loved so dearly." They touched foreheads, and as the Emissary straightened, they continued. "Know he loves you still and watches over his little mouse." Madison's eyes went wide. The Emissary gently cupped Madison's chin in its hand. "Your quick mind and innovation will serve humanity in the coming years."

Next, they turned their golden-eyed gaze on Birdie. "Daughter of Fire, soothsayer, keep trusting your instincts, for they will guide you to the truth. You possess a creativity that the world will need to sustain it as the tower crumbles. During the time of chaos, your creations will add both beauty and hope as the people turn towards the light once more." They touched foreheads, and then the Emissary spoke to Gideon.

"Scholar, you have chosen your path well. I entrust you to keep the stories of your people safe and to share them with all who will listen." Gideon merely nodded, and when the Emissary pulled away after touching foreheads, Gideon reached for his mother's hand and gripped it tightly.

Then the being looked to the edge of the circle, and Lizzie inhaled sharply, her heart lurching in her chest when she spied Wren and two other Fey.

"Members of the Fey, we are in your debt for coming to the aid of the humans and for your role in keeping the daughters safe while they performed their hallowed duty. When you return to your world, tell your leaders what transpired here today. Tell them how valiantly these humans fought to keep *your* world safe. Open your people's hearts so they may work in concert with the humans to create a great benefit for both your worlds."

"We are honored to carry out your wishes," Wren replied. Then he and the other two Fey executed deep, reverent bows.

The Emissary nodded their head in acknowledgement, then turned to Lizzie, taking up her hands in theirs. "The time has come for us to return to our place with Gaia and our sacred responsibility to which we have been entrusted. But before we leave, we would offer you a gift in gratitude. Whatever you desire, we shall make manifest."

Lizzie gazed up into the Emissary's golden eyes, warmed by the comfort of their touch. "Everything I desire, I already have, right here." She looked around at the people surrounding her, then smiled up at the light being and placed her hand on their chest. "My family."

"Family," they said, their delight radiating from their energetic body, touching all who gathered there. "Twice we have offered you a boon, and twice you have refused, choosing love of your family over material gain." They closed their eyes and placed a finger to their lips. "Yes," they said, opening their eyes to look at Lizzie. "There is still time. So, we offer you a gift and return to you that which we stole." They held their hands out as a pulse of light shot through the air.

Lizzie felt it move through the ground beneath her, too. And then she felt him, their connection re-establishing itself in a wave of the purest joy.

"Bear!" She whirled around just as he materialized at the edge of the clearing. The rest of the group let out gasps and exclamations of surprise as he ran to her, jumping up and placing his large paws on her shoulders, tail wagging furiously. She hugged him, burying her face in the thick fur of his ruff, inhaling that peculiar dry hay smell that was uniquely his. "I thought I'd lost you." She cradled his head in her hands, looking into his eyes. Laughing, she turned her head to the side as he started to cover her with wet kisses. When he dropped down on all fours and leaned into her, she laced her fingers in his fur, needing to feel him, to hold onto him. Then Bear sat up straight, cocking his head at the Emissary. Their eyes locked, and in the silence, something passed between them. The Emissary blinked slowly and gave a slight nod of their head.

The Emissary looked around, stepping back from Lizzie and Bear, putting some distance between them. "Farewell, Elizabeth."

"Goodbye, Em," Lizzie replied, suddenly filled with sadness.

The Emissary placed their hands on their heart, their energy expanding and pulsing, the air crackling with electricity. And in a blinding flash of light, the Emissary shot up into the sky.

Everyone craned their necks, following the Emissary as it blazed higher and higher, streams of light radiating outward like wings, a tail of energy fanning out in shades of blue, yellow, red, and green. It shot like a comet streaking fire across the sky. Before it disappeared from view, a pulse of energy boomed through the air, and then the Emissary was gone.

The group stood silent, dazed, ears ringing, knowing deep in their bones that something momentous had been set in motion, shifting timelines and altering the destinies of both worlds, the humans' and the Fey's, forever.

CHAPTER TWENTY-EIGHT

The jubilant calls of two hundred ravens finally broke the spell of those still looking skyward.

"Mom," Gideon's voice broke with emotion as Vivienne held him close. "Are you okay? Are you hurt?" He squeezed his eyes tight as he held onto her, his words coming out in a rush. "I was just leaving the Kelowna Chapter House for Vancouver when the team you'd sent for came back. They said you'd rescinded the order, and I knew you'd never do that. Even if you'd captured the warlocks, you would have still wanted the team there. And then—and then when you weren't answering my calls, I knew something was wrong. You always pick up when I call. So, I turned around and came here, and when I saw your SUV overturned in the ditch...." his voice broke, "I was so scared, Mom. I was so scared something had happened to you." His shoulders shook, tears escaping from the corners of his eyes.

"It's okay, Gideon, it's okay," she murmured into his hair, rocking him back and forth. "We're all okay."

While mother and son held each other, Bear made the rounds, greeting everyone he could, his tail wagging in delight, finally weaving his way back to Lizzie's side. In the midst of the exuberant cacophony, Lizzie found herself wrapped in the arms of Madison and Birdie. Laughing, she extricated herself from the middle of the group hug, finally getting a good look at her friends.

"Oh my god, oh my god," Birdie cried as the three women stepped apart. "Did you see it? The Emissary looked like a phoenix. The phoenix from my vision."

"It totally was," Madison agreed. Turning to Lizzie, she

asked, "How did you do it? How did you get the Dark One to change? To get the Emissary to remember who they —" she stopped abruptly.

Lizzie was about to say how it wasn't just her, that it was all of them and their memories that did it, but she couldn't find the words. Like the way a dream fades once you awaken, the detailed events of all the women's lives were now just vague impressions, and, with every passing moment, they were evaporating like wisps of smoke from her grasp. "I took Em into the in-between, and from there, it is all a bit hazy."

She rubbed her eyebrows, desperately trying to recall the details of what had happened. When Bear leaned his weight into her leg, she reached down, automatically stroking his head, instantly feeling calmer.

She looked from Madison to Birdie, who were both now staring intensely at her. "What? Is it my hair? Is it like yours now?" She laughed, running her fingers through it. With the exception of a single black streak down the left side, Birdie's hair was a silvery white, while Madison's curls were completely frosted, making her look like a wintery snow queen.

"No, it's still brown. It's not your hair, it's your eye. The left one."

"What's wrong with my eye?" Lizzie gingerly prodded the area around her eye with her fingertips. It felt fine. There was no tenderness, and her fingers came away clean. She blinked. Her vision was clear.

"It's gold like the Emissary's," Birdie said. "Does it hurt?"

"No, it doesn't feel any different than my other one."

"I guess we all have souvenirs to remember this day, not that it's likely any of us are going to forget what happened anytime soon," Madison grinned. "So back to how you zapped yourself and the Dark One into the in-between, I'm dying to know the details."

Madison started rapid-firing questions at her, but Lizzie no longer heard her as every fiber of her being hummed, resonating to his energy as she felt him draw closer until he was standing directly behind her.

"Elizabeth."

Trembling, she slowly turned around. "Wren."

Bear whined softly at her side as she marched towards Wren. A tsunami of emotions churned inside her, her body continuing to shake, as everyone and everything around her fell away until it was only Wren she saw. She wanted to run into his arms, to feel the warmth and strength of his embrace, and at the same time, she wanted to lash out at him for what he'd done to her.

His eyes went wide. "You remember."

"Yes, I remember everything." She clenched her fist.

"The counter spell worked," he said just as Lizzie hauled back her arm and punched him. She didn't put any magick into her punch. She just wanted him to know, without a doubt, how angry she was.

She was aiming for his shoulder, but unfortunately for Wren, that was the moment he bowed low to begin the atonement ritual of his people. So, instead of Lizzie hitting his well-muscled arm, her fist slammed into his nose with a sickening crunch. Caught off-balance and off-guard, Wren fell backwards, landing hard on his rear end, his legs splayed out in front of him, his hands flying to his nose.

"And if you ever use magick on me again without my knowledge, I'll give you more than a punch in the nose." She stood, chest heaving, hands on her hips, when what he said finally hit home. "What do you mean the counter spell worked?"

He raised one eyebrow, looking up at her. "The one I sent with Bear when he came through the portal to tell me the memory spell failed and how it was causing you harm," his voice muffled through his cupped hands. When Lizzie saw the blood seeping through his fingers, she dropped to her knees beside him on the damp ground.

"You're bleeding," she cried, gently prying his hands away from his face. She winced at the sight of so much blood. "I'm so sorry. I didn't mean to hit you in the face. I was angry, and I didn't expect you to bend down."

"It was the least I deserve. I'm just grateful you didn't have any magick behind that punch."

"Is it broken?" She didn't wait for an answer as she placed her hands on either side of his face, sending her magick into him. To her relief, she discovered his nose was just badly bruised. Her magick quickly staunched the bleeding, and using the cuff of her sleeve, she carefully dabbed away the blood. Wren reached up, stilling her hand.

"I was wrong, Elizabeth, so very wrong. I panicked when the council brought down their decree. The very idea of them ending your life clouded my thoughts. I could live with the pain of never seeing you again, but not the pain of losing you. You are my heartsong. I was bound to you the moment we met, here, the night of the full moon." He searched her face. "I ask for your forgiveness, but if that is something you cannot grant, I understand. If you wish me gone, I will leave and never return. The choice is yours."

She thought about what she'd been through, what they'd all been through in the last couple of days, and all that she'd learned; that life was never black and white, that the grey areas were where the truth lay. And it was within those liminal spaces where compassion and empathy existed, shedding the light of understanding and illuminating the truth.

Looking into Wren's eyes, the duel colors of deep forests and open skies, of moss and streams, what she saw there loosened the barricades she'd built around her heart to protect herself from all the times she was betrayed and all the ways in which she'd been abandoned, and for all the times she'd betrayed and abandoned herself because she'd believed she was broken, unlovable.

"I understand why you did what you did, and I appreciate that you undid the spell. And I can even forgive you for thinking what you were doing was the only way to protect me. But, if you had told me what was going on from the beginning, from the day we first met, I could have decided what was best for me. I could have saved myself.

"So, what I'm struggling with right now is I don't know if I can forgive you for taking away my right to choose my own destiny and for not believing I was capable of making the right choice." She felt his energy shift, drawing inwards, and watched the light in Wren's eyes dim. She recognized that look. The silence stretched out, so all Lizzie could hear was the blood pulsing in her ears.

Suddenly, he stood up in that graceful preternatural way of the Fey. "Goodbye, Elizabeth. But before I leave you, there is something you need to know."

"Wait, what?" Lizzie reached up, grabbing his hand before he could take a step towards the portal. "Where do you think you're going?" She yanked his arm hard, pulling him back down on the ground. This time, she did use a little bit of magick.

"I was honoring your decision, and so I am leaving."

"I didn't say I *wasn't* going to forgive you. I said I didn't know *if* I could forgive you. There's a big difference."

"There is?"

"Yes, there is. I don't know if I can because I don't really know you, and you don't really know me. I don't know if what I feel for you is just physical attraction or something deeper, because we haven't spent enough time in each other's company. And in order for us to figure that out, I want you to stay, and I want answers."

The light returned to his eyes. "I would like that also. What do you want to know?"

"I have so many questions, I don't know where to begin."

"Begin at the beginning." Wren gave a crooked grin.

"Okay. Is Wren even your real name?"

"Yes, or the closest your language comes to it. Although Maxwell isn't. I made that up as we don't have an equivalent of last names as you have here. Next question."

"The one thing that's been puzzling me is, how did you come to be here in the first place? If Grandma Faye was right, and your people sealed all the portals between our worlds eons ago, how did you get through it the night we met?"

"Because this particular one," he indicated to the open portal still snapping blue light, "was never sealed. Its location was either never recorded, or the record was misplaced and, over time, forgotten.

I had reason to suspect its existence and spent most of my life looking for it. Then, on Beltane night, I heard your heartsong and followed it. And that's when I found the portal. I stepped through it for the first time just as you appeared through the forest."

"Heartsong? What do you mean you heard mine?"

"Surely you felt it. You must have. Otherwise, how did you find me the moment I stepped through to your world? Do you not feel it now?" He gently placed her hand on his chest.

"Yes," she whispered, "I feel it, and that night I did too. It sounded like singing, like the earth and the air were calling me to come to the circle."

"What you heard was my soul calling to yours as yours was calling to mine. In my world, when you meet your heartsong, it is usually followed by a formal courtship so they can deepen their understanding of each other before deciding to bond. Because even though a heartsong is a sacred relationship, bonding is always consensual and always by choice. Our bonding, as exquisite as it was, was a bit unusual." He trailed a gentle finger down her cheek, her skin tingling where he touched her. "And considering all that has gone before, I never hoped I would have a chance to court you. Or, as you say, get to know each other. That is the same thing, is it not?" He glanced down at her lips, and she leaned in closer.

"Yes, pretty much," she replied breathlessly.

His lips sought hers, tentative at first, but when she hungrily returned his invitation, he threaded his fingers through her hair and deepened the kiss.

"My beloved," he murmured as he nipped her ear, then moving down to plant kisses along her neck.

She bit back a moan as desire sparked every nerve ending, a delicious longing tugging in her lower belly. She yearned to feel the heat of his skin on hers, to feel the weight of his body pressing down on her. Her hands fumbled with the fabric of his tunic, desperate to get him naked.

Bear shattered the moment when he barked, pushing the bulk of his body between them and forcing them apart.

"You are right, old man," Wren chuckled, sitting back and giving Bear a scratch behind his ear, "He says the others will be returning soon, and perhaps we could hold off mating until later." Bear, satisfied the lovers wouldn't continue, settled himself down beside them.

Lizzie's cheeks now burned with embarrassment instead of passion as she twisted around, expecting curious stares. She was shocked to discover they were alone. "Where did everyone go?"

"Shortly after you laid me flat with your right hook, everyone seemed very eager to be anywhere but here," he chuckled. "I believe Grandma Faye and the one she called

Vivienne took to the cottage to see to a child there. Lachlan and Isla headed off into the forest with the remaining group to assist in repairing a water line. Quinn flew off with them."

"We should probably see if they need help with the repairs." But when she made the move to stand up, Wren laid a hand on her arm.

"Elizabeth, wait. There's something you need to know. Something I need to tell you before the others return. It's about your mother."

"My mother?"

"I knew her."

Lizzie stared at him for several minutes, trying to make sense of what he'd just said before she replied. "But, how could you? You said you only stepped into my world for the first time last month, and my mother's been dead for over thirty-five years."

"I knew her when I was young." He hesitated, then started again. "There's so much I need to tell you. I don't know where to begin."

"Begin at the beginning."

Wren nodded, then took a deep breath. "I first met your mother, Lillianna, when I was about seven or eight at the Library of All Knowledge. I was hiding from my older brothers," Wren's lips curved in a crooked grin, "in the one place they'd never step foot in or think to look. I chose the least used wing of the library, the human history wing, to secret myself away. She found me several hours later, fast asleep in an out-of-the-way alcove. Instead of sending me away, she introduced herself and then brought me a book. She let me stay, hidden in the alcove, until the library closed for the night.

"I have a very large, very loud family, and I escaped to her section of the library whenever I needed some quiet and calm. Very few people ever wandered down that way, and I think she must have been eager to share her knowledge and her love of the documents under her care with someone, anyone, and so she shared them with me. She showed me ancient texts, illuminated manuscripts, scrolls, and maps from your world, and it wasn't long before I became just as curious as she was about the mortal world."

"She was a Fey," Lizzie stated, trying to make sense of what Wren was telling her. He nodded. "But why do you think she's my mother?"

"I suspected the connection the second day we met, and I noticed the necklace you were wearing. It was hers, given to her by her brother on her eighteenth birthday, and she wore it always. It was missing the dragon tears that were part of the necklace, but the design of the cross is distinctively Fey, as were the wards placed on it. Wards that were designed to protect only you."

Lizzie's hand went to her throat, her fingers touching the area where the cross used to rest.

"But it wasn't just the necklace that convinced me. It was what I felt in you; you have Fey power running through your veins alongside your human magick."

As improbable and impossible as to what Wren was saying, she knew deep in her bones it was true; her mother was Fey. It explained why she always felt different, like she didn't quite belong. "And my mother, she was a librarian?"

"Yes."

"Of course she was," she said more to herself as she thought of the Jane Austen books her mother had left her. But how did she end up here? In my world?"

"Because she found this portal, and she went through it. She never told me how she found it or where it was. And I never would have known about her travels had I not snuck into the library late one night. I had yet another argument with my older brother, and I couldn't sleep, so I went to the only place where I could be by myself and think.

At that time of night, I should have been the only one there, but I heard someone else moving about in the dark. I followed the sound and discovered her carrying an armful of books down an unused corridor. I startled her, and she dropped them. I went over to help, and even in the half-light, I could tell the books were nothing like the ancient texts housed in her section.

"We were both crouched down in the darkened library, the books in a tumbled heap between us, when I picked up the closest one. It was *A Study in Scarlett* by Sir Arthur Conan Doyle. I flipped it open and looked at the publication date. I knew then she'd somehow traveled to your world. She didn't say anything, just stared at me, waiting to see what I would do. And I simply handed the book back to her, wished her a good evening, and left." Wren looked off into the distance.

"For several years, she traveled back and forth bringing back books from your world, sharing them with me and telling me stories of the things and people she encountered." He returned his gaze to her, the emotion in them turning his eyes the color of a midnight sea. "Until one day, she didn't return. She would usually be gone for two or three days at a time, four at the most, so when a week went by, I started to worry. By the second week, I was in a panic. I didn't know what to do. The only family she had was a brother, and he was off on an expedition and wasn't expected back for months.

I knew if I told the High Council where she'd gone, their only priority would be to locate the portal and seal it. They would not have sent anyone to look for her, leaving her trapped with no way to get back home." He looked down at his hands, his voice unsteady. "For the longest time, I thought, if only I had told someone after that first time she went through, put a stop to her travels, she wouldn't have disappeared. She would be safe in her own world." He paused. "But if I'd stopped her, you wouldn't be here. I would never have met you. And both our worlds would have been at the mercy of the Darkness."

"How old were you when she left that last time?" She asked, placing a comforting hand on his thigh, but he wouldn't look at her. She spread her energy towards him, enveloping him.

"Ten."

"And you spent the rest of your life searching for the portal, searching for her?"

"Yes. I told her brother what I thought had happened to her as soon as he returned from his travels. And since then, we've both been looking for the portal in secret."

"I have an uncle," she whispered.

"Yes, his name is Malcolm. I told him about you, and he desperately wants to meet you. And I told him of Lillianna's death when I returned her necklace to him. I found it that night you were shot, lying on the forest floor."

She could feel his grief and realized although she had a lifetime of coming to terms with the death of her mother, Wren had only found out recently. She also felt the guilt he had carried, still carried, and her heart ached. Two memories flashed in quick succession; one was when the spirit of Emma, the first witch of Rose Cottage, came to her aid and spoke the words, *reveal your history, heal his sorrow*. The second message was from the spirit of her mother.

"Wren, I don't know why things unfolded the way they did or how fate and destiny play a role in our lives, but I do know one thing for certain. My mother wouldn't have wanted you to feel any guilt about *her* choices. You were just a child. She was an adult, and what happened to her was never your burden to carry. And I know this beyond a shadow of a doubt because her spirit came to me with a message for you."

His head snapped up, a single tear escaping from the corner of his eye and rolling down his cheek. Cupping her hand to the side of his face, she used her thumb to gently brush the tear away. "She said, Tell Wren it wasn't his fault." And as she spoke the words, the hairs on her arms rose. She sensed a deep, abiding love fill the clearing and wash over her.

She smiled as Wren looked around, searching. "You feel her, too, don't you?"

"Yes," he replied, a smile spreading across his face.

"Tell me about her. Tell me what she was like."

And so, he did. As they sat in the stone circle and the sun moved below the treetops, he spoke of Lillianna and his memories of her. Of how smart and kind and funny she was. How she possessed a soft voice but a raucous laugh. Wren told her how he would know Lillianna returned from one of her journeys by the mischievous twinkle in her eye, even before she would show him the books she'd brought back. On Lizzie's prompting, he recalled Lillianna's favorite color was a deep forest green and that she was obsessed with a drink called coffee.

Wren spoke of his remembering, bringing Lillianna to life until the shadows stretched long and dusk approached. And they would have continued to sit there oblivious to the passage of the hours if it weren't for the return of the Fey and humans from the forest beyond.

CHAPTER TWENTY-NINE

After saying goodbye to Lachlan and Isla, Lizzie closed the portal, and those remaining trouped back to the cottage, where they were met by Grandma Faye. She stood in the doorway of Rose Cottage, her hands on her hips as Cathy peered out from behind the old woman's luminous skirt.

She beamed a smile. "Perfect timing. I was just heading to my place to gather supplies for dinner and feed the animals. Vivienne and I have decided it would be best if we all stayed here for the night, if everyone agrees?" When everyone either gave a nod or voiced their agreement, Grandma Faye continued. "As many hands make light work, Madison and Birdie, I'll need you two to follow me over to the cabin in Birdie's car. You can both wash up at my place."

Birdie looked down at her mud-caked clothes. "I don't have anything to change in to."

"Not to worry," Madison draped an arm over Birdie's shoulder. You can borrow some of my clothes. You'll just have to roll the pant legs up a bit." She looked down at Birdie, sizing her up. "Okay, maybe a lot, but we'll make it work."

Grandma Faye turned to Gideon. "Could you see what you can do about getting the SUV out of the ditch? And bring in your mother's luggage. It's still in the back of the car," Grandma Faye said as she led Cathy down the stairs by the hand. "You may have to use a winch. I'll just add that to the list of things to bring over."

"Honored Grandmother," Wren interrupted, "I would like to offer my assistance to Gideon if you give me leave to."

"Your help would be much appreciated, and you will be

staying for dinner, of course."

"It would be my pleasure," Wren said, bowing towards the old woman.

"And what do you need me to do?" Lizzie asked.

Grandma Faye bustled down the porch steps to where Lizzie stood and patted her on the cheek. "I think saving two worlds from being overrun by Darkness is enough work for one day, don't you?" She didn't wait for Lizzie to reply. "I've seen to your chickens, and Vivienne and I have re-established the wards around your property. She's already used the shower and is busy on the phone, checking in with the Order. So, go on in, get yourself cleaned up, and then pamper that dog of yours." She gave Bear a good scratch behind the ears, then motioned to Madison and Birdie, "Come along ladies, the sooner we see to everything, the sooner I can get dinner on the go and start the celebration because tonight we have much to celebrate." Grandma Faye headed towards her truck. "Now Cathy, how would you like to help me feed the goats?" she said as she boosted Cathy onto the front seat.

Lizzie stood with Bear on the porch steps as she watched everyone disperse. She smiled when she heard Wren ask Gideon, as they walked down the driveway, if he thought Grandma Faye would be serving coffee with dinner.

***

Lizzie hated to admit it, but Grandma Faye had been right. By the time she'd showered, changed, fed Bear, and started a small fire in the fireplace, she barely had the energy to shuffle the few feet to the couch, where she collapsed lengthwise, leaning up against the armrest. Bear joined her, stretching out his body along her legs, placing his head in her lap, and promptly falling asleep.

When everyone returned to the cottage, and Vivienne joined them after concluding her phone call with her team at the Mother House, Lizzie roused herself. But when Grandma Faye insisted she remain where she was, she was more than happy to do so. From her vantage point on the sofa, she'd watched in amusement as the old woman happily bustled about preparing a ham for the oven, all the while assigning the rest of the meal prep to the others, so by the time Grandma Faye slid the clove-studded ham into the oven and took a seat on the rocking chair with Cathy on her lap there was nothing left for Lizzie to do even if she'd been able to muster the energy to help out.

Instead, she snuggled deeper down into the couch cushions and closed her heavy lids as she absently stroked Bear's head, listening contentedly to sounds filling the cottage; the rustle of turning pages as Grandma Faye quietly read out loud to Cathy, the thump-thump, thump-thump of the rocking chair legs, the crackle of the fire, the rush of water filling a pot, the scrap of a chair being pulled out from the kitchen table, the rhythmic rattle of a wooden rolling pin being drawn in long strokes, the rise and fall of easy conversation punctuated by the occasional laugh.

When a log popped loudly in the fireplace, Lizzie opened her eyes, stifling a yawn as she looked around at Grandma Faye and Cathy in the rocking chair, Vivienne standing at the kitchen counter rolling out a round of dough, and the rest of them seated at the kitchen table, peeling and cutting potatoes and shelling peas. It looked like a Rockwell painting of a family if that family had included five sisters of the light now sporting white hair, a being from another realm who she was currently dating, a bird who commanded a legion of ravens, and a dog with magickal abilities.

"An unhappy alternative is before you, Elizabeth," Grandma Faye quietly read aloud to Cathy from Lizzie's tattered paperback copy of *Pride and Prejudice*, "From this day, you must be a stranger to one of your parents. Your mother will never see you again if you do *not* marry Mr. Collins, and I will never see you again if you *do*." Grandma Faye looked down at Cathy, her eyebrows raised in mock concern. "Well, what do you think of that? Should we find out what Elizabeth will do? Will she marry that nasty Mr. Collins, or will she hold out for the lovely Mr. Darcy?" The child looked up at the old woman, her eyes wide, and nodded solemnly. Grandma Faye kissed the top of Cathy's head before continuing.

Lizzie's smile broadened. It didn't matter that Cathy didn't understand the words being read. What did matter was the strong protective arms holding her and the love even Lizzie could feel encircling the little girl.

"Gideon," Vivienne called over her shoulder as she expertly slid a perfect round of pastry into the bottom of a pie pan, "Grandma Faye said you managed to pull my car from the ditch. Is it driveable?" She turned around to face him, brushing her hands on the front of her apron.

"No," Gideon said, looking up from writing in one of Lizzie's new journals, a mound of unpeeled potatoes piled high on the table in front of him. "The engine turned over, but the steering wheel is locked. We only managed to get it up the driveway because Wren floated it off the ground while I pulled it up the drive with a chain attached to the other SUV."

"I could take a look at it in the morning," Madison volunteered. She sat at one end of the kitchen table, quartering a peeled potato, then scooping up the pieces and plopping them into a large pot filled with water. Quinn perched on the back of her chair, methodically preening her ice-white curls. "It could be a number of things that's causing the problem. I'll know for sure once I get a look at the chassis."

"That would be great, thanks," Vivienne said as she turned back to the counter to add cinnamon, sugar, and flour to a bowl of sliced apples.

"What?" Madison demanded when Gideon shot her a look. "Just because I'm a woman doesn't mean I don't know about cars." She dipped her fingers into the pot of water and flicked her fingers at him.

"Hey," Gideon snapped, swiping the water droplets off his face.

"And just because you're a man doesn't mean you get out of kitchen duty. Those potatoes aren't going to peel themselves." She jabbed a finger at the pile of unpeeled potatoes in front of him.

"You know about automobiles? How they work?" Wren asked, his voice filled with excitement as he methodically shelled peas into a stainless-steel bowl.

"Yeah, my dad was always working on cars, and I loved spending time with him while he tinkered under the hood, so I learned by watching, and then when I was old enough, I learned even more by doing."

"Do you think I could observe you working on the automobile?"

"I can do one better. If you can levitate the car like you did earlier and save me the hassle of jacking it up so I can get underneath it, I'll take you for a spin in one of the other cars."

He gave a puzzled look over at Lizzie. "Spin?"

"She means she'll take you for a car ride," Lizzie replied.

"Yes, I would like very much to be spun in a car. And it would be my pleasure to assist you in the repairs."

"Don't you have cars in your world?" Gideon asked, half-heartedly swiping the vegetable peeler across a potato.

"No, no cars or any industrial mechanisms or machines to speak of. We chose a different path than your world, one where we use magick and live in harmony with the earth and her cycles." Wren continued to shell peas into a large earthenware bowl, his long, elegant fingers quickly popping open the pods and removing the peas without looking.

"So, no labor-saving devices like electric ovens or hot and cold running water?" Madison asked.

"We have hot and cold running water, and we can and do use magick to help with work, but sparingly. My people honor the time, physical effort, and craftsmanship required to make things, whether that is plowing a field, making a delicious meal, or crafting a fine diary as you have there," he said, pointing to the journal Gideon had been writing in and was now resting on the table. "May I?"

"Sure," Gideon said, handing it over.

Wren brushed his fingers along the cloth cover, then reverently opened the journal, examining the inside, his fingers brushing across the paper. "This is expertly done with such attention to the binding, to the quality and weight of the paper, and the precision of how the end papers were glued down. Whoever created this diary is as skilled and talented as any I know."

"Birdie made that," Lizzie said. When Gideon and Wren had returned from hauling out the SUV, Gideon had asked her for some paper because he wanted to write down something Wren had told him. She'd happily given him one of Birdie's journals she'd bought at the market. "Black Bird Bindery is her new business."

Wren turned his full attention to Birdie, whose face had gone a bright crimson. "You have created a thing of great beauty. Do you take commissions?"

Birdie nodded as she clutched a forgotten pea pod in one hand.

"I have nothing to barter with at the moment. But we could discuss what would be a fair exchange after I have put some thought into what I could offer you that would honor the beauty of your diary. Only if you would be amenable to such a transaction, of course."

Again, Birdie merely nodded, the peapod now mangled in her fist.

"Could we go back to the no car thing?" Gideon interrupted. "Do you at least have trains?"

"No, no trains either."

Wren handed Gideon back the journal, and Gideon quickly abandoned the potato peeler for his pen. Madison rolled her eyes and reached over to snatch the peeler and a potato from the pile.

"But how do you get around?" Gideon looked up from taking notes. "What if you have to travel long distances? I'm having a hard time wrapping my brain around the idea of having to walk everywhere."

"For longer distances or to bring things to market, we use horseback or horse and cart, but for traveling from one end of the realm to the other, there is griffin wing or dragon flight."

"Dragons, you have dragons!" Birdie finally spoke as the other two just stared open-mouthed. Suddenly, Birdie went rigid, her eyes wide and blank, her magick rising so that her skin glowed like firelight. She blinked, her eyes focused as her magick died down.

"You had a vision, soothsayer?" Wren asked. "Were you with the dragons?"

"Yes," Birdie whispered, her eyes shimmering, "I was soaring on the back of the most beautiful dragon, his scales the color of copper and firelight. And I wasn't scared at all. He told me his name is Ruaidhri. And…and he said that he is mine and I am his, but I have to wait for us to meet. I could feel him, here." She pressed a hand on her heart.

"Birdie, your arm," Gideon pointed.

Birdie stared down at the image of a dragon now emblazoned on her left forearm in colors of bronze, gold, and copper.

"Does it hurt?" Madison asked, leaning across the table to get a better look. Birdie traced the outline of the dragon, shaking her head. She looked up at Wren, her face lit with wonder. "What does this mean?" she whispered.

Wren sat back in his chair regarding Birdie. "Griffins and dragons chose their riders, and he has reached out to you because you have been deemed worthy of such an honor." He looked up, speaking to everyone. "It looks like we have a great deal to celebrate this evening, for no human has ever been chosen to be a dragon rider, and your particular dragon, Ruaidhri," he said to Birdie, "sits on the High Council. In choosing you, a human, he has announced his choice to allow our worlds to know each other again. His opinion holds a great deal of weight, and I have hope that the rest of the council will side with him before long, and the portals will be opened again."

"And you said there are Griffins who live in your world. Like, the creature that's half eagle, half lion? Do you have unicorns, too?" Gideon asked, pen poised.

"Yes, to the Griffins, no to unicorns as they existed in your world alone."

"Hold on a sec, you just said you hoped the portals would be open again, but there's a portal open right now, here," Madison said.

Wren looked over at Lizzie, a question in his eyes. She nodded her permission.

"To explain how this particular portal remained open, it is best that I begin," he gave Lizzie a slow smile, "at the beginning." Wren settled back in his chair. "When I was eight years old, I snuck into the Library of All Knowledge...."

And as Wren retold the story of how he found the portal, Lizzie shifted on the couch, using her power to levitate her sleeping dog just enough so she could sneak out from under him. He half-opened one eye as she gently lowered him back down, then quickly fell back asleep.

As she moved quietly around the table, her presence largely unnoticed by those enthralled by Wren's tale, she put the pot of potatoes on the stove to boil, prepared the shelled peas to be steamed once the potatoes were done, then joined Vivienne, who was leaning against the counter listening intently. She smiled at Lizzie as she wrapped her arm around the younger woman's waist, drawing her closer to her side, then turned her attention back to Wren. Lizzie rested her head on Vivienne's shoulder, her eyes suddenly misting.

She had spent her whole life searching for a place where she belonged. When she found Rose Cottage, she thought she'd found her home in its grey stone walls and blue-painted door. But, the cottage, as lovely as it was, had only ever been a house until now. For home wasn't a place but the people she held close to her heart, whether two-legged, four-legged, winged, or of the Fey who now gathered within its sturdy walls. She sighed with contentment as she realized, without a shadow of a doubt, that she had finally found a home with her family, not the one she was born into but the one she belonged to. And perhaps that was even better.

CHAPTER THIRTY

In the room under the eaves of the little stone cottage, Bear lay curled up at the foot of the bed, relishing the solid feel of being in a body again. He'd been shocked and unprepared when The Dark One had flung him against the tree, completely severing his spirit from his physical vessel. He barely had time to anchor himself in Elizabeth's world between worlds before he would have been pulled into the light and lost to her forever. And even then, his hold in her in-between had been tenuous, taking all of his will to keep him there. So, when the Emissary appeared before him and offered Bear the choice of returning to the mortal plane or into the light, he chose the former without hesitation.

He raised his head to look over at his Elizabeth and Wren, her mate, both who were fast asleep. Even in slumber, they were entwined in an embrace, their breathing in unison, deep and slow. He was looking forward to seeing what magick the two of them would create in this world and in others. He slowly stood up, careful not to jostle the mattress, and instead of jumping off the bed, he simply opened a portal and stepped quietly through it.

He exited the portal down in the hallway just outside the main bedroom. The door was slightly ajar, and he nudged it open with his nose. He peered in at the four humans sleeping there. Gideon was snoring from his makeshift bed of cushions and blankets on the floor by the fireplace. The two older women slept on either side of the bed, curled inwards like parenthesis, bracketing the young girl who slept sprawled on her back, her legs and arms splayed out like a tiny star, her one hand held in Grandma Faye's.

Grandma Faye, the healer, the bone mother, the crone. Her skills would be needed in the coming months, and her knowledge of root and branch, of healing herbs and tinctures would be invaluable. Vivienne, the mother to many not born to her. She was just opening up to her true power contained in the nurturing water that was her element. He had no doubt she would open her heart to love again and be loved in return.

He stepped back through the door, leaving the humans to their slumber, and padded soundlessly down the hall. As he passed the kitchen, he could smell the peanut butter dog cookies he loved so much, and his stomach growled. Perhaps he would retrieve a cookie. He smiled to himself. Lizzie believed his ability to create portals came from her when she'd healed him with her magick, but she was wrong. Creating portals was what he was born to do. It was what his clan was known for, what he and the ones who had come before him used to search for The One Who Walks Between the Worlds and, once found, to guide and to protect her.

But Lizzie wasn't completely wrong. She *had* given him a new ability, and he delighted in the fact he could now move things with his mind, like water taps and lids off cookie jars.

For now, he ignored the cookies and made his way through the living room to where the two young women slept; Birdie on a cot, Madison stretched out on the couch. Although both maidens possessed strong magick, it was the kindness that dwelled in both their hearts that gave Bear hope. Because when he returned to his body, he found he wasn't beneath the tree where he'd fallen but inside the cottage, tenderly laid out on his dog bed by the fire. When he'd asked Madison why she and Birdie risked their lives to do such a thing, she'd simply kissed his nose and told him because it was the right thing to do, the only thing to do because he was family. His kind had always been solitary by nature, and he was surprised at how much he liked the feeling of having a family and a place to call home.

He would tell his people all they needed to know tomorrow when the new day dawned, and the results of their magick would begin to spread. But for now, he would give his family a night of peace.

Creating another portal, this time through the closed front door, he joined Brother Raven on the front porch. Quinn was perched on the railing, looking up to the night sky. He turned when Bear appeared, acknowledging his presence with a dip of his head, then returning his gaze to the stars.

Before taking a seat himself, Bear gave an enormous shake that rippled from his head to his tail. Energy shimmered around him as he grew in size, his snout elongating, his plume of a tail shrinking down to a small nub that curved around his backside. His fur, while the same color as it had been moments before, grew thicker and coarser. His curved claws clicked dully on the wood beneath his massive paws as he took a seat on the top step. Leaning his broad back against the handrail, he sat on the stoop in a very human-like fashion with his back paws resting on the step below and his front paws resting on his thighs. He groaned in pleasure as he scratched his back against the porch post before leaning back, the wood creaking slightly under his weight.

Bear and Raven sat in companionable silence as they had done many times before, through many turnings of the wheel, but this time it felt different. Bear marveled at this new feeling burgeoning in his heart. He searched its texture and resonance as it flickered to life. His lips curled up into a smile when he realized what it was. Call it a knowing. Call it faith. It didn't really matter. What mattered was the people now asleep in the cottage, his family. It was their commitment to each other and to the Light that gave him hope that this time, the majority of humanity would choose kindness over cruelty, generosity over greed, collaboration over conflict, and freedom over tyranny.

But before Gaia could fully awaken and humanity could choose their path, all that darkness had created would end, and with its ending, chaos would follow, creating space for something new to rise. Bear raised his black snout to the clear night sky, awed by the vast beauty of the universe, as he waited with his brother for a different kind of storm to arrive.

EPILOGUE

"Lizzie, they're ready," Birdie called out jubilantly from down below.

"I'll be right down."

Lizzie stretched her arms above her head, working out the stiffness in her shoulders. She wasn't used to sitting for so long after months of traveling by portal magick. But, much to her surprise, she'd come to look forward to her time spent with pen in hand in the relative peace and quiet of the converted barn loft, the light from the stained-glass window on the back wall throwing pools of soft pink and green light across the floor; the only sounds those of typewriter keys striking the platen, the scratch of her pen on paper, the flutter of book pages. *Scriptorium,* she silently corrected herself as Gideon insisted on calling the loft space he shared with her, going as far as hanging a wooden plaque over the railing at the top of the stairs.

It had only been a few years since the Phoenix event changed the world forever, and humanity was just now emerging from the destruction and chaos of the aftermath. The Emissary's words had come to pass; the warlocks and the elites who benefited from subjugating the Emissary and siphoning off the light being's power discovered there was no bunker deep enough, no island remote enough to escape from the burning light of the Phoenix's flight. Within months of the Emissary remembering who they were and taking to the sky, governments fell, institutions crumbled, and then the grid went down.

And in the midst of the old falling away, sparks of light

ignited across the land as humanity, jolted out of its slumber, began to awaken to the magick rising in the earth and inside themselves.

For months on end, Lizzie, Wren, Vivienne, and Bear walked the world through the portals Lizzie created, first to all the international Orders of the Triple Goddess to organize and deploy teams to the hardest hit areas, mostly the big cities, providing basic needs, medical care and establishing magickal training centers to teach people how to use their new abilities. There were still those who chose darkness over light, and special teams were sent to root out the small pockets of black magick to stop it from gaining a foothold in the new world.

Although the Fey and its High Council were still reluctant to open the portals to the human realm, they didn't hesitate to send their own teams during the first months of the collapse to disarm the nuclear warheads and safely deactivate the nuclear reactors when the grid failed. Additionally, they sent magickal communication stones and scrying mirrors, which Lizzie and her group distributed on their trips that kept the lines of global communications open. And finally, they dedicated all their librarians to scour the Library of All Knowledge's human history wing to find as many documents with ancient human magicks that would be of use.

During the worst of it, when what Lizzie had seen on her travels, the images of burned-out buildings, empty neighborhoods, the vacant-eyed stares of people who, in the flash of magick, had their world turn upside down, the safe, comfortable life they once led gone forever had left her hollowed out from grief and guilt she would lie awake at night as Wren slept next to her.

And in those dark moments, she would take herself off to her in-between. And there, sitting on the stoop of the cottage with Bear at her side, she would watch the golden web connecting everything, hum with life, with magick, and with the Light. She found, if not peace in those times, solace and acceptance with what her choices had let loose across the world and what the alternative would have been if The Dark One had risen to power and consumed not only her world but others.

On one such visit, when she'd been at her lowest point when her own dark thoughts couldn't be put to rest by Wren's love or her new family's shared understanding, she'd glimpsed a flash of golden eyes peering from the shadows of the forest and heard a voice riding on the breeze whisper to her, "All shall be well, Elizabeth. All shall be well."

She still had dark days and sleepless nights, but those moments occurred less frequently, replaced by the simple joy of spending time with her family, sharing a meal, planting a garden, marking the changes of the season, or just being in each other's company.

Carefully closing her journal and capping her fountain pen, Lizzie glanced over at Gideon, who sat opposite her at the writing table, typing on an old Olivetti. Next to his typewriter was a beautifully illuminated manuscript, a Lemurian grimoire, cradled in a book pillow he'd made to protect the ancient tome. Gideon used a small translation stone, another gift from the Fey, which allowed him to easily understand and translate any language. He'd hand off his translated copies to Birdie and her apprentices in the newly running printing press and bindery housed below in the expanded main floor of the barn. With her team, Birdie would produce two copies of the translation, for now, one to be housed in their newly built library, the other sent with Wren through the Fey's portal to The Library of All Knowledge.

Gideon's long-term goal was to have every ancient document on humanity's forgotten history and magicks the Fey had returned to them, translated into several languages, and distributed worldwide for everyone to have access to.

"Are you coming down?" Lizzie asked as she pushed back her chair and stood up.

Gideon looked up distractedly. "What for?"

She'd become used to how deep Gideon's focus would go when translating a book, so she merely smiled. "Birdie, just let me know the first copies of the Ravenwood Chronicles are hot off the presses, which means Wren and I need to be leaving soon. Did you want to come and see us off?"

"Oh, the book! Yes, yes, of course. Just let me secure the grimoire, and I'll be right down."

"Sounds good." Lizzie headed towards the stairs and glanced over the railing. Birdie stood in the rotunda, backlighted by the clear light flooding in through the wall of glass behind her. The summer sunshine refracted through the huge chandelier that hung suspended from the vaulted ceiling, shooting colored rays across the floor below. Lizzie marveled at the suspended rough-cut crystals and the hum of magick flowing through them. In her vision, she'd mistakenly thought the crystal structure was a light fixture when in reality, it was what powered the lights and HVAC system, not just to the barn but to all the outbuildings on the property.

The Fey librarians were the ones who located the knowledge and spells specific to the human realm that were used to infuse the crystals, creating an endless power supply, but it was Wren and Madison working tirelessly that made it a reality and not just an idea on paper.

Around where Birdie stood waiting, several women moved purposefully, carrying baskets filled with fresh herbs. Lizzie could smell the rosemary and lavender even from up in the loft. The herbs had come from her garden, and the women were headed to the apothecary and distillery in the basement of the barn, where they would fill small amber bottles with the essential oils, medicinal tinctures, and potions to be added to Grandma Faye's healing supplies.

"You coming?" This time, Lizzie directed her question at Bear, who had been curled up on his dog bed in the corner. He answered by standing up and then lowering the front half of his body in a deep downward stretch, before trotting over to join her, his plume of a tail waving happily back and forth.

Poking his head between the spindles, he looked down, not at Birdie, but off to her left into empty space and barked. Lizzie followed the direction of his gaze, the air just to the left of Birdie rippling, and, for a brief moment, the outline of a person shimmered before the air smoothed out again. Bear withdrew his head from between the spindles and looked up at her. Giving him a knowing smile, she gave a scratch behind his ears before she headed down the stairs. Bear, on the other hand, blinked out of sight to reappear down below before Lizzie hit the last step. He sat before Birdie, his tail thumping on the concrete floor.

"Hold on a sec, I think I have one in my pocket," Birdie said to Bear, handing Lizzie one of the two books she was holding before digging in her pocket and pulling out a dog treat. When she held the treat out, the dragon insignia on her inner arm flashed copper fire in the sunlight. Bear took the cookie delicately between his teeth and then gulped it down. "Bear," Birdie laughed, "Did you even taste that?"

"Oh Birdie, it's exquisite," Lizzie said, running a finger lovingly along the gold embossed title on the spine. Birdie had wanted to call the series The Odyssey of the Bad-ass White Whites and World Walker of the Light, but eventually agreed with the rest of the women to call the first book in the series, *She Who Walks Between Worlds, Book One of the Ravenwood Chronicles*.

When the Fey High Council had formally requested written accounts of what had happened the day they defeated The Dark One and detailed biographies of everyone involved to add to their library's collection, Lizzie had wholeheartedly agreed along with the rest of the women to fulfill the request. It was the least they could do to repay the Fey for the help they'd given to humanity over the last few years.

She assumed Gideon would be the one to do the actual writing, but after he'd read her notes and the brief outline she'd given him, he handed them back to her with one of Birdie's blank journals.

"I'm a scribe, not a storyteller. It was clear to me, even just reading your notes, that that's your gift, not mine. And it's not my story to tell. It's yours."

So, Lizzie reluctantly began to write up her story, the process she found both terrifying and exhilarating in equal measure. And when she'd shared her rough draft with Vivienne, Grandma Faye, Madison, and Birdie, she was surprised and mostly panicked when they all nominated her to not only continue writing her part of the story but to write their biographies, too. But, the more she wrote, the more she discovered how much she enjoyed the process and the more she missed it when she was called away to her other duties as a world walker.

"Thank you." Birdie beamed with pride. "How's the second book coming along?"

"Good, now that Wren solved the mystery of where the scroll containing the counter spell to release the spirit of Emma Hawksworth from my cellar came from." Even when Lizzie knew who and what Wren was, it never dawned on her that he was the one, after sensing the dark magick in the cottage, who found the counterspell in the Fey library and left it for her to find on the fireplace mantle, nor that it was Bear who returned it to him. "Now that I have that missing piece of information, I should have the final draft ready for the printing press in a couple of weeks."

"Great, I'll make sure my apprentices will be ready. Will

you be leaving soon?"

"Yes, now that I have the book, I was just going to gather the others and head off. Are you coming?"

"Wouldn't miss it for the world. Oh, wait, I almost forgot." Birdie dashed back into the book bindery, returning with a metal tin secured with an elaborate bow. "Would you mind giving this to Ruaidhri?"

"It would be my pleasure," Lizzie said, tucking the book under her arm and taking the tin.

Birdie looked at her shyly, "I hope he likes it. It's an apple spice cake sweetened with honey. Vivienne showed me how to make it, and Grandma Faye supplied the honey from her beehives."

"I may not know what Dragons like to eat, but having had the pleasure of tasting Vivienne's cakes myself, I have no doubt he will enjoy it."

Suddenly, Birdie's eyes darted towards the stairs leading up to the Scriptorium, a definite blush coloring her cheeks. Lizzie did her best to stop her lips from curving into a smile as Gideon joined them, and Birdie handed him a copy of the book.

His eyes lit up as he mirrored Lizzie's gesture when she'd first held it by running a finger slowly across the spine and then the cover. Opening the book, he then studied the marbled end papers before carefully turning several pages, holding the book up to his face to examine the quality of the print. Finished with his inspection, he reverently closed the book and held it to his chest. He looked up at Birdie, a mix of awe and longing in his eyes.

"You're beautiful," he blurted out, his own face suddenly going beet red. "I mean—" he stammered, "the book," He held up the book, waving it frantically, "the book is beautiful, not you. That's not what I meant. Not that you aren't because you are, I mean—"

Lizzie couldn't help the laugh that escaped her. "Gideon, seeing as Wren and Madison installed the circulation desk yesterday, wouldn't now be a good time to show Birdie where you want the sign-out ledger to go so she can get the correct dimensions?" She asked, coming to his rescue.

"Right, yes, the sign-out ledger. Do you have time to come and look?"

"Do I?" Birdie asked Lizzie.

"Of course, you do. Why don't the two of you meet up with the rest of us at the circle in, say, fifteen minutes?"

"Sounds good," Birdie replied, heading for the large oak doors just to the left of the staircase, a slight bounce in her step. A small brass plaque affixed to the wall next to the double doors proclaimed in a simple yet elegant script, *The Audleian Lib*rary.

Gideon scrambled to catch up with her, reaching the door seconds before Birdie, swinging it open, and holding it for her as she passed through. The strong scent of newly varnished wood drifted out into the rotunda before Gideon shut the door behind them.

Lizzie smiled as she stepped out into the summer sunshine. If the two of them hadn't made it to the circle in fifteen minutes, she'd leave them be as she had no desire to interrupt the budding romance between those two.

With Bear at her side, she crossed the yard, slowing her pace as she took in what the little parcel of land her cottage sat in had become in such a short period of time. A place her family had christened Ravenwood in honor of the hundreds of ravens who decided to make the forest around the stone circle their permanent home. With Madison acting as interpreter, the ravens announced they would be pleased to remain and take up permanent guardianship of the portal.

Along with her stone cottage, now there was a small cow barn and dairy, the jersey cows a gift from Anna. With every member of her family pitching in, they expanded the garden, planted an orchard, created the apothecary and distillery down in the old grow-op, and built a workshop for Madison where her inventions, marrying crystal energy technology, magicks, and already existing machines, could be tinkered on and perfected.

Rose Cottage was still Lizzie's home, and now it was Wren's, too. The rest of the group either lived on the property or close by, the eight of them routinely gathering to share evening meals and to celebrate milestones.

Grandma Faye, Vivienne, and Cathy lived in the old woman's cabin down the road, that now boasted the addition of two more bedrooms. At first, Gideon bunked down in the hayloft until the Fey High Council expressed their intention of returning all of humanity's lost histories and magickal texts to the care and keeping of the Daughters of the Earth. When Gideon proposed the idea of housing the Audleian Library in the barn, he also requested a compact studio space be built connected to it for his use. Madison and Birdie shared a room in Rose Cottage until just recently, when they moved into the newly built white clapboard cottage strategically placed between Madison's workshop and Birdie's printing press and book bindery.

On market days in the village, with the help of Lizzie's portal magick, Madison and Grandma Faye took their surplus food, Madison's latest inventions, and Grandma Faye's medicinal supplies to barter for things they couldn't make or grow on the farm. And it was on those days, as Grandma Faye and Madison manned their stall, that they were approached by people wanting to learn how to make plant medicine or how to plant a simple garden.

So Ravenwood also became a place that welcomed anyone who wanted to learn what Birdie affectionately dubbed 'Granny skills.' The old woman taught her eager students about growing and preserving food, animal husbandry, and herbal and plant medicine. Vivienne taught baking and the culinary arts when she wasn't using all of her diplomatic skills during her meeting with the Fey High Council through the scrying mirror. And before long, both Birdie and Grandma Faye found they had willing apprentices both in the apothecary and the printing bindery.

As if sensing Lizzie's gaze on her, Grandma Faye looked up from hoeing a row and smiled.

"We'll be heading to the circle in a few minutes," Lizzie called out.

"I'll be right there," the old woman replied before quickly giving out instructions to the young men and women working alongside her. She wound her way through the garden, side-stepping the contented chickens that scratched and pecked in search of grubs and worms.

Quickly untying the large garden apron she wore, she hung it over a nearby fence post and gathered up a basket laden with vegetables. Before joining Lizzie, she detoured over to two young girls riding bareback on a large shire horse through the orchard. The horse whickered when Grandma Faye approached and lowered his head to receive a gentle stroke on his cheek and a fresh carrot the old woman plucked from the basket she carried.

"Cathy, I'm just going to see Lizzie off. When you and Allachka are finished your ride, you can feed Handsome a flake of hay like I showed you."

"Will do, Granny. And I'll make sure to give him fresh water and give him a good brushing and check his hooves for stones."

"That's my good girl." Grandma Faye patted the young girl's leg affectionately. "When I get back, the three of us can make ice cream if you want? I think your first sleepover deserves a special treat to mark the occasion."

"Yay! Ice cream, I can't wait," Allachka said, "Can we save some for Bear? He likes ice cream, too."

"Of course, but just a little taste. Now off you go and have some fun." Grandma Faye beamed as the two young girls rode through the trees, chatting and giggling as if they'd known each other all their lives.

As Grandma Faye came alongside Lizzie, she took the basket from the old woman and handed her the book.

"Well, now," Grandma Faye said admiringly, "Birdie has done a fine thing. She definitely has a talent for creating beauty. Where is she, by the way?"

"With Gideon checking out the library," Lizzie said with a smirk. "They may or may not be joining us."

"Oh, I see," she said, unable to stop her own knowing smile. "All I can say is it is about time."

The two women strolled over to where Grandma Faye's truck was parked near the cottage, its hood raised. Wren was behind the wheel, Madison chest deep under the hood, adjusting something with a wrench.

"Okay, Wren, give it a try," Madison said, straightening up and taking a step back. Wren turned the ignition key, and the truck roared to life, then the engine spluttered and died. "Damn, we were so close." She tossed the wrench in her nearby toolbox and fisted her hands on her hips.

Wren slid out from behind the wheel and joined Madison to look inside the hood. She reached in and detached something, holding it up for Wren. He plucked the large egg-shaped crystal wrapped in copper, turning it in the light.

"I think if we add a stabilization rune right about here," he pointed, "that may do the trick." He looked up as Grandma Faye and Lizzie approached. He smiled at Lizzie, his eyes lighting up. Handing the crystal back to Madison, he took the basket from Lizzie and gathered her up with his other arm. Lizzie's heart fluttered as he kissed her soundly on the mouth. When they broke from the kiss, he kept his arm wrapped around her waist.

"Hey, is that the book?" Madison asked as Grandma Faye held it up for her to see. Madison reached out to grab it but noticed the grease smudges on her hands. With a flick of her wrists, she used her magick to remove any grime from her hands and took the book from Grandma Faye, turning it over and then flipping through the pages.

"Wait for us," Birdie called out as she rushed down to join the group, Gideon following in her wake.

"Excellent work, you two," Madison said, holding up the book. Her eyes suddenly narrowed at Gideon, and she barked out a laugh. "You missed a button, lover boy." She pointed to Gideon's chest where his shirt front sat askew.

Gideon looked down, then whipped around to quickly unbutton and re-button his shirt. When he turned around, he scowled at Madison, who ignored him and handed the book to Lizzie.

Linking arms with Birdie, Madison pulled her friend towards the path in the woods. Quinn flew after her and landed on her shoulder. "I have no idea what you see in him, but I promise not to hold it against you," she grinned. "Anyway, I think I may have figured out how to get that ancient behemoth of a printing press of yours running without having to use the hand crank. I'd like to try a chunk of charmed ammonite and a tesla coil," Madison's voice trailed off as they headed further into the forest on the well-worn path to the portal, the rest of the group following behind.

"Is Vivienne coming?" Madison asked as everyone stood next to the open portal, its blue light snapping and buzzing with energy.

"Yes, I'm coming, I'm coming," Vivienne said, slightly out of breath. She held a biscuit tin in her hands. "Sorry I'm a little late. I was in conference with Councilman Rendric, and you know how he can ramble on." She handed the tin over to Lizzie, who wedged it next to Birdie's tin of cake in the vegetable hamper. "Those are the blueberry muffins I promised him. It never hurts to appeal to someone's stomach if it helps our negotiations.

"Oh wait," Vivienne said, her hands going under her apron as she rooted around in her pockets. She pulled out a letter sealed with her personal seal, not the official one she used for her role as human ambassador to the Fey. Lizzie took the letter and added it to the hamper. The letter more than confirmed her suspicion that there was definitely something going on between Vivienne and the dapper Fey ambassador.

Bear chuffed.

"He says we need to stop dawdling," Madison said, "because the faster the three of you leave, the faster you can get back, and he says he doesn't want to be late for dinner. He heard rumors there may be ice cream for dessert."

Madison hugged Lizzie and Wren before stepping back to let the rest of the group wish the couple and their dog a safe journey. Grandma Faye kissed Lizzie's cheek, "There is no need to be nervous. You've spoken to your uncle several times over the scrying mirror. He's going to be just as excited to meet you in person as you are to finally meet him."

Lizzie nodded, her smile a bit shaky. Wren squeezed her hand affectionately, then picked up the hamper. He looked down at Lizzie and smiled. "Ready?" He asked, his eyes the blue-green of a tropical sea, radiating the joy Lizzie felt welling up in her heart.

"More than ready," Lizzie replied as all three of them stepped through the portal and were gone.

The rest of the group stood watching until the portal snapped shut, each one lost in thought about what lay on the other side. Then one by one, they drifted off in separate directions; Vivienne to the bake house to make an apple pie to go with the ice cream for dessert, Grandma Faye back to the garden and the children under her care, Madison with Quinn riding on her shoulder, to follow Wren's suggestion determined to have the truck running by the time the two of them returned.

Gideon and Birdie were the last to leave the stone circle. Birdie gently tugged Gideon's hand as he frowned at where the portal had been. "Birdie, did you see that?"

"See what?"

He was about to tell her that just before the portal closed, he could have sworn Lizzie's dog, Bear, had suddenly grown in size, his feathered tail shrinking down to a nub. He turned from the portal and rubbed his eyes. "Nothing, it was nothing. I probably just strained my eyes from spending so much time at the typewriter."

"Why don't we stop by the apothecary and pick up some eye wash, and then you can finish showing me around the library?" she looked up through her eyelashes at him. "If you want?"

Gideon swallowed hard, all thoughts of seeing Lizzie's dog transforming into a white bear flying from his thoughts as he eagerly followed Birdie through the forest.

Acknowledgements for The Light Bringer

To Jasmine Kabernick, I am so grateful for your friendship and for being the most dedicated and insightful beta reader any writer could hope to have. Thank you for your encouragement and inspiration that helped me see this final book through to the finish line.

Thank you, Karen Fuller, for publishing Lizzie's story, for your patience, and for your wonderful editing to make my books the best they can be.

And to you, dear reader, for taking the journey and giving me the extraordinary gift of sharing my stories with you.

Lora Deeprose is a curiologist, a devotee of morning coffee, and author of *The Ravenwood Trilogy*. When she's not writing, she can be found prowling thrift stores for enchanted jewelry or spending time in nature looking for faerie stones and portals to other realms.

She currently lives with her sister and Dragoncat, Steve, in the Fraser Valley.

www.ingramcontent.com/pod-product-compliance
Lightning Source LLC
Chambersburg PA
CBHW020603260626
47157CB00003B/847